HOPE AT HARBOR AND DIVINE

Book Two of the Harbor and Divine Series

HOPE AT HARBOR AND DIVINE

A STORY OF LOVE, HEALING, AND HOPE

by T. W. Poremba

XULON PRESS

Xulon Press
2301 Lucien Way #415
Maitland, FL 32751
407.339.4217
www.xulonpress.com

Paperback ISBN-13: 978-1-66285-406-4
eBook ISBN-978-1-66285-407-1

For

Cathy

Table of Contents

Books by T.W. Poremba

The Harbor and Divine Series
Book One:
2021
*Sfumato**
A Story of Love, Loss and Hope

Book Two:
2022
Hope at Harbor and Divine
A Story of Love, Healing and Hope

Book Three:
Coming Soon in 2023
The Meeting House
PTSD Stories of Love, Healing and Hope

Chapter 1

Annie, Dr. Z and the Starbucks Cheer

Annie Dunlop got up extra early that morning for work at her real estate agency. She planned a head start on her day's work so she could take an extra long coffee break to meet with Dr. Melanie Zurkos at the two-story Starbucks in downtown Cleveland. Dr. Zurkos was a long time friend and mentor of Gary Siciliano, Annie's heart throb. With the early start, lots to do, plus her excitement to meet Dr. Zurkos, the morning flew by. After she had taken care of her on-line listings, returned a few calls, sent texts and e-mails, chatted with her agents when they stopped in and scheduled several home showings, she was ready to make her way downtown.

Originally, when Dr. Zurkos had called to invite her to coffee today Annie was really nervous, even though this was just coffee and scones at Starbucks. "That's ridiculous," she scolded herself as she began closing up the office.

"Yeah, but she is a *doctor*, for crying out loud," Annie said aloud arguing with herself. She looked around to see if anybody heard her and saw no one, so she continued fussing at herself, Annie #1 v Annie #2.

Annie #1: "So? What are you, chopped liver? You own Dunlop Realty, the fastest growing realty on the West Side. Besides, she's Gary's friend, not yours. Settle down."

"Yeah, but that's just it," argued Annie #2, "I want her to like me, *because* she's Gary's friend. Dr. Z practically grew him up as an artist — she and that high school art teacher Val. But Val died ten years ago, so she hardly counts as a friend today."

"Whoa! That's harsh," retorted Annie #1. "Don't ever say that in front of the guys, especially Joe and Gary. Joe especially, since he and Val were married, even though, you're right, that was ten years ago. And Gary, well, you know, Dianah just died like, what, five months ago."

"Come on, get a grip, Annie."

"Yeah, get a grip. Oh, this is stupid." And for the first time Annie #1 agreed with Annie #2. With her conflict sort of resolved, Annie took a deep breath to push away the edge of tears. Falling in love with Gary Siciliano was like walking on eggshells every single day. Every day she had just wanted to throw herself in his arms for him to have his way with her, but she'd never done it, because she knew how tender he was in his grief at Dianah's tragic death. Annie wouldn't hurt him for the world. But still, her heart ached for him. And, besides, the truth is, she was afraid to meet his beloved mentor, Dr. Zurkos.

Then suddenly, with a lightning bolt of genius, she jerked her head up, smiled and declared, "I know what I'll do!" Sporting an eager smile Annie started to lock up and walk out the door.

Two things still intimidated Annie about Dr. Melanie Zurkos: Number one, Dr. Zurkos was fourteen years older than Annie, and held a very responsible job at the Cleveland Museum of Art (CMA) where she currently worked with Gary. Again!

Again! because16 years ago she had also supervised Gary's Master of Fine Arts project, Old Tony, using Leonardo Da Vinci's *Sfumato* techniques like those he used on the Mona Lisa. Dr. Z actually mentored Gary in perfecting those *sfumato* techniques for which he became famous, and for eight years, she guided him to complete his award winning painting.

Dr. Z knew a lot. Dr. Z *knows* a lot! And that's intimidating.

Plus number two, she's a DOCTOR! Of something or other. Art? Who knows? But still, Annie felt compelled to genuflect and call her 'Doctor.'

Oh yeah, and number three, yes, three, Gary liked and admired her. Hmm. "Got to get over that, Annie," she told herself. "There is absolutely no romance there at all. Pretty sure; pretty sure. And definitely no competition. She's like his big sister. And maybe mine. Hmm. Good thought."

But that's it. That's really all Annie has ever known about Dr. Melanie Zurkos.

Plus, get this: even though Gary had years and years of history with her, he never shared much of anything about Dr. Zurkos with Annie. Zilch. Nada. Dr. Zurkos was a mystery woman. An intimidating mystery woman. Until today. Today Annie felt more excited than intimidated to meet her, thanks to the argument she had just had with herself that flipped a switch inside her heart. As she left the office, she suddenly decided to "have fun" at 'Coffee with the Doctor' by pretending in her make-believe mind to be a private investigator on a due diligence assignment scoping out Dr. Who? No! Dr. Z! It was the kind of silly fun Annie loved, and, for her, it turned an intimidating coffee with the doctor into the high adventure of a snooping detective on an imaginary hunt for the *real* Dr. Z.

"Oh, yeah! Fun, fun, fun!" she said aloud to herself, pretty convinced it would be true. Well, at least Annie #1 and Annie

#2 were not going at it. "That should count for something," she told herself conclusively.

Right at 11:00 she finally zipped out the door, locked the office, hopped in her car and headed downtown.

Dr. Zurkos had already found a parking space on the street and sat waiting with the car running, the heater blasting and the radio chattering with NPR know-it-alls Dr. Zurkos loved. When Annie saw a woman parked on the street with the motor running, she guessed she might be Dr. Zurkos, so she parked in a nearby lot. Walking toward that running car, she peered into the windshield and waved until Dr. Zurkos saw her and waved back. The waves turned to smiles, and when Dr. Zurkos got out of her car to meet Annie, the smiles turned into joyful greetings.

"Hi, there, I'm Melanie Zurkos. Are you Annie Dunlop?"

"I sure am," replied Annie with way more enthusiasm than she anticipated. Surprise! "Nice to meet you, Dr. Zurkos"

"Oh, please, Mel will do just fine."

"Alrighty then! Thank you. Mel it is. Or Dr. Z?"

"Dr. Z? Some of the younger museum interns actually call me that already. I sort of like it. Mel or Dr. Z, Annie, you choose."

"Then I choose 'Mel!'" she smiled. And down went the anxiety along with *doctor intimidation*. 'Hallelujah!' Annie cheered within. Still smiling, Annie asked Mel, "Did you have a good ride into town?"

"I did. How about you?"

"Way better than I expected. I'm still surprised that traffic in downtown Cleveland is so much lighter than when I was a little girl."

"A good thing?"

"I suppose, except I used to love the holiday rush of folks coming in for Christmas shopping at May Company, Higbee's and the rest. You know, a hundred people crossing the street on every corner at every traffic light change, mothers shepherding their young children and eight-year-old boys running after the pigeons. And the buses! Oh my, eight or ten buses with their diesel perfume filling the air waiting for a turn to let out and pick up riders at lots of bus stops around Public Square."

"I'm with you there. We're just not a big city any more, are we?"

"Guess not. Oh, speaking of which, where are we going in this not so big city? Where is this grand, two-story Starbucks we seek? I saw no star to guide me."

Mel laughed, "I know it's Christmas time, but Annie, only *men, wise* men at that, get the star. And there aren't many more left — wise men, that is. Still lots of stars!" That crack sent Annie into a surprise of apoplectic laughter.

Mel stepped in and said, "Annie, not that funny!"

"Oh, yeah it is. I'm divorced, and I know about the dearth of wise, really wise men, let me tell you! But, truthfully, where is this Eden of Coffee Heaven?"

Mel laughed. She was already getting to like this Annie Dunlop. "It's just down Euclid almost to East Ninth. Maybe you can see it from here. Take a look."

"Oh, yeah, I can."

"All righty then. Shall we?"

"Indeed! I'll follow you anywhere as long as you spout wise-cracks like that one about wise men."

"Hear, hear! Annie, I'm beginning to believe that we have much in common."

Smiling, with sisterhood established, Annie and Mel locked arms and verily skipped down the yellow brick road to

Cleveland's Emerald City of coffee, Starbucks. There in the holy shrine of high test, the wizards of joe mix up concoctions that cast delicious spells of vigor and chatter. And all that without eye of newt or tongue of toad.

Not intimidating at all!

As they got closer to St. Starbucks (no real skipping, just happy steps), Mel suddenly remembered, "My ex and I used to hit this exact same Starbucks three, four times a week, when it first opened. And, believe it or not, those were happy times — mostly. Like this one time we got feeling really silly and we made up a Starbucks Coffee cheer while we stood in line, chanting it back and forth to each other. The people around us started laughing, then all of a sudden they began chanting it with us:

'**Starbucks coffee picks us up; edgy vigor by the cup;**
Chit and chatter all the day; Starbucks coffee,
shout hooray!'

Even the baristas joined in. What a hoot! And then when we got to the register to pay, the manager told us it was on the house!"

Annie laughed and was so taken by Mel's story of Starbucks joy, that she started chanting it along with Mel, right then and there, like a couple of teenagers:

"**Starbucks coffee picks us up; edgy vigor by the cup;**
Chit and chatter all the day; Starbucks coffee,
shout hooray!"

And *deja vu*, it happened again! Smiles spread from face to face around St. Starbucks, and the two story coffee shop in downtown Cleveland began rocking with holiday joy as everybody chanted the Starbucks Cheer. Lots of people even stood up, some began dancing, and everybody started clapping their hands and stomping their feet, led, of course, by a giddy Mel and Annie who were nearly breathless.

By the time they got to the station to pick up their hot mochas and pay, wouldn't you know, it happened again. "Ladies," said the manager, "that was an absolute blast! You made me feel like I was 16 years old again. Thank you! Thank you! AND for lifting all of our spirits, your drinks are on the house, plus here's two gift cards to boot! Come back and cheer for us any time!"

"We will! Gladly! Thank you!"

"Oh, no! Thank YOU!"

As they settled around a high table in the corner still laughing, Annie told her new sister-in-fun, "Mel, that was awesome! You are so much fun!" Two young girls on their way out the door stopped when they overheard what Annie told Mel, and one said, "You can say that again! You two are my sisters-in-coffee! And I hope when I get older I can laugh and cheer and hop around just like you!"

"Yeah! Right?" said the other. "You ladies are my new heroes!"

And they cheered and chanted themselves out the door:

"Starbucks coffee picks us up; edgy vigor by the cup;
   Chit and chatter all the day; Starbucks coffee;
shout hooray!"

And once again the whole place cheered and hooted.

"I think we made some friends," said Annie.

"I think you're right!" agreed Mel. "Plus I don't feel like I'm a day over sixteen!"

"Me either!" laughed Annie. "And to think I'm over 40! And you?..." She paused as Mel gave her the stink eye warning, making Annie laugh even more, saying, "...and you are too! Isn't that exactly what you *thought* I was going to say?"

Mel choked out a laugh and said, "Yes! Exactly!"

They started to sit, but the chairs were too tall for them to actually sit *down* causing them to laugh all over again realizing that they had to sit *up*.

And then, once they got situated, to their surprise, Annie and Mel unexpectedly just quietly stared at one another as if they had just looked in the mirror and seen someone else's face.

"Annie," Mel began, "I think I'm making a friend."

"Really?" Annie asked. "Tell me who."

"Oh, you silly girl. *You*."

Annie felt the same way, but still was amazed by Mel's words, by her candor, yes, but even more so by her transparent affection for a younger sister whom she had only just met.

"Good," Annie said thoughtfully with a confused look that took Mel by surprise.

"Good? Just good? Like a hamburger is 'just good?'"

"No, no, no. Mel, your candor took me by total surprise. Blew me away! Because, Mel, I feel the same way. And know what?"

"No. What?" And they giggled again like kids at their homophones.

"I think silliness makes friends, even after forty. I love being happy enough to laugh."

"Even after FIFTY, girl, but I'm so glad *you* didn't say that!" And they both laughed again.

Smiling at one another like friends do, they sipped their coffee.

"But I admit," confessed Annie, "I haven't always been this happy. Not even close."

"Hmm," Mel cogitated. "Want to talk about it?" she asked.

"A little bit. Do you mind?"

"Not at all. That's what friends are for, Annie. Right?"

"Right. But still, thanks. I mean, I haven't had a girlfriend for a long, long time. Like in forever."

Mel nodded her head and said, "Me too, Annie. Me too. Trusted girlfriends are hard to come by, starting all the way back in junior high school."

"Amen to that! True friends are slippery, hard to hold on to. And happiness is elusive, hard to see, hard to find and hard to keep. And, Mel, I think right now in my life I've got both, friends and happiness — even love. And you know what?

"What?"

"It scares me to pieces," Annie confessed. "It worries me, troubles me, even frightens me that I could have all three of those elusive joys all at the same time."

"So, Annie, if it makes you so happy why in the world are you so frightened?"

"Well, can I start with what is making me so happy these days, and then why it worries me, frightens me? Troubles me even. Has happiness ever troubled you?"

"Whoa, whoa," said the Mel the PhD counselor, not used to being counseled by the counselee. Let's take one thing at a time. First, you tell me, my new friend, what is making you so happy?"

"Well, in a word, 'Gary.'"

"Ohhh. Tell me more, tell me more."

"A 1960's song."

"Right, and it's about the very conversation we're having, except I think there were more girls involved, and they were a LOT younger! Nevertheless, tell me how Gary makes you so very happy, and then why it troubles you so much."

"Mel, I feel so happy when I'm with him that I want to giggle, laugh, shout, cry and jump his bones all at the same time. I've never felt that way about any man."

"Not even your husband? Sorry, ex-husband?"

"No, I'm sorry to say."

"Not even a little?"

"Oh, sure. Maybe a little. Enough to get married, I guess. But he never set my heart to thumping like Gary does just by smiling at me."

"And that's what troubles you?"

"Well. Yes. I mean, I've been divorced for ten years, so falling hard for Gary is a fabulous gift. Except." Annie took a beat.

Mel stepped in, "Except what, Annie?"

"Except," Annie began, but was interrupted by unexpected tears. "Except Dianah, Gary's wife. Dianah just died what, five months ago."

"I know. Such a tragedy."

"Well, yeah. But it's just that I think it's wrong to take advantage of a raw, grieving guy desperate for love no matter how much my heart thumps for him." At that, no longer able to hold them back, Annie let the tears flow until they turned into heart-wrenching sobs, converting what just a few minutes ago was the epicenter of Starbucksian cheers and laughter into a brooding corner of weeping remorse.

"My tears have been my food both day and night," Annie quoted.

"Psalm 42?" Mel asked.

Annie nodded her head.

"But, Annie, that's not how things end in the Bible, is it?"

"No, but that's how I feel now.
Unreasonably happy
while at the same time
disturbingly distressed."

Chapter 2

Coffee Talk

M el paused and then decided to jump in with both feet. "Want to tell me more?" she asked tentatively.

"Yeah," Annie answered shyly. "I do. Do you mind?"

"Annie, that's what friends do. That's what big sisters are for."

"Right. But Mel, it's just been so long since I've had a friend, a real friend. And I've never had a big sister."

"Well, you've got both now, so just dive right in. What in the world is sucking the joy out of you? I mean just five minutes ago we were leading the Starbucks Cheer. And, yes, Gary was grieving Dianah, also five minutes ago. Correct?"

"Yes. Oh. I see. Since nothing substantial has changed, what makes me unhappy now?"

"Yes. I have a hunch it's more than Gary stealing your joy. Just what it is I don't know, so it's something you're going to have to tell me. Like, are you afraid of something?"

"Oh, yeah! Big time. I'm totally afraid I'm going to completely screw it up — and not in the good way." Instantly Annie's face turned beet red, so she back-tracked with "Oh, I'm sorry. Did I really say that?"

"You certainly did, and being divorced myself, I understand completely—that you meant both."

Although one might think it a total impossibility, Annie's face turned even redder, so red, she was certain she was on fire. Which, to tell the truth, she was.

"Oh, Mel," Annie laughed, "how did you do that? You described it per-fect-ly! Both. Exactly. And it's so embarrassing."

"Why so embarrassed? Annie, look, you are a caring person, but also a very beautiful woman. Of course you want to care for Gary in his grief, mother him. But you also want to be *that woman* in his life, the siren that turns him on." Then Mel took a beat when she saw Annie tear up at 'that woman,' and she comprehended the unspoken truth in Annie's tears.

"Oh, Annie, I'm so sorry." They instantly connected in their souls.

"One day Mr. big shot Dale Dunlop just walked out. Found some hot little number at a...," and she made air quotes, 'a realtors conference' downtown. Right there in fact." She pointed to the hotel right across the street from where they sat. "Right f-ing there in that building, right across the street from St. Starbucks."

Mel gasped at her *faux pas* in meeting Annie at this particular two story Starbucks. "Wow. Annie, I am so sorry I brought us here. Actually it seems like both of us have dark memories hiding in this place, or near by. This is also where my ex told me we were done. In this very place. And then he just left. Just left. Rotten jerk."

"Whoa. Maybe we shouldn't have cheered so loud, you think?"

They both snickered. "Maybe. But it sure brought the joy back in the place, didn't it."

"Sure did, sister."

By that time Annie had sniffed back her sobs over old anger, and then admitted, "Mel, can I trust you? He, Dale Dunlop, was the last human being I trusted with my soul. 'Soul mates,' he called us, yeah, right. And then he just ran off. He took my soul, my love, betrayed my trust and left behind anger, fear, longing, distrust, loneliness, sadness, depression all to take up residence in the hole in my heart, and, Mel, I don't want to lose Gary that way. I want to be hotter for him than any woman he'll ever know or see or want to know. Ever! Except, you know."

Mel nodded. "Except Dianah."

"Exactly. She's my saint as well as Gary's. Our Dancing Bear. It's just so hard figuring it out. Oh, we even laugh about it. One day he called the realty office and I saw it was his number, so when I answered I put on this deep, sultry voice, you know,

'Helllllowww, this is Annie Dunlllop.'

"He said, 'This is Gary.'

"I said, 'I knooowwww, big fella.' And he hung up."

"For real?" Mel shouted out a horse-laugh.

"Yep. He called right back and asked for Annie the Realtor."

"No way."

"Yeah way. He's a sweet, sweet guy."

"Annie, this guy sounds like a keeper, girl."

"I know. For real, I do."

"But then what did you say?"

"I said, 'Just a minute, I'll get her.'"

"NO! You didn't."

"Yep, I did. And I apologized. And then he apologized. It was awesome, and I don't ever want to lose him."

"Annie, it sounds like you two are made for each other."

"Yeah, I think so too. Always did."

"What? What do you mean by that?"

"By what?"

"*Always* did."

"Oh." Annie took a soul-deep pause for a deep down look at things kept secret, never before shared. "Mel, can I trust you again? I mean, deep down inside really trust?"

"Yes. For sure. But, Annie, I think you already have trusted me. And I plan to keep that trust, so help me God, I do."

"Thank you, Mel." Annie smiled a little rascal smile, and said more in jest than for real, "I feel like right now we ought to lock little fingers like the young girls do and take a pinky swear, or prick our fingers and become blood sisters."

Mel feigned frightened alarm, "Oh, help us, Huck Finn, not in the age of blood-born viruses!" and broke the dead serious mood with laughter.

Annie picked up the conversation, "So, I grew up in Cleveland on the Near West Side, and I actually knew Gary–from a distance–in high school. I was a freshman and he was a senior at Lincoln-West. So a couple of months ago I straight out asked him if he went to Lincoln-West, because, to be honest with you, I had a crush on him even then. Ever since then."

Mel interrupted, "Ever since? Even while you were married?"

"Well, not an active crush. But I did pay attention whenever I heard or read his name, like when he became a famous artist. But no, I never went chasing after him — even in my heart. It was more a stowed-away-in-a-secret-safe-place crush."

"I understand those. But then *he* called *you*?"

"Yeah, from Colorado, and I about fell out of my chair. But since then, after hearing his story and knowing my own, I've been wondering if this is how God works healing, sending blessings, making wrong things right? Is it? Because, if it is, I am amazed. Mel, it's like a dream come true for me. It's like living in a real life fairy tale. And, Mel, I don't ever want to wake up from this dream or the fairy tale. I don't ever want to lose Gary, or lose this incredible blessing from God.

"So that's how it is that I am both happier than ever and afraid at the same time. Like I said, I don't ever want to screw this up."

"Thank you, Annie, for trusting me. But I have a gnawing hunch that there's even more to your story. Is there?"

"You are incredibly perceptive, Dr. Z. And the answer you deserve is this: 'Yes, there's more.' I grew up in an abusive family. But perhaps that's for another time."

"Well, then, perhaps at that other time you and I can share my childhood abuse stories as well."

"Oooo. Deal. Oh, and Mel?"

"Yes?"

"Thank you for listening to my story, my rants and my tears."

"Oh, Annie, you are already a treasure from God in my heart."

"As are you in mine."

Mel took a beat, then asked, "But before we leave, is it okay to change topics, like to Saturday's dinner that I invited you to?"

"Sure. Tell me what's it all about?"

"Well, if you recall, when we first talked about coffee today, I also invited you to supper on Saturday with me and DJ and Gary, because I suspected there were enough wounds among the four of us that together we might find God's healing. You know, grace and hope in a small fellowship of the broken friends."

"Right, because together we'd be four wounded people with wonderful chances at new life, throwing life lines to one another, wiping away tears and celebrating victories. Still sounds awesome!"

"Good. But I just got a text from DJ and now there's one more wrinkle."

"What's that?"

"Well, DJ said that a friend of his and Gary's..."

"Joe?"

"Yes, do you know him?"

"I do. He and Gary have gotten to be good friends, plus Joe directs The Mission at Harbor and Divine in the church buildings across the street from Gary's house. And, as your probably know, Gary was hired to be a part time outreach worker there as well as working with you in the art museum."

"Right! So that's where Gary will be doing his art outreach! Good to put two and two together. I'll get things straight eventually, especially once Gary and I figure out exactly what his outreach work is going to be. So Joe's in charge of *that* mission?"

Annie nodded. "Yes."

"Huh. We have all kinds of connections! I want to say, 'What a coincidence,' but DJ tells me there are no coincidences, it's all God at work changing and saving lives," Mel said. "But, anyhow, you're right. That's the guy—Joe. And DJ says Joe has met a woman, like *just met* a woman, whose husband ran out on her and her daughter ten, twelve years ago."

"What's her name?" Annie asked.

"Carmela."

"Carmela. Hmm. Well, good for Joe. Joe's wife died of cancer ten or eleven years ago. Right? I'm happy for him."

"Right," Mel affirmed. "And get this—I know Carmela. Her daughter will be in Gary's Old Tony studio. And we'll be playing match-makers for Joe and that Carmela. So now DJ is asking Gary to host our dinner this Saturday, now a dinner for six."

"Oh, my. Mel, I did not get *that* memo."

"Don't blame Gary. I just got it in a text from DJ. He wants to know if it's all okay with you and me. What do you think?"

"Well, I guess, if it's okay with Gary," she said.

They got on their coats and started walking out of Starbucks to their cars while Mel was still talking. Annie had a *thinking look* on her face that bordered on a scowl.

Mel picked up on the look and asked, "What's up, Annie?"

"What?"

"The sort of a scowl," Mel answered gesturing with her own face.

"Oh, nothing really. I just need to talk with Gary. Seems like nothing is ever as easy as it could be. I'll be okay if Gary is."

"Ahh, one of those scowls." And they both chuckled.

"But as far as the dinner goes, I'm definitely in if you still do the cooking," promised Annie. "And I'll help Gary get his house together."

"Perfect! I love to cook. Actually for me this gets better by the minute. Literally."

"Yeah, I'll say—the *last* minute. Oy. Men."

Chapter Three

See You in a Few...

Annie called Gary's cell before she even got to her car. "Hi, Annie! Boy, am I glad you called!"

"I'll bet you are. This is all pretty last minute stuff, isn't it?" Annie said a bit more snarky than, perhaps, she wanted.

"Whoa. Well, yeah," Gary said not quite sure what was up with Annie. He decided to go on, but to tread lightly. "We just thought Joe and Carmela would find it easier getting to my house on Harbor Street than winding their way to Mel's home through that maze of streets and traffic circles in Shaker Heights. And, besides, Mel is still going to do the cooking. Right? Still? I mean, you gals just talked, right? And you and she are still all in. Right?" Gary asked uneasily.

"She is, and she's still really excited about it." Annie took a breath and paused a beat to settle down–from what she wasn't really sure. "I promised her I would help her out as much as she needed, as well as help you out too, like, you know, having enough places for six people to sit and eat. I mean, Gar, you do need more furniture."

"Yeah, right, for sure. Four chairs for six people is a little too cozy, and dinner on the couch can get pretty messy. Besides, I've been meaning to get more furniture anyhow. So, Annie, what do you think? Want to right now? There's that Discount Furniture Warehouse they advertise on sports talk radio south on West 41st Street near I-90. It's like ten minutes from my house. Want to? I mean, you're not mad, are you, with all this last minute stuff?"

"Surprised, yes. But mad?" She did still have the remnants of that scowl Gary couldn't see. 'Easier to hide things on the phone,' she thought, then said, "At you? Not a chance. And, actually, Gary, it sounds like fun. *I'd love* to. But, Gar, you know what else?"

"What?"

"I'm surprised you're not creeped out," Annie said with a half smile creeping into her scowl, also which he couldn't see, "because it really sounds an awful lot like nest building to me, buying furniture and all. Are you sure you're up for that?"

"Nest building, huh? No, not really up for that." He paused, thought then said, "But up for outfitting a man cave? Oh yeah! You up for *that?* We could still go to the same furniture store. If the sports talk guys advertise it, well, they've got to have some 'man cave' stuff. Right?"

Gary's boyish enthusiasm finally just flat out turned Annie's scowl into a big old smile. "Right. When you put it that way I sure am. With you, Gar, it all sounds like fun. And Gar?"

"Yeah?"

"Maybe they've even got some cowboy stuff. D'ya think?"

"Great idea, Annie! We could have a western theme!" And he switched into his cowboy drawl, "Well, Ma'am, would you care to meet me there in, say, twenty minutes?" Gary asked.

"Well, cowboy, I'd rather drive to your spread to study the lay out with cowboy furniture and decor in mind."

"That's a good idea. Together we can see if we're on target with the man cave cowboy motif," he teased, grinning and winking into the phone as he cheered, "Yee-hah!"

"Right, Mr. Cowboy. Then," she said with that sultry voice that always turned Gary's knees to mush, "maybe some day, cowboy, I'll have a chance to soften it, just a bit, with a woman's touch."

The air went deadly silent for a few awkward moments as Gary recomposed himself from the impact of that voice he loved and dreaded at the same time. No. Not dreaded. Loved and feared.

Unsure of how to respond, if at all, Gary finally said sweet and low, "Maybe... some day, ma'am, maybe some day," followed by another short silence.

Thrilled in her heart with Gary's response, Annie responded softly,

"See you in a few then, cowboy."
"Okay. In a few."

Chapter Four

But I Had My Seat Belt On....

After forty minutes Annie still hadn't arrived. Gary called her cell phone, but no answer. He left a message, but no response. Then every few minutes he called again, though he stopped leaving messages after the third call. Finally, after more than two hours, with Gary in near panic mode, Annie called.

"Annie, Annie! Are you okay? What's happening?"

"I'm okay, but I think my car is a wreck, and I'm in the ER at Fairview Hospital. Gary, I'm so sorry."

"What?! Oh, Annie! But you're okay? You're really okay?"

"Yes, they're still checking me over. The ER doctor wants me to get a head scan and body x-rays and then, he said, he'll know more. But, Gary, would you come sit with me? Please? I'm achy and woozy, and scared."

"Annie, I love you, and I'm out the door on my way right now."

"Thank you, Gar. Could you stay on the phone with me?"

"Absolutely," he promised.

"Oh, shucks, I guess not. They're prepping me as we speak to go somewhere. Let me ask?" She turned to the ER staff, "Where am I going?"

"To get a head scan, ma'am. First you'll have to change into a hospital gown, and then we'll get you scanned. It will only take about fifteen minutes. Then if all is normal, we'll take you for a full set of x-rays. That will take about an hour. Evidently you flew around in your car a bit and lost consciousness. We just want to have a look-see to make sure you have no broken bones, internal bleeding or brain injuries."

"But I had my seatbelt on," Annie whined.

The nurse asked for Annie's phone. "I'll put it with your purse and car key. Want to say 'good-bye?'"

"Bye, Gar. I love you too. See you in a little while."

"Bye." He blew a kiss, but the line had already gone dead. "She wouldn't have seen it anyhow," he said sadly, with fears from Durango sneaking into his heart.

"But I had my seat belt on,"
she said again sadly to no one in particular.
The nurse heard.

Chapter Five

Deja Vu?

In a flash Gary hopped into his SUV and sped out toward Fairview Hospital. But in his mind's darkness he was on his way to Dianah and Lily from the Durango airport to their dream home on Durango Mountain. Their beautiful log home was smack in the path of a sixteen thousand acre wildfire propelled by 30 mph winds driving the blaze through the dry aspen forest right toward Durango Mountain.

Gary's mind raced backwards to five long months ago. Fire marshals had already evacuated Dianah and Lily safely two days earlier, but Dianah begged to go back to the house to save some art that she had left behind following the first evacuation order. "The blaze is less than an hour away, ma'am," the ranger manning the blockade warned her. "This road is closed."

"Ten minutes," Dianah pleaded. "We'll be right back."

"All right, but absolutely no more than ten minutes, ma'am."

"Tops," she confirmed. Tops....

However, in only five minutes a 50 mph updraft propelled the firestorm up the mountain side and over the crest engulfing Gary and Diana's dream home trapping mother and daughter in a blazing inferno. Gary arrived at the same ranger road block twenty minutes later. Twenty minutes too late.

Now on his way to Fairview Hospital, he was speeding like a mad man. That mountain fire tragedy that had haunted him daily, driven him into darkness for the last five months, now suddenly, once again, enveloped Gary in its darkness. Angry at the darkness, Gary shouted with vituperative rage, "Stop! This is not Durango, Gar! Settle down. It's Fairview Hospital, and Annie's in good hands."

He slowed down his SUV and his mind, forcing out the darkness. Surely nothing else would happen to Annie before he got there. Surely! His phone rang and scared him silly. "Uh-oh. The hospital. Oh no. Can't be." Deep breath. "Hello, this is Gary," he answered frantically. "What's happening?"

"This is Rachel Durough. I'm a nurse at Fairview Hospital. Annie Dunlop asked me to call you. She is all right," Nurse Durough assured Gary.

Gary let out the huge breath he had unwittingly been holding in out of fear for Annie. "Oh, thank you, thank you thank you, Lord."

"Really, she's okay. Typically I don't make phone calls for patients, but she told me what happened to your family five months ago, and that you might need some assurance about now. She was right. And Mr. Siciliano, you've got quite a catch there, sir, a woman in distress herself who thinks about you first. Wow. So let me tell you one more time, Ms. Dunlop is okay. She just got out of the MRI. The radiologist reading the scan told me that so far everything looks just fine. Right now Ms. Dunlop is on her way to get a full set of x-rays to detect any bones broken or organs damaged. That will take more than an hour not counting transport time, so you can slow down. You should be here in plenty of time to get all the results in person.

But, Mr. Siciliano, really, she appears to be just fine. And we'll take good care of her for you."

Gary took a giant breath to force back the encroaching sobs. Somehow he managed to say, "Thank you, Nurse Durough. You're an angel to call me. I'll slow down and still should be there in fifteen minutes, and I'll be sure to thank you in person."

"You're very welcome, Mr. Siciliano. But really, take your time, you've got plenty, and we'll see you soon."

Four more deep breaths. "Thank you, thank you," he said quietly. He felt a giant, dark weight lift from his shoulders with Nurse Durough's assurances. A few more stress-freeing breaths slowed down his breathing, his mind as well as his driving. Once he got down to the actual speed limit, he put a half smile on his face, but he couldn't stop the tears from flowing until he pulled into the ER parking lot. Briefly, Gary imagined how everything might have been so different had he found Dianah and Lily safe and sound in the Durango Hospital that day. "Don't go there," he scolded himself. "Anyhow," he said, "Annie is just fine...just fine."

Nevertheless, once he had parked his SUV, he sprinted into the large ER waiting room. Getting control of himself, Gary walked toward the smiling, peaceful-looking woman at the check-in desk. She got the information she needed from Gary, smiled, thanked him and said, "If you'll have a seat, Mr. Siciliano, we'll let you know as soon as you can see her. It shouldn't be much longer."

"Thank you," he replied, amazed how that woman's peace settled him down. He picked up the recent issue of Discover Magazine from the magazine rack, opened it up to somewhere in the middle, stared at the pictures and took a seat. Too worked up to read, he pulled out his cell phone, walked just outside the door and called DJ to tell him what's been happening. In four short months Rev. Dr. DJ Scott had become Gary's pastor, his confidant and his best friend. They talked for a few minutes, and then DJ prayed for Annie and Gary.

"Thanks, DJ. Your prayers always calm me down, and I appreciate them a lot. Appreciate *you* a lot."

"You're welcome, Gar. Will you call me back when you get the updates?"

"I sure will."

"And, Gar, what about her car?"

"Annie said it was really wrecked, the adjuster labeled it totaled."

"They know that already?"

"I guess. She gave the police her insurance card. The officer called the insurance company; an adjuster came right out, took one look and judged it totaled. They've already hauled it away. I'll drive Annie there to see the wreckage and pick up her things. And you know what, DJ?

"What?"

"She was on her way to help me pick out furniture, so we have places for everyone to sit Saturday night. Would have been fun."

"Ya. Well, let me know, okay?"

"Sure will, my friend. Bye."

"God bless you both, Gary. Bye."

After an hour and a half of snoozing, worrying and playing musical chairs with those confounded, uncomfortable waiting room chairs, Gary heard the receptionist quietly call, "Mr. Siciliano, you can go back to see Ms. Dunlop now."

"Great!" he said as he jumped out of his chair.

"Just go through those doors to room 118," she told him smiling at his wonderful, loving enthusiasm. "He's a catch," she said to herself.

"Thank you," Gary said already halfway through the door to find Annie. A few steps later he found room 118, knocked on the glass partition and called through the curtains, "Annie?"

A nurse came out, pretty, middle aged and tired-looking. "Hello, I'm Rachel Durough and you must be Mr. Siciliano."

"Yes, I'm Gary Siciliano, and I'm pleased to meet you, Nurse Durough. Thank you so much for helping Annie and me."

"You're very welcome. Sorry to say she just fell asleep not two minutes ago, but she really wants to see you. So how about you sit quietly in that chair near her bed and wait. That might be just enough to gently wake her. Do you mind waiting?"

"Oh, my, no. I don't mind at all. But she looks bruised, is she okay?"

"She's a little bit bruised, yes. But considering what she went through, she is doing very well. I'm going to check on another patient. Call me if you need me."

"Thank you. I will." And Gary sat alternately watching Annie breathe and scanning the monitors for her vitals. She looked peaceful and beautiful. And, he thought, alive. Yes, alive. His eyes moistened again. He found himself saying quietly, "This is so different. Praise you God. Thank you. Thank you." It was only just then that he noticed the wires and tubes and oxygen mask, even though they had been in plain sight all along. And more bruises. "Poor Annie. Poor Annie." And in thirty seconds, exhausted from his emotional roller coaster, Gary fell asleep sitting straight up, listing a bit to the leeward side.

"Gary. Gary." Gary heard an angel voice far off. He stirred, but didn't wake despite his awkward left-leaning position. "Gary," Annie called again. He recognized that voice, vaguely. "Poor Gary," she said.

At that his eyes shot open. "Oh. Hi, Annie. I guess I fell asleep waiting for you to wake up. I'm sorry."

"I don't mind. I'm just so glad that you're here." She reached for his hand, and he reached for hers but stopped at the sight of the IV stuck into and taped onto her left forearm. Instead of grabbing her hand, Gary offered Annie his pinky finger and a smile. Annie smiled back. Biting her lower lip she studied the situation for a second or two with love soaked eyes and then hooked her pinky in with his. She raised her head and smiled even more to see that Gary had been watching her with smiling, loving eyes of his own. It was so good to see him. So good. "Hi," she said not knowing what else to say. "I'm a mess."

"You're beautiful."

Two hours later the ER Dr. Sabar released Annie, telling Gary, "We see no internal injuries and no brain damage, but she has mild concussion symptoms. Nothing too serious, but," and he looked directly at Annie, "you must take it easy for forty-eight hours and be sure someone is in the house with you at all times just in case. I've sent two prescriptions to your pharmacy. But if you have any severe headaches, dizziness or vomiting, you come right back here immediately."

"Thank you, Doctor Sabar," Annie said. "That means I can go home now?"

"Yes, as long as you're not driving."

"Oh, no problem there," Gary said, "she'll ride with me."

"Ms. Dunlop, it sounds like you're in good hands then."

"I am," Annie agreed smiling.

"Well, then, good night."

"Good night, Doctor," they both said.

"Knock, knock. Can I come in?" It was Nurse Durough. "I'm here to help Ms. Dunlop get ready to go home."

Gary pulled the curtain aside for her. "Absolutely. Please, come in. I'll step out so you can help Annie get situated." And to Annie, "I'll be right outside in the waiting room. See you soon." He smiled.

"See you soon." She blew him a two fingered kiss. Gary melted. Annie smiled. He was so predictable, much to Annie's delight.

Ten minutes later Nurse Durough wheeled Annie out to Gary. After "Thank-you's" and "Good-nights" Gary wheeled Annie to the reception desk. "Do we have any more paperwork?"

"No, sir. You are all set."

"Thank you very much for all your help."

"You're very welcome. Have a good night and drive safely."

"Yes, ma'am. Good night."

"Annie, I'll go get my car and come back for you in a minute. Okay?"

"Okay. Gary, how is my car?"

"Totaled."

"Oh." She teared up. "That's not good."

"No. But I'll tell you about it on our way home."

"My home?"

"That's what I was thinking. I can sleep on the couch if that's okay with you."

"I'd like that."

"Good. I'll be right back."

Gary parked in front of the main ER doors, wheeled Annie out, carefully helped her into his SUV, took the wheelchair back, climbed behind the wheel and asked, "How are you doing?"

"Good, Gary. Thank you for being so good to me."

"My pleasure. You know how glad I am that you're still here for me to be good to."

"I know."

He leaned over and they kissed.

"Ready? Seat belt on?"

29

"Ready. Yes. And, Gar, I did have my seat belt on."

"I know. Praise God. If you hadn't this might have turned out quite a bit differently. But let's not even think about that."

And off they drove to Annie's house.

Chapter 6

Nurse Gary

Gary's ring tone came on playing "If You're Happy and You Know It." Since the fire it had always sent Gary off the rails to hear Dianah, Lily and Gary singing their favorite road trip song. But, surprisingly, not so much these days. Annie noticed the difference, especially when Gary asked, "Annie, would you get that for me, please? It might be DJ."

"Sure. I like talking to DJ." And, indeed, it was DJ. She put him on speaker phone. "Hi, this is Annie."

"Annie? Great to hear your voice. How in the world are you?"

"Hi, DJ. Good enough that I'm on my way home thanks to my chauffeur and nurse all rolled into one awesome man."

"Super. Praise God. I've been worried about you, praying for you and just happy to hear your voice."

"Thanks, DJ. Good to hear your voice too."

"Are we on speaker phone?"

Gary chimed in, "Yep. Hi, DJ."

"Hi, Gar. So, I'm thinking maybe now we need to adjust our dinner? What do you think? Date, location or both?"

"Have you talked to Joe about it?" Gary asked.

"Yes, and he's okay with whatever."

"Well, what do you think, Annie? If it's okay with you, I'd like to change the date and keep it at my place. Annie's nodding yes. She has to stay put for forty-eight to seventy-two hours, concussion protocol, so I'm actually driving her to her place right now, and I'll stay with her until she's out of danger. That means anywhere Saturday is out for us."

"So what are you thinking? Next week sometime? Saturday?"

"That's Thanksgiving weekend," Gary said. Annie shrugged more of a *no*, so Gary kept talking, "My mom and dad invited us over for Thanksgiving Day, so we'd be good for Saturday or Sunday, but it'd be a busy weekend. How about Mel? Is she cooking Thanksgiving?"

"Yes. I'll have to run that by her. How about that next Saturday then, December whatever-it-is?"

"You know, DJ, I think that sounds better yet. It's December 6th. Annie will have more time to heal, I'll have time to get some furniture and we'll both feel a lot less stressed. DJ, Annie, what do you think?"

DJ answered, "That sounds good to me, and I won't have to check with Mel about that. Or Joe. Dinner at six for six on, what is that, you said, December sixth? Dinner at six for six on the sixth. Ooo. That's a sign for sure, and maybe not a good one. How about Sunday? Dinner at six for six on the seventh. Sound better?"

"Annie's nodding 'yes.' We're good for the seventh at 6:00."

"Excellent. Annie, be a good patient now. Gary, be a good nurse. See you sometime next week."

"Okey dokey. Bye."

"Good plan, Gar," Annie told him.

"Glad you like it. Almost home."

32

"Hooray. I'm exhausted and sore. And sad that my car is smushed."

Gary parked in Annie's parking spot and helped her into her house.

She got ready for bed in no time, said good night to Gary and was asleep before her head touched the pillow. Gary made himself comfy on the couch, turned on the tv low and watched home improvement shows until he fell asleep thanking God for Annie and his new friends.

Chapter 7

Angel of Hope

Saturday morning Joe Whitehorse sat fixing a bike on the stone steps leading to the old church's side entrance hoping people would stop by to chat and eventually say, "Hey, I have an old rusty bike. If you think you can fix it up, I'll just give it to you if you want."

To which Joe would say, "That sounds great, can you get it right now? I've got a kid looking for a bike, and this one's already taken."

Unfortunately, it was a slow day, especially for a Saturday, and no one had even stopped by for a chat let alone to offer an old bike. So he kept on working on the three-speed in front of him, an old blue C.Itoh bike donated a couple of days ago by the old lady who lived across the street past the Dari-Delite.

"My husband and I bought matching blue bikes when we were first married," she had told him, "and we haven't ridden them in decades. This is mine, his is still in the garage. I heard you fix them up and give them away to kids. Is that right?"

"It sure is."

"Well, do you want them? They're both old and rusty, kinda like we are. We'd love to see kids get some good out of them."

"I would love, love, love them," answered Joe mimicking some of the women he hears on HGTV. "After I fix them up, they'll be as good as gold to the kids around here. Thank you!" Joe reached over to take her bike. "Oh, my name's Joe. I'm the outreach pastor here at The Mission at Harbor and Divine."

"I'm Sandy Korver. I live right over there with my husband Donald, Dr. Don. Retired now. And you're welcome. Should I get his bike too? Right now? It's really dirty. I cleaned this one up a little, but not that one. We both stopped riding bikes when he broke his hip years ago."

"By all means, bring it. I'll clean it up. Or better yet, you and I can clean it together."

Sandy smiled at the offer, a bicycle date with a handsome young pastor. "That sounds like fun," she announced. "I'll be right back. Maybe I'll get Donald to come back with me. I think he'd like cleaning up that old bike together and giving it to a neighborhood boy."

"From better to best!" Joe cheered.

True to her word, Sandy returned leading her husband who, with some effort, was pushing his dirty, old blue bike with two flat tires, rusty wheels, a rusty chain and spider webs in the spokes.

"You didn't lie. That baby is *really* dirty."

"I told you it was."

Joe stuck out his hand as he said, "Hi, I'm Joe, and you must be Dr. Don."

Dr. Don grabbed and shook Joe's hand. "Good to meet you, Joe. And I am Don, but just Don unless you need your spleen removed. Then I'm Dr. Don." Joe laughed, Don continued. "I see you've got a new name on the sign. When did this place become The Mission at Harbor and Divine?"

Joe chuckled. "Actually just a couple weeks ago. The Hispanic church moved out about two years ago and the Methodist district, who still owns the buildings, just sat on it until about a month ago when they finally decided to keep it open as an outreach mission for the community. The superintendent and the bishop appointed me here to be the pastor."

"A pastor with no flock, huh?" Don joked.

Joe laughed. "True. Not yet. But God will provide."

"Amen."

That was a couple of days ago, and both Sandy and Dr. Don had returned to help. Neither one was there at the moment, but earlier in the morning they had brought their own lawn chairs, cleaning supplies for Sandy, and Don's set of metric wrenches including three varieties of ten millimeter wrenches, which were the most used tools for a bicycler next to a folding Allen wrench cluster. Together Joe, Sandy and Don cleaned, disassembled, lubricated, de-rusted and shined those old bicycles into respectable, almost beautiful condition.

"You know, Sandy," Don said admiring their spruced up ancient bikes, "maybe we should buy these babies back and start riding again." Seeing Sandy's tight-lipped sympathy smile, Don quickly rethought his idea and said, "Although, we really haven't ridden at all since we moved back to the Near West Side." He sighed in defeat, "Darn broken hip."

Joe jumped in. "Do you really want to buy them back?" he asked like an over-eager used car salesman. They smiled and shrugged their shoulders. Joe continued, "Either way you help the mission. Donate them and I give them away to kids; buy them back, and you give me cash money to buy bike supplies. It's all good."

Sandy jumped in, "I think we should keep them donated, Don. It will be thrilling to see children riding them around the neighborhood."

"You're right, of course," admitted Don. "Though, I've got to tell you, after two years of recumbent bicycle rehab, I'm feeling a little frisky for a real bike ride."

"We can talk about it." End of conversation.

Joe turned to dip into his small stash of tires and inner tubes and spent Saturday morning finishing up the rehabs. He had them ticketed for the Montoyas, a neighborhood single parent family with mom Serena and her son and daughter who lived just around the corner on Divine Street across the street from the Korvers. Preteen kids, Carlos and Carlita would be getting the two bikes. Actually, although Joe had already given away several ready-to-go used bikes, these blue babies would be the very first of his personally restored bicycles given to neighborhood kids. So after months of planning The Mission at Harbor and Divine with District Superintendent Rev. Dr. DJ Scott, giving away these first fully restored bicycles was quite a milestone for the mission, especially since neighborhood residents not only donated the bikes but they also helped restore them as well. Joe let the happy retired couple know that the Montoya family would be coming at 2:00 that afternoon to pick up their *new* bikes.

"Would you both like to come to the presentation party?"

"You bet!" Dr. Don confirmed. "2:00 it is! See you later, Joe."

Later that morning DJ called Joe to let him know that he was bringing over a young lady, discovered by folks at the Cleveland Museum of Art, to interview to be a neighborhood outreach worker for the mission to teach art and faith to kids on the Near West Side.

"Great!" exclaimed Joe. "So, hey, as long as you're going to be here, how about coming to our bicycle presentation of the very first bikes totally refurbished by mission staff, namely me and volunteers, at 2:00 this afternoon?"

"That sounds awesome, Joe! I'll bet Angelina would love seeing that the mission is already changing lives. Wow! Plus I'll bring my very best camera phone to send pics to the <u>Plain Dealer</u> and <u>cleveland.com</u>. This will be great!"

Joe caught DJ's excitement, adding, "How 'bout I order a few Mamita's pizzas, Coke and napkins to cap off our first ever mission party?"

"Perfect, Joe! And you're going to love meeting Angelina."

"This is gonna be so cool!" cheered a grinning Joe. "See ya later, Boss." Pumped up from his phone call with DJ, Joe dived in to finish mounting the tubes and tires in less than an hour, just as Sandy and Don walked back from home oohing and aahing at the finished bikes.

"Those are beautiful, Joe," Sandy gushed.

"I'll second that," Don added. "Joe, you did a great job!"

"WE did a great job, Don. All three of us. Oh yeah! And get this, my district superintendent called to say he's coming to join us for the bike presentations, plus he's bringing with him a candidate to be our first community outreach worker for the mission. In fact, there they are right now. AND here come the Montoyas too! Fabulous!"

"Buen dia, Serena, Carlos, Carlita!

"Buen dia, Pastor Joe," they all said back.

Joe began introductions saving DJ and his guests for last. "And this is my boss, Rev. Dr. DJ Scott and his guests."

DJ took the lead. "With me today is Angelina Anderson and her mother Carmela. Angelina is applying to be our first community outreach worker."

Serena Montoya, still elated over the bicycles for Carlos and Carlita, was so over the moon to see that a Latina could be the first outreach worker for the Mission at Harbor and Divine, shouted out, "*Excelente! Maravillosa!*" jumping up and down like Angelina's own cheer leader. Everybody caught her festive spirit and cheered right along, sharing congratulations, greetings, hand shakes and hugs just as the Mamita's Pizza delivery car drove up. Joe paid for the food and set it down on the folding table he had been using, up until that very moment, as his bicycle shop workbench. It certainly was not the cleanest of tables, but a bicycle workbench as the lunch counter added authenticity to the celebration.

"Hang on, everybody! Food second! Bikes first! This is our first ever presentation of Harbor and Divine Mission rehabbed bicycles worked on right here in our outdoor workshop by Don, Sandy and myself for Carlos and Carlita Montoya!" Everyone clapped and cheered. Serena wept and said, "Thank you, thank you. You are so wonderful to my family."

Joe gave the bikes to Carlos and Carlita and said, "Go ahead, try them out!" And away they rode to even more cheers as Joe served the pizza and coke. The two kids, though, were back in such a hurry, Joe was stunned.

"Why are you back so soon? Something wrong with the bikes?"

"No! Nada. The bikes are wonderful, thank you very much!"

"So.... ? What's up?"

Carlos and Carlita confessed together with shy, slightly embarrassed grins, "We didn't want to miss out on the pizza!"

Everybody laughed, and a laughing Pastor Joe rushed over to the kids with their pizza and cups of coke. Everyone else chatted away as if they were one big, happy family or at least old friends. It was a perfect beginning for The Mission at Harbor and Divine as well as for Angelina who might soon begin her new job on the corner of Harbor and Divine.

As the party died down the Montoya family left for home with the kids riding their new bikes. Dr. Don and Sandy, though, hung around, seemingly waiting for something.

Joe was curious, so he walked over to ask them, "So, Don and Sandy, what do you think?"

"Oh," said Don smiling, "the presentation was perfect, the party was wonderful fun and the Mamita's pizza was delicious. Hooray for you, Joe." Don paused, Joe jumped in.

"Bu-u-u-u-t? Something on your mind, Doc?"

"Yes. Sandy is hoping to talk with you, Rev. DJ and Angelina for a minute or two, if you're willing."

"Not for long," Sandy added.

"Sure, let's walk over to see if they've got time. Is this a secret?"

"You'll see," Sandy answered smiling, but keeping her cards close to the vest.

As they walked up to Carmela, Angelina and DJ, Sandy cleared her throat and began her talk that no one in a thousand years would have ever expected.

"Excuse me. I'm Sandy Korver. My husband Donald and I moved just down Divine Street a few years ago, because, well, forty-five years ago I was a community outreach worker from this church, which back then was called the Wesley United Methodist Church. I worked with children and families, and I want to tell you, Angelina, how pleased I am that you will be picking up that mantel of serving children on the Near West Side."

Mouths dropped open, eyebrows raised up, because every-single person was amazed and stammered out words like,

"Whaaaat?" and

"You've got to be kidding!" and

"That's samaaaazing!"

"I never even knew this was a mission church way back then!"

Joe started clapping and cheering for Sandy, and in a flash, everyone else joined in.

As the joyous mayhem subsided, Angelina, in her sweet, soft voice asked, "Sandy, what did you do?" Others jumped in. "Yeah, tell us Sandy." "Sandy, Sandy, Sandy!"

" Okay. Okay. I'll tell you if you'll walk with me one block up Divine to West 45th Street. I'll show you something and tell you my story. Want to?"

"Absolutely! Of course!" cheered Angelina, Carmela, Joe, DJ and, of course, Dr. Don.

"Let's go!" DJ called out.

So off they went, and on the way they passed the Montoya kids riding their new bikes smiling and waving at Joe and the group following Sandy to watch her show off her surprise to everyone.

As they walked Sandy recalled for them the glory days of the West Side Ecumenical Ministries (WSEM), the United Methodist Cooperative Parish, the West Side Community House, St. Patrick's Catholic Church and all their work to help people in need, especially children and their families. Sandy continued to tell the backstory as they turned south onto West 45th Street, walked up two houses more and stopped directly in front of a large, mostly vacant lot. Not messy or overgrown, just empty except for remnant evidence like an archeological excavation of a past civilization.

"This was my big project," Sandy explained, "the Tot-a-Lot."

It was rather underwhelming for the others. "Oh." "Uh-huh." "Interesting." Undeterred, Sandy went on. "This was an overgrown, rock and varmint-infested vacant lot with plenty of suspicious-looking leafy plants, furry critters, needles, rubber gloves and a reputation for drug dealing, sex trafficking and general after-hours trouble making."

"Ooooh." "Yuck!" Everybody got the picture.

"Exactly. The neighbors complained constantly to their Cleveland City Council woman because of all the nasty, illegal activity and because the property was then, like now, city-owned. Eventually the council woman invited the Near West Side pastors and church leaders to meet with her and come up with a solution, which, miraculously they did. They agreed that the City of Cleveland should maintain ownership of the land, but they decided to turn the care, use and development of the property over to the pastors of the five Methodist churches, their congregations and their District Superintendent if they would promise to join with neighborhood residents and other churches to build together a children's playground on the site.

"That's when they hired me, telling me, 'Sandy, we want you to organize the neighbors to turn this drug-infested rats nest into a playground for families and little kids.' And that's exactly what we did. Tons of volunteers showed up on organized work-days with especially large crowds from the burbs on Saturdays to dig up the weeds (pun intended), rake up the broken beer bottles, latex gloves, used needles and other trash, rototill the rock hard ground and rake it level for walkways, play areas and picnic tables. Families with little kids, church folks, single people and old geezers like Donald and I are now, literally dug in so that in six weeks we had a ribbon-cutting. Even our Cleveland mayor at the time came in a bus with his entourage of cronies and reporters to celebrate what neighbors can do when we work together for the good of our neighborhoods. We ran daily programs for little kids, weekly family events and even field trips to Edgewater Park and the Natural History Museum.

"I like to think lives were changed, families strengthened and that I had a hand in making that happen. The church also hired a guy named James, actually a high school and church youth group friend of mine, to organize activities for teen and pre-teen guys including a wrestling camp in the church parlor (believe it or not) and bus trips geared for older boys. It was a great summer job for a college student like me and a just-married seminarian like him. Even Don came to help a few times before we got married.

"Angelina, you can make a difference in people's lives here, and have a blast doing it. I'm so proud of you, and I don't even know you yet, but it's a big, beautiful step in faith. Are you taking the job?"

"Honestly, I still wasn't sure when Mama and I got here that I even wanted it. But, Sandy, after the bike give-away, listening to your story about Tot-A-Lot and then witnessing first hand your over-the-top enthusiasm to make a difference in families' and children's lives, I'm sold — that is, if the church will hire me, which, now I hope they will, even though I have no clue how to do such a job. So, Sandy," Angelina said shyly, "if I get hired, will you mentor me along the way?"

Sandy's face lit up. "WILL I? I'd love to, Angelina, just love to. Working with you will give me a re-do of a job I loved forty-five years ago when I was your age. God is so good."

"All the time," Angelina chimed in.

"And all the time," Joe continued.

Everyone, even the Montoya kids, finished it up, "God is Good!" accompanied by cheers and "Amens."

"Sandy, one more thing, my mama and my friends call me Angel."

Joe spoke up, "Does that mean you'll take the job?"

"If you'll hire me, I will."

"What do you say, DJ?" Joe asked the man with the money.

"I'd say she's hired!" exclaimed the superintendent.

Hoorays, applause and "Atta girl's!" broke out with smiles all over the place.

Sandy raised her hand for quiet, looked at Angelina and her mama, and proclaimed, "You are our Angel of Hope, young lady."

More cheers, more "Amens."

Then DJ prayed them all home.

DJ left for his office in the Holy Oil Can, that church on University Circle that looks like an oil can. The Montoya family walked and rode new bikes home, but Joe, Angel, Carmela, Don and Sandy kept chatting.

A grateful Joe told everyone. "I'm just so glad DJ gave me a heads up about this yesterday. Angel and Carmela, it's been great to meet the two of you. And, Sandy, your story about the Tot-a-Lot was simply inspiring, especially standing together across the street from its archeological remains! What a great touch to your presentation. You are three awesome women! So how about we skip across the street and celebrate Angel's new job—actually two jobs, right?"

Angel's face lit up, "Right! This one and the Old Tony Studio. I am so excited, I can't keep the smile off my face!"

"So let's go celebrate with some Dari-Delight ice cream, my treat!"

"If you're buying, I'm eating!" cheered Dr. Don Everyone else agreed and across the street they skipped.

"Angel, with those two jobs you'll earn enough to live on. Do you think you'll move over here to the West Side?"

"Never know," she answered with a big smile. And off she went leading the skipping for ice cream.

After chatting, joking around and enjoying ice cream they all said their good-byes and see-ya-laters and went to their homes. Except Joe, who walked into the mission talking to himself.

"I've got to call DJ. Something fishy going on here." He punched in DJ's cell number.

"Hey, DJ here."

"DJ, Joe.

"Hey, Joe! Wasn't that great today?"

"It was. It's going to be great working with Angel. And her mom is kinda cool too. We all decided to have some Dari-Delite."

"Sounds great."

"Absolutely. Except one thing: what's this about dinner Tuesday night at Mel's with Gary and Annie but without me?" asked Joe.

"Hey, Joe, no offense, but it's a couples thing."

"Ohhh really? No offense, huh?"

"No, no. But how do you know about it?

"Oh, a little birdie told me. But, DJ, so now I have to have a date to eat with you guys?"

"No, only for this one. It's a couples counseling sort of thing."

"Oh, couples. Putting on the pressure, are we?"

"No, no, it's not like that."

"Yeah it is. It's exactly like that!"

"Huh." DJ conceded, "Yeah, I guess you're right."

"So what if I bring Carmela?"

"WHAT?"

Chapter 8

Carmela

Carmela was floored the next morning when Joe Whitehorse asked her to dinner with his friends, his very upscale white friends. He had called her after the bicycle give-away at the new mission where her daughter, Angelina, had just been hired as a community organizer. Well, they call it being an outreach worker. Whatever, she thought. It's still a good job, especially added on to Angel being chosen to be in that art museum studio with world famous artist Gary Siciliano, who actually grew up on the Near West Side. It was like God just opened up the floodgates of heaven and dumped blessings all over that girl. "Lawd have mercy," she said aloud at the very thought. And now *she*, Carmela Anderson, was actually going to have dinner with that famous artist and two white Methodist preachers. Not that she was awed by white preachers. Never. Her papa ran a mission for children, an orphanage, in Ciudad Juarez across the Rio Grande from El Paso. And over the years dozens of white American preachers came down with mission teams from their churches to work for free on whatever her father, Mateo, asked them to do. She remembered this one retired preacher — an old guy with white hair — worked on a roof during the day, then preached awesome sermons after dinner. Raffa, one of the older boys, translated for him. That preacher paused in all the right places, but still Raffa had to hustle like a chihuahua after a rat to keep up with the old guy. In fact, one time Raffa had to hold up his hand to stop the preacher because he was laughing so hard because it was so much fun. Then, when the preacher finished his teaching, hard to call something that much fun a *sermon*, he turned, bowed to Raffa and applauded him for his awesome job of translating and keeping up with him. He actually said that. "I'm amazed how well you kept up with me!" Truth is they made a wonderful team and, obviously, had a lot of fun doing it. Carmela was positively certain that the preacher must have had lots of experience with Mexican translators, because he and Raffa worked together so seamlessly as a team.

Plus, the Americanos always brought building contractors and lots of money to buy materials, pay the cooks, give tips, and buy their own food for the week for themselves and–get this– for the whole orphanage — kids and staff! No, Carmela was not awed by the preachers, but rather totally impressed with their character, their generosity and their servant hearts. Even when they had time off, they'd take their teams to her mama and papa's *buy-anything* store to spend hundreds of dollars on gifts and souvenirs to take back home to Ohio, all to support the orphanage and her family.

In addition, the fact that her new friends were Americans delighted her most because she too was an American, that is, with Mexican/Indian parents, but born across the river in the USA. Their family doctors were in El Paso near their El Paso second house, so when babies came, her parents would drive over the border and make sure their children were born in America, with American birth certificates and an El Paso address. Oh, yes, Carmela loved Americans and loved American preachers.

But after she graduated from college in the states and moved up to Ohio to attend the churches who supported the mission, she was surprised that not all Americans were as egalitarian as the ones on the mission teams who helped at the orphanage. In fact, some were more racist than the Anglo-Mexicans in Juarez. That surprised her. Disappointed her. The only young American men who would ask her out in college or on a date in Cleveland were brown skinned men, which delighted her since those guys found her honey-brown skin more beautiful to their eyes than the white guys did. Mostly white men steered clear of her, unless they wanted her as a prostitute, which turned her stomach so much that she actually spit in one man's face when he tried to hire her out like a horse to ride. She laughed to herself remembering how angry he had been. Good thing she was with a large group of friends, including several large, strong young men, or, and she was pretty sure of this, that guy would have raped her on the spot. Or tried to anyhow. She was pretty sure she could take care of herself.

She did, however, find a wonderful man to marry, an African American guy, Melvin Anderson, from E. 93rd Street. They moved to their honeymoon house on E. 51st Street, had a fabulous marriage, birthed a baby girl together, but then, after ten years, things just fell apart, all because of PTSD. Just before they were married Melvin served in the Marines in the early years of the war in Afghanistan. Unfortunately, after each one of his three tours of duty, he came home progressively more wounded in body and increasingly more scarred in his soul. That he had PTSD never bothered her, not the night terrors, not diving for cover at loud noises, not becoming terrified in the midst of loud crowds, not even when she had to hold him in her arms to calm him after he, for no apparent reason to her, just fell to his knees in uncontrollable sobs. But when Melvin told her gruesome accounts of women and children being mutilated and murdered by the Taliban, and then one time actually by two American Marines who were court-martialed, drummed out of the Marines, and sent to prison, she shook with anger.

"How could they do that?" she had screamed.

"I don't know," Melvin answered, "but I do know how war will twist and pervert a good young man's soul, derange his decision making and demonize his character. Those wounds of the spirit are deeper and linger long after wounds of the flesh have healed."

"But you, you didn't do any of those terrible things, did you?"

"I did terrible things, Carmela, but none to women or children. I promise you that. None."

But the wounds of his soul tormented him mercilessly.

He regularly woke up yelling and crying, eyes wide open, reliving those terrors as if they were happening at that very moment right before his eyes. "Get down, Carmela! Get down, girl!" he yelled at her one night. And then broke down in tears crying, "Oh, oh, little girl, I'm so sorry. I tried to tell you. I tried. I did. I did. Why didn't you listen to me and get down?" That night he held Carmela in his arms weeping over her. And she just let him, weeping along with him, praying for the healing of the soul of her wounded warrior.

More than a few times it was she who held him while he wept and she assured him of her love and loved him back to sleep. The VA had given Melvin lots of counseling and drugs for PTSD, but after ten years he became too ashamed to keep putting his wife and their daughter through his troubles. It's not that he ever physically or emotionally took it out on them in particular. He never got violent with Carmela. Never. He just.... he just felt like he wasn't man enough for her. Not good enough for her, even though she told him time and again, "Melvin, you are all the man I want; you are all the man I'll ever want or ever need." And then he'd cry some more. So she'd tell him again, "You are such a good, good man, Melvin Anderson. You're the only man I'll ever need. You!" And she'd kiss away his tears.

"No, no. I'm not good enough. I don't deserve you, Carmela. And you deserve so much more than a broken down, hollowed out wreck of a man, lucky to have a job that pays dirt worker wages. You deserve more, girl, so much more."

Then one day, he just left. Not for another woman. Oh no. Melvin would never do that. He left because he was ashamed.

"Can you imagine?" Carmela once asked a VA doctor. "Can you imagine a man, a Marine Corps sergeant for heaven sake, who offered his life for his country, can you imagine that man feeling ashamed? Such an honorable man. Such a good, good man." Then she asked, "Doctor, do you think the stress of having a baby girl to protect, to keep safe, triggered his increased worry, depression and flashbacks after all the little girls and women he saw abused and murdered?"

Her counselor sadly shrugged and said, "Maybe. But you just never know what trigger will set off a man with war-time PTSD."

She remembered the time his VA doc had upped his drugs to help him get past the worst of the night terrors, but Melvin's first doses of the higher-powered stuff turned him into a total zombie with slurred speech, a stumbling walk, dizziness and no mind to think. He hated himself even more then, and he told her so. Sure, the docs eventually adjusted his meds, but for Melvin it was just one more slide down an endless slope into darkness, one more proof that he wasn't good enough for Carmela. Or any woman. Huzzah? *Semper fi?* Ya, right. That's when he left. That's when Carmela and their little Angel cried for weeks, nearly non-stop. For months.

It took five more years for Carmela's heart to heal, maybe not heal, but at least to scab over. Five years of praying to God. Five years of loving the sadness out of Angel. Five years of hoping, praying, begging God for a miracle for her daughter, for herself and for her good, good husband. Then God answered. "And don't be telling me God don't answer no prayers," she'd say to anybody who would listen, especially her lady church friends at the Abyssinian Baptist Church "God answered, I'm telling you! God...is...GOOD. He answered my prayers."

"Oh, Lordy, did He ever!" she'd say adopting her friends colorful spiritual language.

Now for the first time in her life in America a white man—well, mostly white—has asked her out. And it's not that Carmela was dark skinned either. Her neighborhood friends on Cleveland's East Side called her a light-skinned woman. And when she and Melvin first moved into their home on East 51st Street and started attending church, the old church ladies would fuss over her and tell her, "You know, girl, you're so fair skinned that in the old days you coulda passed. Oh my, you coulda. You're a beautiful young lady. And that Melvin Anderson, he is a lucky man."

For ten years he was. But then Melvin left. And for the last ten years Carmela had grown to doubt and then resent any hopes she ever had no matter how the church ladies tried to encourage her. "When there seems to be no way," they'd tell her, "God will make a way!" And then she'd preach that to herself. That's how preachers said it. And, praise God, after ten years He did make a way. And not just *one* way, but many ways. And all at once it seemed. Blessings flowed like an avalanche of goodness. "Praise God!" she'd say aloud.

And then, then she continued to think not about Melvin but about Joe Whitehorse.

Joe Whitehorse was not just any ordinary white man. No, he was more like Melvin. Just as Melvin was a Marine, Joe Whitehorse was an Army warrior, willing to give his life for his country. Joe was a full-blooded Navajo warrior. Joe Whitehorse was a man of high character, a mission pastor who cared about poor people, children, hurting people of *any skin color*. That high character Joe Whitehorse took care of his dying wife until she went to Jesus. He cares about his run down community, like the American preachers who sacrificed money and time to help her father care for the orphans in Juarez. He's a man like her father and like those American preachers, with his life goal to bring hope to discouraged people, and to demonstrate the love of God by treating every single person as important, as someone whose life matters to him and to God. Carmela would never admit it, not yet anyhow, but she already admired Joe, respected him as a man, just like she did Melvin. And for Carmela, that was a big, big deal. For Carmela to respect a man is one short step away from love.

She realized that even the men Joe hangs with are cut from that same high character cloth, so for her, anticipating that dinner with Joe brought more excitement into Carmela's life than she had experienced since Melvin left. Melvin. She couldn't stop herself from comparing every man to Melvin, because, now, there was a good, good man, that Melvin. Strong. Caring. Fun loving. A fabulous lover. Hard worker. Willing to give his life for his country. And he did. Really he did. Yet he felt ashamed, because of the way war took his life — not to the grave, no, but to the darkest holes ever in his spirit. Carmela admired and respected Melvin for his service to his country and then even more so for the dark price he had to pay, the invisible price that no one else ever saw. Just Carmela and Angel — and his doctors.

And fie on those idiots who laughed at him when he dived for cover on E. 65th street that day a car backfired. Laugh they did, laughed out loud and pointed. Yes, they did. And Carmela rose up. Oh, rose up with fire, she did. She stood high on her toes and shouted, "How dare you laugh at my hero! He's five times the man you'll ever be, you sacks of shit!" And she fell to her knees on the concrete and wailed.

One of the men, feeling ashamed, walked toward her.

"You — you get away from me and my good, good man!"

"Ma'am, I am so sorry. He must be a good, good man for a fine woman like you to weep over him."

"You don't know nothing! Just get away!"

"Yes, ma'am." He turned to leave, then paused and turned back. With quiet respect he asked, "Afghanistan?"

Instantly Carmela stopped crying and turned for the first time to look at the man's face, into his moist brown eyes. "Yes. Afghanistan," she told him softly. "Three tours. Broke him."

"I was also there, ma'am, but only one tour. It's a hell hole for sure. When he comes out of it, please tell him thank you for me. And, ma'am, thank you too. He's a lucky man to have you."

She stood up. Her backbone straightened. "Marines. Sergeant."

"Then I will salute him." And he snapped to it, executed a classy salute, a drill perfect about face and then marched off When he got to his friend across the street, who fully understood what had just happened and had held his own salute until then, with the silent communication of comrades in arms, they both turned to face Melvin, clicked their heels, snapped off two more picture perfect salutes, stood at parade rest, as if Melvin had been inspecting them on parade, which, in fact, he had been, and they now waited to be dismissed.

Melvin hadn't missed a thing, but he missed his chance to dismiss them, to properly thank them with his own salute, and they walked away. Melvin, from the ground hurried to return a wounded soldier's salute, just at the very moment the first man turned back for one last look. He nudged his friend, and they both spun about face, returned Melvin's salute and nodded their respect. Then they walked away hoping they had tempered Melvin's shame with respect and honor.

They had.

Carmela treasured that memory. Still, it was not nearly enough to heal the great big holes in her heart from Melvin's leaving.

But Joe's dinner invitation bloomed the very first flower of promise, of hope for healing, Carmela had felt since that day Melvin left. Then when she added Joe and Dr. DJ hiring Angel in their mission, plus their artist friend, Gary, inviting Angel into his art museum studio, she couldn't help but think a miracle was happening. Pure and simple. Put that all together and surely the heavens had opened wide for her as well as for Angel with the love of Jesus to pour down blessing upon blessing.

That's why these days now every morning she woke up expecting a blessing, thanks to Joe and his friends. Thanks to God.

If those three men could bless the lives of other people on the Near West Side like they'd already blessed her's and Angel's, then, God willing, she would be a witness. Like when Joe gave away those bicycles to the Montoya kids. She would love to be a witness to see and tell how God is working through those men to bless Cleveland's Near West Side. Like the preachers call out, "Can I have a witness? Will somebody stand up and be a witness today for the love of Jesus?" Yes, Carmela had the spirit to stand right up and shout at the top of her voice, "I'll be a witness. I'll stand and shout how I see God at work!" And yes, she thought in her heart, 'I want to join God in that work on the corner of Harbor and Divine. Yes, even if it means moving to the West Side, Lord have mercy.'

So much to be thankful for.

So much, so much.

Now, Carmela was not a crier. Not by a long shot. She'd seen too much tragedy and sadness in her life for her to cry much about anything any more, like the beautiful little children dropped off by their parents at the orphanage in Juarez. Often the parents were strung out on drugs and just did not want to be bothered by their *guaguas,* the insulting Latino/Indian word for unwanted children which more literally meant "stinking brats." But they weren't stinking brats, they were beautiful golden-brown-skinned angels, who looked just like Carmela, every single one a gift from God. So much sadness she had seen even as a little girl.

So much tragedy. Like when her uncle Marcos was gunned down in Juarez right in front of his house, only two blocks away from the orphanage in broad daylight. Right in front of his house! *Muy barbaridad!* Drug thugs in her homeland of Mexico. *Carumba!* Even in America. So much tragedy had dried up her tears. She had no more left. Only anger. Anger at drugs. Anger at war. Anger at racism. Anger at hatred. Anger at poverty in a land of plenty. Anger that the only gifts her Melvin carried with him from his courage and selfless acts as a Marine were shame, fear, darkness and sadness that robbed him of his upright character and his manly courage.

But these days, these days? These days as she thought of all the ways her life was changing, hers and Angel's, her old anger was giving way to a flood of hope in her heart. At times, hope overwhelmed her so much that she could no longer keep at bay the waters of joy and thanksgiving she found cascading down her cheeks.

"Thank you, thank you, thank you," she said to herself, then scolded herself as she dabbed away the strange but not unwelcome tears of happiness, "You silly woman."

That's when her phone rang. It was Joe. She gasped, then whined, "Oh my goodness, I just knew it. He's going to back out of that dinner with me." She immediately got herself worked up into a poison ivy attitude, and answered the phone with the poison in full bloom. "Hello. This is Carmela. What's up?"

"Hi, Carmela. This is Joe. You okay?"

"Not if you called to back out on our dinner date with your friends."

"No way! Never. What ever gave you that idea?" Silence. "Carmela?"

Dismayed at how quickly old anger could retake possession of her heart, she could only squeeze out, "Nothin'." "Except," she confessed, "I'm still amazed you asked me out in the first place."

"Well, prepare to be amazed again, girl."

'Whoa,' Carmela gasped to herself still saying nothing to Joe. 'Melvin calls me that — girl.'

"Do you suppose you and Angel might meet me at the art museum in about an hour so you two can tell me about what Angel will be doing there with Gary and his Old Tony Studio? We could eat lunch together at the cafeteria. My treat. What do you think?"

"I think I'm a fool." More tears; she hated that. "And I think you're amazing." Angel got her attention. "Hold on, Joe. Angel's talking at me." She answered Angel so Joe could hear her. "It's Joe, and he wants to treat us out for lunch at the art museum and hopes you and I, mostly you, will give him a tour of what you'll be doing in that studio you're in."

Joe heard Angel's "I'd love to, Mama."

"Did you hear that?"

Joe chuckled. "I sure did. See you in an hour then, at the welcome desk? Okay?"

"Yes. That will be just fine, Joe Whitehorse. Just fine."

She ended the call,
wept more tears of hope and joy,
glad that nobody could see her
crying like a baby.

Chapter 9

Joe Whitehorse

When Joe was growing up in Columbus, Ohio, his friends most often called him by his last name. "Hey, Whitehorse, want to ride bikes to the Scioto and jump in?" He didn't mind. He was proud of his first people's heritage and liked his distinctive name, Whitehorse. Born to native American parents in the small New Mexican town of Truth or Consequences just south of the Four Corners area of the Navajo nation, he learned a great deal about Dine` (Navajo) culture including lots of stories about the legendary, and even divine, White Horse, the *Caballo Blanco*. In fact, they actually lived in the town of Truth or Consequences which was on the shore of the Caballo Reservoir. They were so poor that in a few short months they had to move up to Farmington near his father's family who could help them make ends meet.

Unfortunately their being there was too much for his grandparents meager income, so his father, Eddie, got a job as a groundskeeper in Columbus at the Ohio State University. That's where every single one of his friends called him Whitehorse, not Joe, which pleased him to no end.

"Heck," he told himself one day when he came home from church near his home in Columbus, "there's even a White Horse in the Book of Revelation that the Savior will ride in the last days! Imagine that: a Whitehorse in the Bible!"

Similarly, he found out from his Asian-Indian friends, there's a White Horse ridden by Kahli, the tenth and final incarnation of Vishnu, when he will come to save the world. But a more historical character was the Kiowa Chief named Tsen-tainte–White Horse. Renowned for his daring and strength as a warrior, Chief Tsen-tainte fought victorious battles in the late 1800's, stories of which his admirers told around campfires for generations.

And lastly Joe's father, Eddie, told him stories of Caballo Blanco the legendary White Horse of the Tarahumara Indians of the Copper Canyon in Chihuahua, Mexico. The people of that Indian nation were renowned for their tireless long distance running chasing down deer until the deer drop from exhaustion. Included in the tales of Caballo Blanco is a twentieth century incarnation of the Anglo long distance runner, Micah True. To run along side the famous Tarahumara Indian runners in the rugged terrain of Copper Canyon was a high privilege for an Anglo runner. But the Tarahumara welcomed him, shared their wisdom with him, their skill at crafting running sandals as well as the nutrition of their simple food, which Micah True discovered was better for his running than anything he had ever eaten up until then. They even dubbed him, knighted him, *Caballo Blanco*, the "White Horse" of the legend, because, as the stories of near legendary status go, this anglo *Caballo Blanco* would seemingly miraculously appear to help struggling, injured runners unable to safely navigate the rocks and crevasses of the steep canyon walls. Then once he had helped them, *Caballo Blanco* would just as mysteriously disappear into the Copper Canyon rocks, feeding the legend.

Of course, there are also the ever-popular stories of white horse- like unicorns of Greek Mythology and the legendary Lone Ranger, lone survivor of ambushed Texas Rangers. He was mysteriously masked, riding his white horse Silver with his Indian companion, guide and friend, Tonto, saving people in distress and giving out silver bullets as mementos of their valor.

Every story, every legend, every spiritual prophecy Joe learned built inner pride and gratitude that his last name was Whitehorse, as was Eddie's, his father, before him. It was in learning about his Whitehorse heritage that Joe's father told him he had some Anglo blood in him too, that made him look more white. Eddie never explained it any more than that. Joe never asked. Not once. Who cares?

He was a Whitehorse!

Chapter 10

Eddie Whitehorse

Eddie Whitehorse, Joe's father, moved his family from the Four Corners to Columbus to accept a job on Ohio State University's outdoor maintenance crew, a better job with more pay than a Navajo man would ever have gotten in the Navajo Nation. But what a wonderful surprise for Eddie when they moved to the Short North neighborhood of Columbus and actually found a Navajo 'chapter' meeting to attend, which excited Eddie and all his family. In fact, the first time Eddie attended a meeting, he took his whole family to introduce them, and when he did, when he said, "My name is Eddie Whitehorse," the elders of the chapter oooed and ahhed and even applauded.

"Oooo. Whitehorse!" they cooed. Then gray haired Everett Kinlachee, who became Eddie's mentor and best friend in Columbus, rose to speak. "That's a fine name," he told Eddie and his family, including young Joe. "It speaks of courage and daring and mystery in your family. *Tsen-tainte. Caballo Blanco.* The White Horse. Yes. A very fine name. We are very pleased to meet you Mr. Whitehorse. You and your family are welcome here." And true to their word, the Columbus Navajo Chapter members drew in Eddie and his family with such love and warmth that the members of the chapter became like relatives, their extended family and their best, most trusted friends. But that's how it is when you are Dine`, "The People," as they call themselves. All generations, all one family, the living, the dead and the yet-to-be-born, all helping one another.

Quickly, though, away from their Dine` roots and their Four Corners Navajo chapter in Farmington, New Mexico, the Whitehorse family became far more Anglo than Navajo. Assimilation was always Eddie's goal for his family, and that's why he moved them away from the Four Corners, out of the Navajo Nation. The more Anglo they became, he believed, the more opportunities would open up for all of them in this Anglo world. And that's exactly how it worked. Within two years Eddie was promoted to be a crew chief over 25 employees who cared for the walks, landscaping and lawns surrounding the Ohio Union, Mershon Auditorium, the Wexner Center for the Arts, three classroom buildings and about two and a half miles of walkways bounded by College Road, West 12th Avenue, West 17th Avenue and the highly visible Ohio State University main entrances on North High Street. It was a huge, prestigious grounds position supervising a diverse crew of men, some of whom were first generation Americans whose families hailed from far off Ethiopia, Nepal, Iran, Pakistan and, yes, West Virginia. A few were Ohio State students of third and fourth generation American families. Eddie respected them all like beloved brothers, his new family, and they loved him in return.

"Imagine," Eddie told his wife one day after work, "a poor Navajo boy becomes the boss man." She was proud. First of all it meant people at Ohio State respected Eddie and his work. Out west, in the Four Corners, Anglo employers seldom granted that level of respect to Native American men, but instead often debased proud, hard working men as wretched, inadequate and incapable of good work. That's why Eddie was all the more surprised and proud that people in his new home-land respected him, honored his work and trusted his ability to lead other men, even Anglos. Plus Ohio State paid him well, very well, more money to take care of his family than he ever dreamed a poor barefoot Navajo boy could possibly make. Ever. When Eddie told his friends at the chapter meeting of his promotion they all cheered—sincerely cheered. In fact, they even stood up, danced Navajo style and chanted like the Dine`, they were. That day Eddie Whitehorse could not have been prouder of his Navajo heritage, nor more pleased with his new home in Ohio.

His heart sang.

"Eddie," his best friend Everett Kinlachee said, "you make us all proud. All of our ancestors are dancing in the Great Beyond to celebrate the honor and respect you, a Dine` man, have been granted. Eddie Whitehorse, your honor is our honor and we celebrate with you."

"Thank you, Everett," Eddie humbly responded. Then, over-whelmed by his friends' accolades, he bowed to each of them one at a time, saying "Thank you, my brother," or "Thank you my father," to each man in his Columbus family.

When Eddie got home that night and joyously told his family how the men at the Chapter had honored him, young Joe chimed in "I'm proud of you too, papi. You're the best father ever, and I'm glad I'm your son." In a flash Eddie embraced his son with such passion and ferocity that, Joe remembered, it took his breath away. But he loved it, and he still loves and cherishes that moment as his best memory of growing up with his father, Eddie Whitehorse.

Like father, like son.

Chapter 11

Lunch in Paris

L unch in the three-story, half acre art museum atrium was always a big deal for Joe, because it felt like he imagined it would be to lunch at a sidewalk cafe in Paris—Paris, Cleveland. He even wore relaxed church clothes instead of his bicycle repair outfit for the occasion. Whistling his way out to his car, he hopped in as happy as a clam, turned on sports talk radio AM 850 and smiled all the way to the art museum parking garage. Thanks to his friend Gary Siciliano's gift, Joe was now, once again, a member in good standing of the art museum, which included free parking. He'd had that privilege once before, when Val was still alive, but not in the last ten years. So this first time back felt pretty good, mainly because now he had a new reason to be there which helped fend off any sadness of not having Val with him.

"Hmmm. Interesting," he mused talking quietly to himself. "I feel like I've won some sort of victory, a second chance. Hmm. Since? Since Val? Since being a drunk? Since the Afghan war? Who knows. But whatever, it sure feels good to be here." So he smiled more broadly, parked, hopped out of his car, walked toward the main level doors, got his parking ticket and headed in to meet Carmela and Angel at the welcome desk, still happy as a lark.

The ladies saw Joe before he saw them. They waved. "Hi, Joe!" "Hey, you made it!," they said with smiles that matched his.

"Hi, Carmela! Hi, Angel! Great to see you both!"

They exchanged 'welcome hugs' and headed toward the atrium. Joe was learning that Carmela and Angel hugged hello all the time, cheek-to-cheek hugs not meant to be provocative, but when Carmela went cheek to cheek hello with him, Joe got all weak in the knees and fuzzy-happy elsewhere. He knew he had to get used to it, but he really didn't want to *get used to it.* He liked the thrill of her cheek on his, and hoped the thrill always would be part of their embrace. Besides, she smelled great. They walked past the main museum gift shop into the huge expanse of the indoor atrium and stopped, just stopped. Even though all three of them had walked through the atrium many times before, they still marveled at its beauty and its size, the largest unseated public indoor gathering place of its kind in Cleveland.

Angel broke the silent reverie. "I love it here," she marveled. "It's an urban oasis, like Eden in the middle of the purgatory of city life. Like Paris. It even smells good, refreshing, welcoming, beautiful and I just love being here. How blessed I feel to actually have a job right here. Praise God."

Joe agreed, "Praise God indeed. I especially love how they built it around that old Greek revival limestone exterior rear wall of the original 1930's museum. They left the windows, columns, cornices and doors all in place for future generations of art lovers to enjoy, but cleaned it all up to look like a brand new old building."

"Plus," Carmela added, "trees, gardens, a fountain, 'outdoor' displays all indoors. My pulse always slows down in the peace that fills this place. Like a cathedral. Wouldn't it be cool to have thousands of people in here for worship?"

"Amen," both Angel and Joe agreed. He loved how outwardly spiritual Angel and Carmela were, and that they drew him into their every-day-for-the-world-to-see love of God. As a newly minted pastor, Joe knew that through them God was filling in a hole in Joe's spirit that really needed to be filled if he was ever going to be a good, effective mission pastor on the Near West Side.

"Well, shall we eat?" Joe suggested. "I'm getting hungry."

"Me too," Angel and Carmela agreed, and off they walked to the cafeteria. "I called Dr. Zurkos," Angel added, "just to let her know we'd be taking a tour. She was thrilled and offered to call Gary Siciliano so the two of them could be available for us if we wanted their expertise."

"Awesome," said Joe. "I love them both. Angel, do you suppose they would like to join us for lunch?"

"That's a great idea, Joe; I wish I had thought of that."

"Well, maybe it's not too late. How about if I call Mel and at least extend the invitation?" offered Joe, who almost always called Dr. Melanie Zurkos by her shortened first name, Mel.

Carmela balked. "How about we just keep it the three of us for lunch, and if we bump into them along the way it would be an added bonus. Would that be okay with you, Joe? Angel?"

Realizing Carmela meant what she had said more as a statement than a question, Joe gladly retreated, "Oh, sure. I'm sorry. You're right, it should be just the three of us today."

Angel agreed, and a relieved Carmela quietly said, "Thank you."

With that settled pleasantly, they moved on to lunch.

Even the name, *The Provenance Cafe,* sounded like a sidewalk cafe in Paris. The setting was elegant, yet informal enough that even jeans and flannels would be appropriate. The hot main dish offerings changed every day ranging from baked cod under steamed squash with garlic and onions to Tandoor international cuisine. In addition they had a daily lunch menu that included pizza, burgers, salads, fries and even gefilte fish and bagels. Eating there was always fun and delicious. The three diners joyfully hopped from one food station to the next collecting their favorites, and Joe picked up the tab like he had promised.

Conversation was limited to "Yum! " "This is delicious!" "Oh, my gosh, I had no idea this was so good!" And then gentle conversation began until it was time to get desserts and start the raves all over again. When everyone was wonderfully satisfied, Angel asked, "Ready for the tour?"

"I might have to get a wheel chair," Carmela joked. "Would you push around your fat, old Mama, Angelina?"

"Oh, hush! You're no fatter than I am!"

"Well, thank you! I'll take that as a compliment any day!"

They pushed back their chairs, stood up slowly, smiled and all three said simultaneously, "That was delicious!" and laughed.

Carmela and Angel added, "Thank you, Joe."

"My pleasure. Angel, you've got the lead."

And off they went.

As they strolled back through the atrium Joe surprised himself by how proud he felt to walk with Carmela and Angel. Had he and Val been able to birth a baby girl he supposed she would have been around Angel's age. And just as beautiful. He smiled at the thought and shook his head.

Carmela saw the smile and asked, "As my grandmama used to say, 'A penny for your thoughts.' What's the smile about?"

"Oh, I was just enjoying the moment."

"Yes, it is beautiful in here."

"True. But actually I was enjoying being here with you and Angel. I found myself feeling proud to walk with you."

"Oh?"

"Because of her cancer, Val and I never had children. If we had birthed a daughter, I was wondering if she would have grown up to be as beautiful as Angel—or as talented. You know, Carmela, God blessed you and Melvin with a beautiful little girl. Yes, He did."

Tears surprised Carmela once again. This man said the darnedest things. "What a sweet thing to say," she told him through her tears.

"Ya, but it made you cry. I'm sorry."

"Don't be sorry. It's just, I thought I was over him—Melvin—after all these years, but I wish he would have stayed with me to watch Angelina grow up. Joe, you get to see her, and encourage her and watch her succeed, but he just walked away. Just walked away. And you...." She stammered, then got it out. "Oh, Joe, I am so glad you're here. You fill the gap in our lives Melvin left empty. You're a good, good man Joe Whitehorse. And you bless us the way a good, good man ought to bless his family." Then Carmela just stopped, tears falling to the sounds of silence. She just couldn't say what she was thinking. Even what she had said was already too much.

Joe said it for her, "But you still love Melvin."

Carmela hesitated, focused her teary eyes upon Joe's good, good face and smiled at him. Not a happy smile, but a grateful smile. It was an I'm-so-sorry smile that came with a furrowed brow and squinty eyes full of confusion. She shook her head "no," but she said, "Yes," with tight lips that fought against the smile.

"Yes, I do still love Melvin. I know that God has put you in my life, but, Joe, I just can't take a step toward you until I know for sure, until I say good-bye to Melvin in my heart and with my lips." She struggled for breath to say more. "Does that make sense to you?"

"Yes, it does. But can I still hang around as your "maybe-guy?"

"Maybe-guy? What a funny thing to say."

"First off, yeah, I get it. It does make sense. For one thing, Melvin's still alive. Not like Val. Val and I got to say good-bye to each other and hug and kiss and cry. And when she died, she was just gone, and I had no choice but to learn to live without her. But Melvin? Melvin's still around. Right?"

"Right. Around. Somewhere. Who knows where."

Joe went on, "No good-byes either way. No farewell kisses. Right?"

Carmela couldn't answer. She just nodded.

"So listen up, he didn't say good-bye to you either. Maybe he still loves you like you still love him. Isn't that possible?"

Another nod and more tears.

"Carmela, what if you're both still desperately in love with each other, and you both want to get back together?"

She shrugged and squeezed out a tearful, "I don't know."

"Well, beautiful lady, I think you really need to find out. Somehow, after all these years, you have just got to find and talk with Melvin and put this thing to rest one way or the other. Maybe you'll fall back in love with each other. Then again, maybe you'll both say good-bye in your hearts and with your lips. Maybe when that day comes, when you say good-bye with your heart and with your lips, maybe, maybe that's where I come in as your 'maybe-guy.' Until you decide about you and Melvin that's really all I can be. If you do get back with Melvin, fine, I guess, for you and him. Although, I admit, not so fine for me. But if you don't, if you don't get back together, then I could turn from being your maybe-guy into your for-sure-guy."

Carmela, set free by Joe's loving common sense, to the astonishment of both Joe and Angel, suddenly threw her arms around Joe, kissed him lightly on his cheek. Then she said, "You know, Joe, for a maybe-guy you say the most wonderful for-sure words a woman would ever want to hear."

"So, it's a deal? I'll be your maybe-guy until you become sure?"

"Deal."

"Just one more thing."

"Uh-oh. What?"

"Would you give me permission to find Melvin for you, tell him that you still love him and bring him back to you for a long overdue reunion or a much needed farewell. Will you let me do that for you? I promise I will be as fair with him as I am with you. Good, honest, straight talk. No B.S."

Carmela couldn't believe her ears. After all these years this man in front of her would fulfill her years of dreams of finding Melvin. "Joe, I can't believe you would do that for me."

"Hey, you couldn't believe I would take you to dinner."

Carmela laughed out loud and punched Joe hard in the arm.

"Ouch! That hurt. You're strong." Then he paused, took a deep breath, looked Carmela straight in the eyes and asked, "But are you strong enough to go through with this, to learn the truth? Because, I want you to know, I *will* find him for you."

"You mean am I strong enough to hear the truth about whether or not he still loves me?" Carmela asked.

Joe nodded yes.

"Absolutely. I want to know if we still love each other enough to get back together. And certainly I'll be strong enough to hear the answer either way. Joe," Carmela continued, "either way I will be a blessed woman."

"Good. That's settled. But one more last thing," Joe teased.

Carmela cocked her head and put on that tough-girl smirky smile she could make. "What now?"

"Will you still go to dinner with me?"

Carmela burst into peals of laughter. "Of course you goofy maybe- guy. I've been waiting my whole life to go out to dinner with a white man who really cares about me, don't you know."

Joe chuckled quietly remembering his Navajo parents. "Good. But I have to tell you, I have totally forgotten that we're different that way. All I know is how beautiful you are, and the shades of your skin are wonderful parts of the package. Besides, I'm not exactly 100% white, what with my Navajo parents."

That earned him a huge smile and another kiss on the cheek. "Thank you. You're such a good, good man, Joe Whitehorse." And more tears. Carmela could never again say she's not a crier. "A good, good man," she said again, because of how very much she meant it.

And Joe? He felt pretty darn good, good himself.

Remembering why they were in the art museum in the first place, Joe took a deep breath and asked Angel, "Angel, ready for that tour?"

Angel had been waiting patiently fascinated by the little drama that had unfolded before her eyes between her mother and Joe. She wanted to talk with them about it, feeling a little guilty that she had eavesdropped on their very intimate conversation. Yet she knew, as the days would pass, they would have time enough to talk. So she stayed focused on her tour.

"Yes, I'm ready. What about the two of you? Are you ready?"

"Ready," they answered together smiling at each other.

And off they went.

Chapter 12

Joe's Hunt

The next day Joe called DJ and Gary to tell them what he was up to as well as to ask DJ for time off from the mission. *And* would they please postpone their dinner. Like the good friends they were — good, *good* friends — they both encouraged him. DJ gave him all the days off he needed. They would also change their dinner once more and help him in any way they could. Huzzah! With work and dinner off his plate, Joe began his hunt for Melvin.

When Joe told Carmela about his plan to find Melvin a few hours ago, he sounded a whole lot more confident than how he really felt now. First off, this guy is a former U.S. Marine Corps Sergeant trained to kill people. But that fear sounded just silly the instant Joe thought about it. Surprisingly he was actually looking forward to meeting Melvin. "After all, Carmela says he's a good, good man. That's solid enough for me," he said aloud to himself.

Secondly, Joe thought Melvin could be anywhere in the world, like that old "Where's Waldo?" game. After all, as a United States Marine Melvin did literally travel around the world. But that worry also held no water. Joe kept on talking it through out loud:

"Naw, he's still here. His VA is here. His doctors are here. His friends are here. And Carmela is here. Plus Angel. Hmmm. Angel! Bingo. She's my wild card. Of course Melvin kept track of Angel. She's got to be numero uno in my hunt!" Joe remembered how Carmela had often said she had absolutely no idea where Melvin went after he walked out of their lives. But Angel?

"Angel never said a word. Huh."

Over ten years Melvin had to have contacted her at least a few times — maybe way more than a few.

He picked up his phone and called the art museum. At lunch yesterday she said she'd be starting her work with Gary in the Old Tony Studio today and gave Joe and Carmela her work phone number and extension. She also said she was looking forward to getting a jump start over all the other studio artists who were older and more experienced than she was, but weren't scheduled to arrive in Cleveland for another two weeks. Ring, ring. Joe had a little case of the nerves. Or was it excitement? The thrill of the hunt. A problem to solve. A way to help Carmela and not lose her to her own self doubt while still loving a man who had walked out of her life ten years ago. Ten years. That's a really long time to keep a flame burning. The phone clicked.

"Hello, Old Tony Studio, this is Angelina Anderson."

"Hi, Angel. This is Joe Whitehorse."

"Oh, hi, Joe. That was so much fun yesterday. Well, maybe not the discussion you and my mama were having. But everything else."

"You heard I'll be looking for your father?"

"Well, yes. It was kind of hard not to. But on another topic, tell me how did you like the set up for the Old Tony Studio? Isn't it cool?"

"Absolutely! It's wonderful. I have a great deal of respect for Gary Siciliano, and I think the two of you will get along famously."

"I think so too. We already are, in fact, with this being my first day. But there is so much to learn. I'm excited, and Mr. Siciliano is as well. We're already sketching Old Tony with charcoal on paper."

"Fantastic," Joe cheered. "Tell Gary, 'Hey!' for me."

"Sure!" She covered the phone with her hand and fake yelled out, "Hey, Gary, Joe says 'Hey!'"

"Tell him 'Hey!' back," fake-yelled Gary who was in truth sitting on a stool three feet from Angel.

"Gary says, 'Hey!'"

"Thanks. He's sitting right there, isn't he?" Joe chuckled.

"Yep," she answered with a giggle. "We're still sketching."

"Well, could you excuse yourself for a few, because I've got something else I want to talk with you about that you might not want Gary in on just yet."

"Sure. Gary, I'll be back in a few."

"Not too long. We've got to keep the artistic fire going!"

Angel smiled in appreciation of Gary's one-track mind and walked out to another studio.

"Thanks, Angel. Your new studio is only part of the reason I called."

"I figured."

"Yeah. You probably already figured that the other part is what you evidently don't want to talk about." Joe took a beat, but Angel said nothing to fill the silence. "Angel, Carmela has told me many times that she has no idea where Melvin went

75

after he walked out on the two of you. But you, even though you were with us during several of those conversations, like yesterday, you never said a thing. And I never thought to ask, until now, that is." He gave her another few beats to gather herself to answer the question she surely knew Joe would ask. "Angel, have you talked with your father or seen your father at all over the last ten years?"

Silence. Joe pretty much knew what Angel's silence meant, but he waited for her to answer the question.

Finally she did. "Yes." That was it. Just 'Yes.'

"How many times? Once or twice?"

"Look, Joe, I've got work to do right now, and this will be a long conversation. Want to meet me at the mission at, say 3:30?"

"Sounds perfect, Angel. See you at the mission at 3:30. Bye."

"Bye." She ended the call, cradled the phone and sighed. "Oh, brother. Here we go."

She shook her head as her eyes teared up knowing that things were now about to get dicey with her mother, who did not have a clue about the many times Angel and her father had talked or met together. Not a clue. Melvin even had a great old man disguise he wore to her away track meets in case Carmela would happen to attend the same meet, though usually she went to the home meets and he the away meets. One time, before he had the disguise, they both attended the same away meet in Shaker Heights. He saw her and turned right around and went home. No need to take chances.

Whatever. Angel still needed to call them both, her father first just for a heads up that Joe would be calling and that her mama would soon know all the times Angel and her father had contact. Nothing he or she could do about it, except to know she wasn't going to lie to either her mama or to him or to Joe.

She got the okay from Gary to tend to family business. Gary knew better than to pry, so he said nothing except "Sure," and moved over to his own work space to get back to mapping out his Laughing Old Tony.

Angel left the studio, walked out to the museum parking garage, got into her car, drove out of the parking garage and started to drive home but stopped. Realizing how emotional she was, Angel pulled into the Natural History Museum parking lot across the circle from the art museum. She found a parking place right next to an armored dinosaur of some sort. The green space around the Natural History Museum was filled with dinosaurs of all sizes. It was a good, private place to talk on the phone with her father, distressed as she was, before she called Joe back. Already fighting back tears, she dialed Melvin's number and he answered.

"Hello? Angel? Is that you?"

She choked out the words. "Yes, Papa, it's me."

"Whoa, Angelina, you all right?"

"No," she answered and cried all the more.

"Oh, little Angel, what's wrong?"

"Mama's friend, that nice man I told you about, thinks you and Mama still love each other and he promised her he would find you to ask you to talk with her about whether you do or you don't love each other. He thinks you two should get back together, or at least talk about it."

"So are you saying he has feelings for your mother?" Melvin asked reading between the lines.

"Yes."

"And she has feelings for him?"

"Yes."

"Is he a good man?"

"Yes. Mama even calls him a 'good, good man like you.'"

"She said that? You really heard her say, 'a good, good man like me?'"

"Yes, I did. I heard her say that a couple of times already. But she already told him that she still loves you and wants you back."

"Really now. So let me get this straight. This good, good man like me who has feelings for your mother, he wants to get us back together? Carmela and me? Have I got that right?"

"Yes."

"My, oh my. It does sound like something I'd do. He really does want us to get together?" Melvin asked almost giddy.

"Yes, he *really* does, Papa. You laughing? Papa, I work with him at the mission on the Near West Side, and he is an upright man. He said he'd back off and be her 'maybe-guy' until you and Mama figure things out."

"For real, now. And you think she wants me back?"

"Yes, Papa, I do. She really wants *you*."

"Huh. I'll be. I always thought she was just blowing smoke when she said that."

"I know you did. But she's telling this man 'no,' because she wants you. She wants Melvin Anderson, Papa. You."

Melvin said nothing for a short minute. "What do you think I should do, Angel?"

"I think you should let yourself be found and go talk with her."

"And get back together?"

"That's between the two of you. I love you both and I'll keep loving you no matter what you decide together." Angel settled her sobs and then said, "But Papa? After ten years she still holds a love for you in her heart. She wants you in her life again." More sniffles.

"Don't cry, little Angel. I never could tell you no. Your mother neither, for that matter. That's why I just had to walk away. I knew I wasn't any good for her, but if we talked about it back then, I knew I'd cave in again."

"Oh, papa, we both love you."

"Well then, maybe it's time. Past time probably. Who knows? I guess I better talk to this good, good man who's like me. You gonna tell him where I live?"

"I'd like to, if you say it's okay."

"You go ahead and tell him, little girl. And, Angel?"

"Papa?"

"You're a good, good girl, and I'm proud of you."

"Thank you, Papa. I'm proud of you too. Always have been."

"I'm glad. Bye-bye, Angel."

"Bye-bye, Papa."

On a roll, now, Angel stayed in the parking lot still next to the smallish armored dinosaur. She actually started talking to the dinosaur through the car window. "Stoney," she said calling the dinosaur by what she figured had to be his given name, "do you think I'm doing the right thing here?" Either it was Stoney or the Lord God, but she felt she got her answer. So she dried her eyes and called her mother, who answered on the first ring.

"Hello. Angel, that you?"

"Yes, it is. 'Are you my mother?'" she asked with loving mischief in her voice.

Carmela laughed. "Now don't you be pulling out your old Dr. Seuss kiddie quotes. I remember them all. Every single one. 'Stars on thars.' 'An elephant's faithful, boiiing, 100 per cent!' What do you think, girl. I probably loved those books more than you did. And to this day, I bet I remember more kiddie book quotes–especially Dr. Seuss–than you will ever know."

"Now don't you be bragging, Mama. You know how bragging leads to a fall."

"Pshah, girl! What we need is a good, old-fashioned, Kiddie Book Smackdown! That's what we need."

"You're on. The five-year-old in me will take you down so fast you'll think you was just whooped by the Black Knight himself."

"Are you trash-talkin' your mama, girl?" Both of them relished a little ghetto talk fun.

"You better believe it, woman! You taught me how."

Carmela burst out laughing so hard she had to pull the phone away and concede that Angel had won that round. No contest. "True that, girlie-girl! So tell me, now that you've got me all happy, what did you really call me about?"

"Joe Whitehorse called me today."

"He did, did he? What did Joe Whitehorse want?"

"Well, I was at the studio, so I couldn't talk with him much on the phone. Instead we decided to meet at the mission. But he did ask me straight up if I had talked with papa or seen him in the last ten years."

"Yes? And what did you say? Because I don't really know the *whole* answer."

"Well, you know he went to my track meets, right?"

"Yes, I saw him that one day in Shaker. I was actually hoping to talk with him myself since there we were, both of us. But I looked around at some shouting going on near me, and by the time I turned back around, he had vanished. I'm telling you, he disappeared like a black ninja! That was the only time I ever saw him, unless he has a disguise or something, ya know."

Angel burst out laughing, "He does! Mama, he does. He has a great old man disguise. Fooled me, even. Did you know?"

"No, I did not. I was just blowin' smoke. A disguise? For real? Lawd have mercy! Now what else did you two talk about besides a disguise?"

"I told him Joe was wanting to call on him and why."

"You didn't." Carmela sounded none too happy about it.

"I did. You know how much I love you both, and I can't, I just won't, deceive either one of you. I had to give him a heads up so he could think about it. And I'm glad I did."

"Why are you glad? I'm not."

"Mama, I even told him that you said Joe was a 'good, good man just like Melvin.'" Silence, and none too comfortable.

"And what'd he say to that?" Carmela was all of sudden interested, invested in this family drama.

"Eventually, after he took a moment, you know, eventually he said, 'Then I guess I better talk to this good, good man who's just like me.' And then he asked me, 'You gonna tell him where I live?' I said I wanted to, if he said it was all right with him. He said it was, and that he was proud of me. And I told him I was proud of him."

"I've gotta say, my little Angel, even though I was upset at first, I'm glad you told Melvin. You did right by him and you did right by your old mama. I'm proud of you too, and proud of Melvin for that matter. And you told Joe?"

"Not yet. I had to talk with you first."

"Thank you for the respect, Angel."

"Oh no!" Angel shouted frantically. "I told Joe I'd meet him at the mission at 3:30! I've gotta go, but can I tell Joe?"

"You have my blessing. But you better hurry! You've got four and a half minutes."

"Bye, Mama. I love you."

Angel started the car while calling Joe on her phone.

"I love you too, Angelina," Carmela said to herself. Then she added as if an afterthought, "My, oh my, that man works fast."

Joe picked up on the second ring. "Harbor and Divine Mission, this is Joe Whitehorse."

"Joe, it's Angelina. I'm sorry I'm not there yet, but I've been in the Natural History Museum parking lot talking to Papa and Mama and the dinosaurs, and time flew. I can be there by 4:00."

"Maybe you don't have to come here if you have time to talk now sitting with the dinosaurs. Do you?"

"Sure I do. And I'm parked right next to that armored dinosaur with the spikes on its back, it's so cute. But that is a great idea to talk right now. I hate driving through downtown at rush hour. And I love sitting next to these dinosaurs. They're my new best friends."

Joe chuckled. More and more he'd begun thinking of Angel as his own daughter. Not that he had the right to, mind you. He just did. "Sounds like a good place to be then." He shifted gears, "So tell me, what did you talk about with your parents?"

"Everything."

"That sounds good. But what is 'everything?' I'm not sure I know. I don't even know, for instance, when or how often you saw or spoke with your father, if ever. Can we start there?"

"Sure can. I did sorta put you off, didn't I?"

"Oh, my, yes, you did, and you did it very smoothly, I might add."

Angel laughed remembering how close to rude she was last time they talked. "Well, to start with, I'm sorry I was rude. And to answer your question, I've seen or talked with my father hundreds of times over the last ten years."

"Whoa!" That news literally took Joe's breath away. "Like every week?!"

"Probably more. Probably lots more."

"Did your mother know before you told her?"

"Yes, but not even close to all of it. She knew he went to my track and cross country meets, the away meets. Truth is, since she knew that, she went to my home meets. I'm pretty sure they never had a formal agreement, it just happened. As a matter of fact, I'm not sure how she knew he went to my away meets. Maybe I let it slip one time. But one time, she told me, she actually went to an away meet hoping to talk with him."

"She told you that?"

"Uh-huh. It was one in Shaker Heights. My dad said he saw her, so he turned right around and went home. She said she saw him too, but got distracted, and turned around the very moment he left. She said he just disappeared like a black ninja. Other than that, she told me, she never chased after him, never saw him or talked with him for ten years. Only pined for him."

"Her words?"

"No. Mine. But her meaning."

Joe continued his cross-examining. "Did you tell her you had hundreds of contacts with him?"

"Not exactly. But I did say he attended all my away meets, though I didn't tell her he went to some of my home meets too."

"Really? And she didn't see him?"

"No, and this is really hilarious, he has an old man's disguise."

"No way. And it worked?"

"Like a charm. First time I saw him in it we walked right past each other and I had no clue it was him."

"Fascinating. So, when you talked with your dad, what did you tell him about your mother and me, and is he willing to talk with me?"

"About you and Mama I told him everything I saw and heard the other day in the museum. He asked directly if you and she had feelings for one another, and I told him 'Yes,' but that Mama told you that she loves him and wants him back even after ten years. And I told him you promised her that you would find him and convince him to come back to talk with her about either getting back together or totally ending it."

Hooked on every word Angel said, Joe asked, "Well, that about sums it up, wouldn't you say?"

"Pretty much. You can ask him about anything else."

"What? Say what? He still agreed to talk with me?"

"I think he is as eager to meet you as you are to meet him. He gave me permission to give you his address and phone number."

"Well, I'll be. I was sure there would be more gnashing of teeth and hemming and hawing. So that's it? I just call him and set up a time?"

"Yep. That's it."

"Anything else you think I should know?"

"Just that he still loves her. I don't think there has ever been another woman in his life. In fact, he might love her so much, that for her sake he'd be willing to hand her over to you. If he likes you."

Joe smiled and snorted, "Son of a gun. We are alike."

"More than you can ever know, at least until you meet him yourself."

Joe took a breath and then said, "Well, I'll be. The more I learn about Melvin, the more I am looking forward to meeting this father of yours."

Angel thought for a second then said, "I just wonder if when you discover you actually like one another, it will make your decisions easier or all the tougher."

Joe nodded sagely. "It might happen that way. Tougher, I mean. But I think that's a good thing. Making a tough decision like that based upon mutual respect can't be easy. Though

I never have heard of two guys loving the same woman and each trying to give her to the other."

Angel got those teary eyes again thinking that just maybe she might end up with two fathers she loves a whole lot.

As if Joe and Angel were thinking the same, very same, thoughts, he said to Angel, "That's crazy Hallmark movie stuff, don't you think? I mean, we could sell this story for a ton of cash and split it!"

"Oh, Joe, you *are* just like my father!"

Chapter 13

Joe Meets Melvin

Once Joe got Melvin's address and phone number from Angel and prayed God to lead, he phoned Melvin.

"Hey, Melvin here."

"Melvin, this is Joe Whitehorse, friend of Angelina and Carmela."

"Oh, yeah. I've been expecting your call."

"Good. I've been looking forward to meeting you mostly because of the wonderful things your wife and daughter have told me about you. Have you got time?"

"Right now, if you want. I'll even karate chop the sofa pillows just for you," Melvin quipped with mischief in his voice.

Joe laughed at the off kilter humor. "I will be so honored! See you in a few."

They both ended the call chuckling at the strange notion they were each about to meet an old friend.

Joe had no trouble finding Melvin's modest bungalow at 421 Wren Street in the Birdtown neighborhood of Lakewood. Lakewood is a west side suburb of Cleveland, and folks call Melvin's neighborhood Birdtown because all the streets have bird names. The ladies would probably call his house cute, but Joe figured he'd keep that bit of wisdom to himself — at least until he and Melvin break the ice.

He parked his car at the curb in front of 421, pried himself out of his Toyota Corolla, stretched his back with pain and vigor and promised himself for the umpteenth time, "Next car's gonna be an SUV, so I can at least get in and out of it without curses or thoughts of visiting my chiropractor." Not that he was all that large a man at six foot and 165 pounds of rock solid muscle (in his dreams.) Still, he always felt twisted like a pretzel when he got in and out of that car.

When Melvin stepped out on his front stoop to greet Joe, he watched Joe grimace and stretch then called out, "I know the feeling. I've got one of them too—a Honda. I hate getting in and out, but I love driving it."

"Same here." Joe walked toward Melvin with his hand extended. "Hi, I'm Joe Whitehorse."

"Pleased to meet you. I'm Melvin Anderson, which you probably have already guessed."

"Indeed. I'm pleased to meet you, Melvin."

"Want to come in to chat?"

"You bet, especially since you went through all the trouble of chopping the pillows for me."

"I'm glad you appreciate a man's work. Right this way, sir."

Melvin led the way into a small living room dominated by a giant TV and neatly furnished with a small sofa, a couple end tables with lamps, a platform rocker and a small recliner.

Melvin chuckled as he watched Joe's eyes go straight to the sofa pillows. Joe laughed and nearly shouted, "Chopped, just like you said!"

"All the effort just for you, Mr. Whitehorse. Impressed?"

"Impressed? Bowled over is more like it."

"Right. Want something to drink? Water, lemonade, tea?" Melvin offered. "I don't drink alcohol, not for ten years."

"I don't drink alcohol either, also for ten years. Lemonade sounds great, thank you."

"Right on it."

Melvin was back in a flash with two glasses of lemonade.

"Thank you. That was really fast," Joe marveled.

"Well, Carmela and Angel tell me that you are just like me. So, I ask myself, 'What would I want to drink if I came to my house?' Lemonade. So before you came I poured two glasses of lemonade just how I like it on a hunch."

"Melvin, you had a good hunch. Thank you again. No ice. Perfect again. Was that part of the hunch as well?"

"Yessir." They both smiled knowing, this-is-crazy smiles.

Joe scanned the room again noting how incredibly neat and cozy it was. "I love your place. Cozy, manly and neat."

"Thank you for not saying 'cute.'" Melvin laughed.

Joe laughed louder and said, "Well, I have to admit, when I drove up that very word popped in my mind as a word the ladies would use, especially the ones who watch HGTV. But for two manly men, "cute" would certainly not be appropriate today. Amen?"

"Amen and thank you. Good instincts."

"You're welcome. But I do confess that, since the minute I pulled up to the curb, before I even walked into your house, I've been scrolling through every description I've ever heard on HGTV about a man's house until I came up with 'cozy, manly and neat.' How'd I do?"

At that, they both laughed deep and long. But then, with the quips all dried up, cold silence crept in, for a full, very uncomfortable, very long minute, until Joe broke the frozen air.

"Melvin, this is awkward, and if you ever feel I'm out of line, you just say so. Or if I wear out my welcome somehow, give me the word and I'll leave. It's your house, you're the boss." 'Besides,' Joe thought, 'you're a tough-looking ex-Marine Corps Sergeant, so you're the boss whether I say you are or don't say you are.'

"That pretty much sets the stage as I see it too, Joe. Thank you for being transparent and straight forward. Joe, we are not warriors here. We are two men who just happen to care about the same woman and her daughter as well as the Lord God."

"You hit the nail on the head again. So since this is your house, how 'bout you pray for us?"

"Just what I was thinking." So Melvin prayed a heartfelt prayer inviting God to be in that room, thanking God for Carmela, Angel and seeking God to lead two godly men, who yesterday were strangers, into a very strange land together.

Joe felt the presence of the Lord as if he were with a fellow pastor or worshiping in church. "Thank you, Melvin. Your prayer was perfect for the day. Makes me feel like we're already brothers."

"I feel the same way, Joe. Unusual for me with a white man, but a welcome blessing for sure. God's already in charge, right?"

"Right."

"So, Joe," Melvin jumped right in like Joe would expect a Marine Corps Sergeant to do, "meeting you has made all the difference in the world for me today. Somehow I already know I can trust you to do what you say. I think I know a man of high character when I meet one, and you are a man of high character. It must be what Carmela thinks too. You have given Carmela and me an opportunity I never dreamed would come our way, not after I walked out without even saying good-bye ten years ago. And it's not that I want to jump right back in and try to make our marriage work again. But talk? Hmm, hmm. Talk with Carmela again? Tell her again that I love her? Embrace her? Listen to her, just listen to her voice? Sit close? Smell her? Eat a meal together? And see, just see, what God does with this love He sanctified in us 20 years ago? Joe, that's a door you have opened, thrown wide open, for Carmela and me, and I just have to walk through it, test to see if God's still in the mix. Like Gideon, we have a chance to put a fleece on the threshing room floor to test if what we perceive is in truth the Lord God's lead.

"And you, Joe? Tell me now face to face, what will you do?"

"Hopefully, I'll do nothing to break your trust. That's my plan. So first off, I'll stand down. I will be working with Angel, but I won't have anything to do with Carmela. In some ways you and I will switch roles. Except this: secondly, I will be cheering you on. Honest, Melvin, I want you and Carmela to succeed in talking this through. But even more than that, I believe the best outcome would be for you two to get back together, back to being married. If maybe you decide otherwise, like I told Carmela, I'll be her 'maybe-guy.' But after meeting you, I have regrets telling her that. She needs to put all her hope-filled energy and love into getting back together with you instead of having to choose between the two of us. Yes, I will be praying that God will lead you both, but in my secret heart I will be hoping God leads you to being married again. I will be pulling for you, Melvin, and I will keep myself totally out of the game."

"Thank you, Joe. You sure lay out a good game plan."

"I hope it is. Now all you have to do is go make the plan work."

"Yes, sir, I can do that. But now that you and I agree, who checks it out with Carmela?"

"That's a no-brainer. You, Melvin. She wants you. She told me that. She told Angel that. And, I believe, ten years ago she told you that." At that Joe got up to leave. Melvin too. Both knew it was time to end the talking and start the trusting—in God, in one another and in Carmela.

They shook hands, patted shoulders and left one another on the same page, feeling respected, hopeful and like they had each just made a new lifetime friend.

Melvin watched Joe walk to his car, and then he smiled, waved and watched Joe fold himself back into his Corolla and wave back.

As Joe drove around the corner, they both smiled, shook their heads and said the exact same thing out loud:

"Now there goes a good, good, man!"

Chapter 14

West 25th Street Blues

Joe finally got home to his small four room apartment at 1779 West 25th Street above *La Cocina*, his favorite restaurant. It once was, years before, Cleveland Indian's short stop Omar Vizquel's favorite as well. Not that Joe had ever really talked with Omar, but a couple of times he did say, *"Buen dia?"* Back in the day, when Joe was getting his Spanish speaking chops back, he imagined having a conversation in Spanish with Omar. In the shower, he'd chat up a storm with Omar *"en espanol!"* But it never happened for real. And lately he had been looking forward to inviting Carmela there for dinner. Hmmpf. Not much of a chance of that happening either. Not now. Maybe he'd better stop planning conversations with people he cares about for dinner in *La Cocina. Ai! Caramba!*

"Oh well," he sighed.

Exhausted, depressed at the thought of having given away his chances with a wonderful woman, he unlocked the street level door and climbed the steep steps to the hall door, also locked. He fished out that key — all three locks were different for security — and unlocked the hall door which took him into the main hall for the four second floor apartments, including his, apartment 2B, the number eye-high on the stringer smack in the middle of the door. He loved that number because he could spin an endless number of goofy thoughts off Hamlet's soliloquy, like "To be or not to be!" In fact, "'To Be' would have been a great song for that old rock group, you know, the Doors.'" he said aloud to himself for the umpteenth time. Unfortunately his jokes never got any better than groaners, so mostly he kept his 2B quips to himself. That's just the way it had 2B. Key in hand he unlocked 2B's door, walked in and took a deep breath of the welcome smells of his home for the last 11 years since Val had died. Blasted cancer!

It was a nice place for a single guy to live. The West Side Market was a three minute walk south down West 25th Street. His bank was across the street. Pic-n-Pay was a ten minute walk west on Lorain. And the mission where he has been serving as its pastor was a 20 minute walk via either Lorain or Divine, depending upon how divine he felt or how divine the weather was. He had quips for everything and everybody. Some were genuinely funny, but most were just odd ways for him to cope with the utter loneliness, anguish, desolation and depression that gripped his life without Val, especially during those first five years or so. "Oh, who you kidding, Joe? Still!"

But it was during those first five years, to cope with his darkness, he rediscovered booze. At first he only drank a bit with new friends he made at the bar next door to the Army Reserve Recruiting Center down the street, two guys in particular who were recently divorced. On their monthly weekends or during the work week, however, they were too busy to get drunk with him, especially the family guys, but that's when, weekday nights, the creeping darkness of depression just snatched him by the throat. Even selling houses, which was his day job, no matter how many he sold, could never keep him busy enough to fend off the dark. So that's when he started, Monday through Thursday, sitting at the bar in *La Cocina* talking with the bartenders, mostly women, in Spanish, of course. They all spoke fluent Spanish, even the ones who weren't Latinas. Thrilled with the company, delighted to improve his Spanish, Joe discovered the longer he sat at the bar the more fluent he got, especially with contemporary idioms and slang. He became particularly fluent at cuss words and sex words, plus the more drunk he got the more hispanic he sounded, or so he thought. Weird.

Even more of an upside was that at the end of the night, when the bartenders either told him to go home or closed up for the night, or both, he was within easy stumbling distance of his apartment, although unlocking three doors and tripping up the steps did prove problematic. Those nights there was no comedy when he contemplated his room number. Sometimes he marveled that Hamlet could even think about killing himself either with a blade or poison. Sometimes, though it sounded like a pretty darned good idea. Eventually Hamlet's own brother used both and took that choice out of his hands, stabbing him with a poisoned blade. On those drunken nights reading aloud "2B or not 2B" haunted him, like Hamlet's ghosts, until Joe scolded himself with, "Unlock the f-ing door, you idiot." He would obey Joe the Scold, stagger in, vomit somewhere then pass out on his bed. No thought at all of Val, 'til the morrow.

But wait! The real downside was that Joe ended up tying-on a six- month bender after which, with some help, he came to his senses with three good decisions: 1. Join AA; 2. Sign up with the Army Reserves; and 3. Attend that Latino church at Harbor and Divine. Actually it was his boss, June Carlson, who helped him make those decision. Forced him was more like it.

WEST 25TH STREET BLUES

Somehow he had kept his job with Carlson Realty, showed up for work every day while being blitzed. AA guys called that being a 'high functioning drunk.' June Carlson, the owner and CEO, grieved her best friend Val's passing right along with Joe. Unfortunately, though, she could see Joe was making a mess of his life and she couldn't just stand by and watch her best friend's guy totally fall apart. So one morning when the two of them were alone in the realty outer office, June called Joe into her office, shut the door and then told him she'd give him six months to get it together or he'd be out on his ear. "I love you, Joe, and because of Val I have put up with you. But I can't have a drunk working for me any more. Even Val would agree with me. She loved you too much to watch you throw your life away with a bottle and vomit."

Tough woman, that June Carlson. But a true friend.

She and Val had been such good friends that the week before Val died, knowing death was imminent, Val had asked June to watch over Joe. June said she would. She remembered Val shouting back though, "But no funny stuff. He's still my guy!" causing both women to laugh and cry at the same time, and gag, especially Val, what with all the tubes up her nose, down her throat, in her arms, almost laughed herself to death that night. No joke. Still, it was a good promise to make. In fact, by June's own admission, it wasn't a tough job at all, because Joe had always been a sweet guy, even when he was drunk. "Plus," she said aloud to no one, "He sells houses. Like crazy! Who would have thought?"

Joe's sales actually went up when he started drinking after Val died. Of course they had hit absolute rock bottom the last two months of Val's life. He had been an awesome, wonderful care giver for Val, and after she passed, he had nothing but time on his hands. So he sold houses. Obsessively. Compulsively. It seemed to June that out of his grief, Joe started treating his customers with the same care and sweetness he had shown to his dying wife. Every woman who walked though the door became a substitute for Val. Needless to say, the customers loved it. Some days people actually lined up in his office, nearly begging him to show and sell them houses they could buy, because he just flat out cared about them. June had always known that the key to success in sales is being kind and honest with people, helping them make the purchase that fits them best, and Joe was already a natural at that. But when Val died he took kindness to a whole new level, especially with older women. Perhaps it was because Val was seven years older than Joe, but still, Joe had a way with middle-aged and older women, and they loved it. Nothing creepy. Just plain kindness and respect. Men too, for that matter. And, again, nothing creepy.

After five months of the six month grace period June had given Joe to straighten up, she noticed he was not making much progress with his alcoholism. She didn't want to fire him in four weeks when his six months ended, so June decided it was time to talk turkey with him. She told Joe not to waste the life God had given him, the life that Val had loved. She told him he needed to dry out with AA; toughen up with the Army Reserves; and get God in his life, go to church. She didn't care where, but she did suggest the Latino church on the corner of Harbor and Divine.

She told him, "With your Spanish skills, you'll fit in easily at that church. I know you will, because I have some clients from that church, and they are folks who care about people as well as about God. But, and more to the point, they have a Wednesday noon AA meeting with a sponsor I think would take you on," she laughed and added, "if you can handle him. Jim, that's the sponsor's name, Jim is a long-haired gray-beard, middle aged guy who loves Jesus, rides a big old Harley Hog and will talk straight to you."

Joe grinned at June's speech. He really like her. Not loved her. Liked her—her style, her straight talk. He couldn't imagine any other boss doing that for him, especially the actual owner of the business. True, June helped and cared for Joe out of loyalty to her dead best friend Val, but also out of respect for how Joe had, with tender love, taken such good care of his dying wife and then his clients. Agreeing with June that he needed a life change, that week Joe took all three of June's suggestions. He joined AA, he signed up with the Army Reserves and he started attending *Primera Iglesias Metodista*, the Methodist church on the corner of Harbor and Divine.

Heeding June's advice surely saved Joe's job, but it could, he realized, possibly also have saved his life. After that Joe came to think of her as his angel from both God and Val, and, perhaps, she was exactly that.

In the next six months with the help of church folks at *Primera Iglesias Metodista* Joe completed regaining the Spanish fluency he'd had as a child. He also started teaching a men's Bible study at church in Spanish, helped run the free clothing center in the church basement alongside a couple of old ('really old,' he said) ladies and, get this, he signed up to explore the call he sensed from God to become a pastor. In addition he completed basic training. Talk about a complete life change. "Praise God!" he said again and again as he started telling people his story. "I'm telling you, that the church at the corner of Harbor and Divine is a place of hope. God changed my life there and God will change your life too!" So, if there was any way to pay forward what June Carlson, Val and God had given him, he was all over it.

Fast forward ten years, including three years of active duty and three years of seminary at the Methodist Theological School in Ohio, Joe had just become the actual pastor of that church, now a mission, on the corner of Harbor and Divine. The Spanish speaking congregation went broke, meaning the church was no longer *Primera Iglesias Metodista.* Instead it became The Mission at Harbor and Divine. With lots of Latino immigrants still living on the Near West Side, Joe joyfully continued to use his reclaimed fluent Spanish along with his love for people and his burning desire to pay forward the blessings that God and others, especially June, had given him.

But now, but now the fly in the ointment was this: he was going to lose Carmela, the only woman he had ever cared for since losing Val eleven years earlier. And to top it off, he was actually making friends with Carmela's ex in order to get them back together. "Am I stupid or what?" he scolded himself. Yet seminary, becoming a pastor, being saved at the Latino church from alcoholism and assured self-destruction, had reshaped Joe's character with put-yourself-last Christian values building upon his already caring, self-giving nature. "Be like Jesus," his ethics profs taught. "Yeah, maybe if I see it that way, being like Jesus, I won't feel so stupid giving her up," he told himself out loud.

Joe decided he'd go talk with his church boss DJ. DJ had gotten Joe through the initial shock of Val's death when DJ pastored the North Olmsted church. Unfortunately that's also when Joe became a drunk. "Well, it's worth a try," he encouraged himself. "DJ hasn't held that against me so far."

He called DJ's office at the Holy Oil Can on University Circle. "Hello, Greater Cleveland United Methodist Church, this is Clara, how may I help you?"

"Hi, Clara, I'm Joe Whitehorse."

"Oh, Joe! That Joe! The friend of DJ and Gary Siciliano whom I have never met. Right?"

"Right on all counts!"

"Joe, how can I help you?"

"Didn't we speak briefly there in your office last summer when I had a meeting with DJ about pastoring the new mission at Harbor and Divine?"

"You know, I think you're right, by golly, we did! Good to talk with you again. So now, what's up?"

"I'd like an appointment to talk with DJ."

"Oh, that's easy peasy! This is your lucky day. How about right now? You know, he might even like the idea of driving out to meet you at the mission and save you a trip. What do you think?"

"Wonderful, Clara, I'd love that."

"Hang on, and I'll run it by him."

Clara wasn't gone for even 20 seconds when the line came alive with, "Hello Joe! Good to hear your voice!" It was DJ himself. "How can I help you?"

"I've got pastor's goo to wade through, and I could sure use your help. Do you have time to talk with me?"

"Oh do I! This is our lucky day! I have nothing but open space on my calendar today. How about I drive out to the mission. I need to get outside and blow some stink off. What do you say? I could be there in half an hour, traffic willing."

"That'd be great DJ! Thanks so much!"

"Oh, but give me a clue. Is this about that business you asked for time off to figure out with — what's her name — Carmela and you and her long estranged husband?"

"You've got it."

"Okay. I'll block out the rest of the afternoon. Maybe we can have lunch together too — at that Mexican restaurant you like so much."

"La Cocina?"

"That's it."

"That'd be perfect! That's where I live. Well, not in the restaurant. Upstairs in an apartment. We can walk there from the mission if you want after we talk. It's about a 20 minute walk."

"Sounds perfect. I'll see you in a little bit."

"Okie doke. Thanks, DJ."

"You're welcome, my friend."

A half an hour later they were chatting in the parish house where Joe had taken over the main floor for his office and workroom. He spent the first 20 minutes telling his story, to which DJ simply said, "Fascinating! Utterly fascinating. So tell me if I've got this right. You're going to give up this budding romance — which is good, because she is married, you know."

"Yeah, I know. But he's been A.W.O.L. for ten years. Eleven years ago, you know, I was a broken man, not fit for woman or beast. Remember? That was the first time you helped me."

"Oh, I remember all right. Till this day that remains one of the toughest funerals I have ever done. You were a great couple."

"I know. And this is the very first time since then that I have let another woman into my heart, all the while thinking, for sure, after ten years of his abandonment, surely they would be getting divorced." He took a deep breath, "But nooooo. They still love each other. It's crazy. And I'm insane for getting involved."

"No comment. At least not yet."

"So do you think getting Carmela and Melvin reconciled and back together living married again is exactly what Jesus would do? Heal 'em up! I need somebody like you to tell me I'm on the right track"

"Keep going," DJ encouraged.

"Here's the thing I'm beginning to understand. Doing someone else a good turn is only half of paying forward the blessings that I've been given. That's the 'forward' half. The other half is the 'back' half, and don't miss the anatomical references. That back half, that's the half that's messing with me. There's a steep, real-time price to pay for the changed life I get from God by giving up Carmela to save her marriage with Melvin. A very steep price. And it already hurts. A lot."

DJ sat back in his chair and thought. "Hey, it's not that bad," he told Joe with a smirk on his face. "Remember the price Peter paid for leading people to Jesus?"

"I do. And for healing people too. But that story about how Peter died is not in the Bible, right?"

DJ nodded, "Right."

"Still, tell me if I've got this right. By Roman Emperor Nero's orders, the Roman soldiers were executing Christians left and right by crucifying them just like Jesus, since that's who they wanted to be like.

"But Peter told his executioners he was not worthy to die like Christ. So the Roman soldiers said, 'Okay,' and crucified him upside down. All for doing good."

"You got it. Just like Jesus. All for doing good."

Joe huffed a couple of times then said, "So, DJ, I've got to tell you, I'm angry, frustrated, and brokenhearted over having to pay a steep price myself, *because* I'm doing the right thing for someone else."

"Right. Goes with the job description, pastor. Becoming a godly pastor has a very steep learning curve, and it all has to do with suffering for doing good. Like Jesus."

"Oy," Joe puffed. "So then, tell me, Rev. Dr. DJ, do you think I will at least get a chance to lead Melvin to Christ as part of the package?"

DJ laughed. "Really? I thought you said..."

Joe interrupted, "Oh yeah, he's already got Jesus. Right. I forgot he's a good, good man." Joe paused, then said honestly, "He really is."

DJ jumped back in. "Joe, look, you're doing the right thing. Carmela is not yours to lose. She's married to Melvin. Yes, he did abandon her for ten years. I can't defend that. But they're still married. By God. And Joe.... by me."

"What?!" Joe exploded.

"Theirs was the second marriage I solemnized a long time ago. Yours was the first, you and Val."

"Holy cow, DJ, that sure brings it home!"

"Yeah, it does, doesn't it," DJ chuckled, "for both of us."

"So, let me get this straight. Whenever I do the right thing or help somebody repent and live a changed life, I must always expect to pay that kind of price?"

"Of course."

"OF COURSE??!!" exclaimed an astounded Joe.

"Well, Joe, tell me, whose life gets changed more, your life or the life of the person you help?" DJ asked knowing how impossible that question would be for Joe to answer.

"I don't know."

"Fair enough. Let me put it this way: When Jesus healed the blind man right smack in front of the Jewish leaders who hated Him, whose life would soon be changed the most?"

"Hard to say. The blind man for sure is one, though not just the blind man. But everyone else who experienced or witnessed Jesus' miraculous life-changing powers. There was Jesus' friend Lazarus whom Jesus raised from the dead, and that political traitor Zacchaeus the tax collector whom Jesus for-gave. Then those ten lepers Jesus healed and who then ran to show the Jewish Sanhedrin what Jesus did, giving them more reason to have him killed. And then, of course, even the rabbis themselves surely had life-changing moments with Jesus. They had him killed as his reward for all the good that he, by his nature, was compelled to do. Crucified because he couldn't—wouldn't—stop helping people, forgiving people, giving broken people a fresh start, because he was God in the flesh. Couldn't change that. So, maybe Jesus?"

"I could not have said it better, Joe. All three of you will lead changed lives by virtue of the godly decisions you are making. And, in my opinion, all three changes will be for the better, filled with hope, love and new beginnings. But, Joe, honestly, especially yours."

Joe nodded and smiled a peaceful, settled smile. DJ recog-nized that look from all his counseling years as the way people smile when they "get it," when they understand and accept the tough road ahead in following Jesus, in doing the right, moral and loving thing.

"Thanks, DJ."

"You're welcome, my friend." DJ took a beat, and knowing God had brought their little talk to a perfect conclusion, he said, "So, Joe, how 'bout I pray so we can get some food at La Cocina? My treat."

"Sounds good, boss. And, DJ?"

"Yeah?"

"Thank you. Again."

"You're welcome. And, Joe, thank YOU for being a man of solid character who walks the high road." Then he prayed.

Ten minutes later off they drove to La Cocina. Yum!

After lunch, DJ left to return to his office in the Holy Oil Can. Joe walked up to his apartment, said, "Hey, Frank," to his St. Francis statue, then called Gary to tell him what was going on with Carmela and ask his advice.

However, unknown to Joe, at the very same time, Angel had been telling Gary how Joe worked to get Carmela and Melvin to talk again after their ten year separation. Gary thought it was a cool story, but also that it was so bizarre he just had to call Joe and tease him a bit. But the moment he picked up his phone, Gary was already on the line.

"Gary?"

"Hey? Joe? What are you doing on my phone?"

"Calling you."

"Hoo-wee-ooo!" Gary laughed as he hooted the Twilight Zone spooky vibraphone hoo-wee-ooo.

"You've got that right!" Joe chuckled. "But I've got something even spookier, and I could use some advice. It's a bit of a problem."

"I heard, brother," Gary laughed.

"What do you mean, 'you heard'?"

"I heard it through the grapevine!" he sang.

"Sing it to me, now!" And they both sang and laughed even more.

Gary interrupted the fun, "But, Joe, no kidding. Angel told me a very confusing, spooky story about how you convinced Carmela and Carmela's ex — his name is Melvin, right? — to talk with her and iron things out. After TEN years. As in 'T-E-N' TEN years! Is that right? Don't answer, because if that is right, and I think since Angel told it to me, it probably is 100% true, then all I have to say is, "Hey, Joe, are you crazy? As in, insane? As in, have you lost your mind? As in, have you gone to outer space? As in, to quote Dr. Phil, 'Joe, what were you thiiiinking?'"

"Ha, ha. Very funny. Look, I'm doing the right thing, all right?"

"You sure?" Gary asked totally serious.

"Unfortunately, yes, I'm sure. She still has the hots for her ex."

"For real?"

"Yep. And Melvin told me he is still in love with Carmela."

"Melvin? Told you? How'd that happen? This gets more like a soap opera with every word. Come on, Joe, 'fess up."

"I told Carmela I'd go talk with him to get him to talk with her about reconciling. You did know they are not officially divorced, right?"

"Sorta. Nobody really came out and told me. Not my business. But, then again, nobody ever told me they actually were divorced either. But, who cares? They haven't shared a bed in ten years! Ten Years, Joe! And, as I understand it, he just walked out on Carmela and Angel one day and never even said 'so long, farewell, *auf wiedersehen*, good-bye-ya,' to misquote an old musical. Am I not correct-o?"

"You are correct-o to a point-o," Joe laughed. "I've still been getting involved with a married woman, and that's wrong, and I've got to get myself out. Period."

"Point taken. But why hasn't she gotten a divorce?"

"Look, Gar, she is so much not over Melvin, that she has no room for me in her heart or in her life. At least not until he tells her it's over and they get divorced. And that's not going to happen as far as I can tell, because he still loves her too. Besides, I don't belong there. Anyhow, they're going to talk together Saturday. That's what Carmela told me. Which all leads me to this: Carmela and I will not be having dinner with you guys. No way, no how. And before you ask, I'm not coming without her."

"I get it. But we could," and Gary pumped his eyebrows a few times for inspiration, "we could fix you up. Annie's got tons of girlfriends... ooo, bad word... *lots* of girlfriends who would love to go out with a stud like you."

Joe laughed again even harder. Gary's goofiness was doing a number on his dark mood. "Thanks, Gar. Really, thank you for brightening up my day. But I don't want to get fixed up just now."

Gary nodded to himself. "Joe, I believe I understand."

"Yeah, Gar, I think you probably do."

"Okay. I'll call and let DJ and Mel know. And, honestly, I don't think Annie is going to feel up to it either."

"She still hurting from her accident?"

"Oh, yeah. Big time."

"You know she hasn't been back in the office since then."

"I know. I've been staying with her. She asked me if I would drive her to work tomorrow. Hey, but, Joe, how do you know that?"

"My boss, June Carlson, is filling in for Annie in Annie's office, and I'm filling in for June in our office. Annie and June are good business friends. But I've got to tell ya, this working two jobs is already getting really tough. I think I'm going to have to make a decision pretty soon."

"Yeah, tell me about having two jobs! Working for you and working for Mel. Well, Annie'll be there tomorrow. But if something comes up, I'll call her office and tell June. Then maybe when she gets back to her office she can give you an 'atta boy' and the rest of the day off. Mmmm, maybe I'll suggest it to her."

"Thanks Gar, although June might be thinking that all on her own. She's a good person too, like your Annie. And, oh, Gar, I want to be the one to call DJ and Mel. It's too complicated, too personal, and I think I should be the one to tell our resident shrinks any new gory details. They already know almost everything else except that we won't be at the dinner. Okay?"

"Okay with me. I really didn't want to anyhow. It's too goofy for me to present it to them in a *positive* light," he explained putting finger air quotes over the phone around "positive." But Joe got the inflection in Gary's voice.

"Oh, hush!" Joe laughed. "I'll talk with you tomorrow."

"Okay. See you soon."

As they disconnected they both laughed not for the situation, but for the honest happiness of their friendship. Still, however, Gary shook his head in dismay saying aloud to himself, "What a goof he is getting in the middle of somebody else's messy marriage. That's really stepping in it with both feet.

"Maybe that's what pastors do when they help out other people.

"Not me. No sir.
That's way too risky. Waaay too risky.
Way too goofy."

107

Chapter 15

Eyes Wide Open
All the Time
(Ode to Johnny C.)

T he next morning Joe got up at 5:00 a.m., read his Bible and the devotional writing from <u>Our Daily Bread</u>, his favorite guided Bible study, then showered and ate. As he cleaned up the dishes he started singing Johnny Cash's "I Walk the Line." He wasn't sure why he picked that song to sing. After all, even though it was one of his favorites, he really did not have a woman in his life that he could say "because you're mine." But when he sang, "I keep my eyes wide open all the time," it hit him like a two-by-four upside the head. "That's it," he shouted interrupting his song — "'I keep my eyes wide open all the time.'" As if they were instructions directly from the throne of God, Joe stretched his eyes as wide open as they could possibly go, and just kept them that wide open as he began walking from his apartment to the mission. Every few minutes he'd stop in the middle of the street then turn very slowly around looking intently at each of the century-old homes that lined the sidewalks of Divine Street. He paused his spin on each house, asked God to bless the people who lived there and then moved onto the next, noticing design and architectural details he never noticed before. It was as if he were an artist, with a new pair of eyes to see details artists see as they get set to paint. Joe's canvas, however, was not a painter's canvas with oils. No. His canvas was prayer. As he turned from house to house, he "painted" a prayer for each person, each family who lived there — until, that is, somebody shoved his shoulder — hard.

"Hey, pal," a stone-faced, bruiser-looking guy said as he shoved the heel of his hand into Joe's shoulder.

"Hey! What!?" shouted back a surprised Joe.

"What-are-ya-doin,' creep, staring into people's houses? You some kind of weirdo? A peeping tom or a pervert or something? Maybe a thief? We've got enough trouble around here without adding a pervert to the mix. Just what are you doing, buddy?"

Surprised and offended at the harassment, Joe had to quickly gather himself, cool his temper, and then tell the guy in a calm, matter-of-fact voice, "Praying." As soon as he said the word, "Praying," he felt instant assurance covering him, urging him to keep talking, which he did. "First off, 'Ouch!' No, not ouch, it really didn't hurt. Just surprised the heck out of me, and it wasn't nice. And second, I'm Joe Whitehorse, and I walk down this street a dozen times a week from my apartment on West 25th Street to that old church at Harbor and Divine. I run the mission there. But, I'm discovering, out of all the times I walk this street, I have never ever actually looked at all the houses as homes of real people, real families. In fact, I've never even thought about the people who live in each one, dealing with troubles just like you and me. So, I don't know, I just stopped here in the middle of the street and started praying for them one house at a time, even though I don't know a single one of them."

"Whoa." The man's hard face softened dramatically as he stared at Joe, simply stared, trying to decide if this peeping tom was actually praying. He took a deep breath, and quickly decided he'd trust the guy.

"Well, you know one now. I'm Gandy, Gandy Martin. Sorry about the shove."

"Didn't hurt. Just unexpected," Joe said again.

"Yeah, I guess it was rude as well as uncalled for. Sorry again. I like to think I'm a better judge of character than that."

"What, are you the neighborhood sheriff?" Joe teased.

Gandy laughed at the tease, and said, tongue in cheek, "Yeah, something like that," obviously not telling it all. "I live right there," Gandy said pointing to a small bungalow, "3615 Divine. See it? Of course you do, you were just staring right at it. That little craftsman bungalow?"

"Sorry about the staring. I love how it looks. It's a beautiful little house, and, I guess I was actually looking at it for a long time. Just wondering. Wondering who lives there. Is there love in the house? What are their struggles? Could our mission help? Maybe I should pray for them right now. Yeah, that's actually the house that got me praying. Don't know why."

"You were praying for me and my family when I shoved you?"

"Yeah, I guess I was, if that's your house. It is, huh?"

"Yeah."

"Hmph. I didn't know who or what I was praying for, only that I needed to pray, HAD to pray. So I was praying for you, huh?"

"Needed to pray? Hmm. HAD to pray?" Gandy stammered, paused and then went on. "Yeah, you were. For us. Thank you. Thank you for praying for us." Gandy paused again to gather himself. "Wow. Talk about being surprised," he said thoughtfully. Then he added, "Yeah, I live there with my wife and our nine year old little girl, Angel. And I'm telling you, Mr. Whitehorse, while we don't need any more creeps around here than we've already got, we can sure use all the prayers you've got."

With that, Joe watched as the bruiser's eyes reddened, a single tear escaped, but Gandy snatched it before it could roll down his face. "Sorry to be such a wimp," he apologized. "Angel, she's such a sweet little girl, but other people say she looks weird and talks funny, you know? She's a Down syndrome girl. Kids make fun of her. Heck, even their parents make fun of her. Damned haters. And they call *her* weird? They're the weirdos. We named her Angel, because that's what she is to us—our angel. So.... I'm sorry again, buddy, for being rude to you before, shoving you and such. I just thought you were one of them, one of those haters trying to creep us out, force us to move. As if these," he said sarcastically as he stretched out his hand introducing all the houses to Joe, "as if these fine, upscale digs are a gated community with a pool, tennis courts and gardeners and such." Gandy took a deep breath relaxed his shoulders, softened his face, let a small, nearly inaudible sigh escape and then apologized again. "I'm really sorry. See, we haven't even been here a year, so I don't even know what neighbors I can trust, if any. I wish I could trust all of them, but I'm not the most trusting guy," explained Gandy, again, not telling all.

"No problem."

"But to hear you say you're praying for us, and you don't even know our names, well that's the nicest thing anybody has done for me and my family since we moved here last year."

Joe stood stunned speechless. He truly believed that God is always at work around us inviting us to join Him in His work, but it still surprised the heck out of Joe when he could see it happening. With his own eyes wide open, Joe could actually see God at work. Now. With Gandy. It's like God was telling Joe, showing Joe all the homes of real people, "Open your eyes, Joe, and look. Now there I AM at work." Joe remembered how Canadian Bible teacher Henry Blackaby taught exactly that: 'When you see God working, that's God's invitation for you to join Him in His work.' Like right now. Of course, 'right now' always means you've got no preparation. 'Right now' always means you just jump up this second, and, not knowing what to do or where to go, you just follow. Follow God.

Henry Blackaby wasn't all that clear on how a person can tell if God is the one leading, except that it looks like something Jesus would do. Still, who really knows? In the Bible they actually *saw* Jesus in person with their very own eyes. Like those fishermen brothers, Simon and Andrew, out working catching fish. *They actually saw Jesus.* And because their friends and neighbors probably had told them about Jesus' miracle healings, when Jesus actually turned to them and said, "Come follow me," they just dropped their nets and followed Him. Two other brothers, James and John did the same thing, only they left their father, Zebedee, standing in the boat. Sure, they didn't have clue one about where he was leading them, what they would do, where they would sleep, or what they would eat. "But at least there he was, in the flesh." Joe said aloud. "These days, though, how do you know if it's Jesus talking in your mind or some dark fantasy screwing with you?"

"What?" asked Gandy looking straight into Joe's eyes with his own emotion-reddened eyes. Joe had not a clue about where this was going. He just knew God was working. Just knew it. Don't ask him how, he could just see it, sense it, feel it. It was like the buzz he got back when he went into the war zones in Iraq, not in charge of a single second—not one second, not one step, not one minute, not one hour, not one day. He just knew at the time to keep your eyes wide open and follow the leads like a little kids treasure hunt. Once you take that first step you'll find the next clue, then the next lead. Those soldiers, the points, the leads, the guys in front of the battalion on a mission like he was had to keep their eyes wide open all the time — wide open, never knowing what was next. 'That's how it is with God,' Joe thought.

Gandy saw Joe's wheels turning, so he simply said, "Look, Mister Whitehorse, thank you. Thank you for your prayers."

'Ahh-hah,' Joe smiled to himself. 'That's it. That's what's next.'

"You're welcome, Gandy. So now I know your name and Angel's name, but your wife...?"

"Lydia."

"...and Lydia's. Okay if I pray for you again, out loud this time?"

"Right here on the street? Some neighbors are watching."

Joe looked around, "Oh, cool! Good for the neighbors. Yes, sir, let's pray right here — on the street. And good for the neighbors. Okay with you if I ask them to come pray with us? See if they will?"

Gandy, caught totally by surprise again, just shrugged, but Joe didn't wait for Gandy's permission. Instead he turned to the folks near by and asked in a louder voice than necessary so everyone else could hear, "Gandy and I were just about to pray for him and his wife and their little girl, Angel. Would you all come and pray with us? 'The prayers of the righteous are full of power.' Come on." And, lo and behold, they came. All of them. Nine. You can't plan those things out. They just happen when God's there working. When the neighbors got there, Joe said, "I'm Joe and this here's Gandy." Everybody else took the lead and shared their names with one another as well as with Joe and Gandy.

Joe then grabbed Gandy's *shoving hand* with his right as well as the hand of Orel whom he had just met, with his left. All the rest joined in the chain, making an unbroken circle. Joe was just about to start praying for Gandy, Lydia and Angel, when Orel turned to him and said, "We heard Gandy shouting at you, so we came out thinking you two was gonna fight." He turned to the others. "Isn't that so?"

"That's what I thought," Orlando said.

"Me too," agreed a few others.

Orel continued, "And here we get ourselves in a prayer meetin' —right in the middle of the street. Don't that beat the band?!"

"Amen," shouted the others. All of them. "Praise God!"

The moment the circle was complete, Joe jumped right in with, "O Lord, our God, please come surround us with your holiness." Even though he knew God had already done that, he said that for the benefit of his new friends and neighbors before he went on to pray for Gandy, Lydia, Angel and everyone there.

Surprisingly, whether it was out of respect, or just curiosity, hard to know, drivers on Divine Street actually stopped their cars to watch this fight-turned-prayer-meeting right in the middle of Divine Street in the middle of Cleveland. Nobody honked a horn; nobody shouted out obscenities or even called out, "Hey, you idiots, get out of the way!" Nobody.

Two people did climb out of their cars though to get a closer look. And when they did, the circle opened up to let them in. Wow! Just opened up. Eyes wide open can see God at work. Joe prayed for a few minutes, then he invited anybody else to pray, not knowing what to expect, but just knowing that was his next step from God. Just knew it. Amazingly they prayed as well. Nearly every single one, including the drivers who got out of their cars, prayed for Gandy, Lydia and Angel, for the neighborhood, for the country, for one another. Hearty "Amens" punctuated each and every prayer, and after everyone who wanted to pray had prayed, more Amens and Hallelujahs led to neighborly handshakes, friendly hugs and lots of folks saying "It was good to finally meet you," along with several invitations and promises.

Joe jumped in with an invitation of his own, "If you want to do this again, maybe we can meet at somebody's house next week? Anybody interested?"

Orel spoke right up, "You can come to our house. My wife and I would love to pray with you all again. Right there. 3620 Divine Street. Same time, same day next week?"

Lots of "Yeps" and "We'll be there's."

"Alrighty then," Orel confirmed and then added, "I'll even put on a pot of coffee for everyone," which lead to a chorus of, "Then I'll be there for sure," and "Thanks, Orel, count us in."

"We were just driving by, can we come too?"

"You bet! The more the merrier."

"Hallelujah!"

For neighbors who never met before, the saying goodbyes took forever lingering over just-born friendships. Goodbyes sounded more like benedictions. Joe walked away feeling twelve feet tall and really proud of God. "Thank you, Lord," he prayed by himself, "for making me keep my eyes wide open all the time, and inviting me to join you in your work." With that, Joe once again stretched his eyes wide, wide open, because now he did not want to miss a thing.

He walked on toward the church, 'the mission' he called it now, and another man walked up to him to ask, "Hey, neighbor, what was going on down there in the street?"

"Oh, a prayer meeting. Evidently God called it."

"Sorry I missed it."

"Oh, Dr. Don! Didn't recognize you. It'll be next week too at the same time at Orel's house, 3620 right down there. You know them?"

"Sure, I know Orel and Becca Freundmann. Okay if I come?"

"Absolutely. Think Sandy would like to come with you?"

"I sure hope so, we're a team, you know. Forty-five years husband and wife. Besides, Sandy loves to be in on the ground floor when things start getting good for Jesus."

"Well said, my friend."

"And, Joe, are you going to be working on bikes this week?"

"I hope to. In the basement though, too cold outside. If you want to join me, I'll let you know when."

"Perfect. Sandy and I are always looking for ways to help people. We'll look forward to your call. You've got our number, right?"

"I do. See you soon, Don."

Joe turned to finish his amazing walk and said to himself, "Wow! So that's how God grew His Acts 2 church!"

As he got to the church building of the mission and turned the corner onto Harbor Street, he reached for his cell phone to call Angelina, thinking she might enjoy meeting Gandy, Lydia and Angel. "The two Angels have just got to get together. God's gotta be in that for sure!" he said with a little grin. However, the instant he was about to tap in Angelina's number she stepped out of her car right in front of Gary Siciliano's house there across Harbor Street.

So he waved his cell phone and said, "Hi, Angel. I was just about to call you."

"Well, here I am in person!"

"Better yet, for sure."

They exchanged a few pleasantries until Angelina asked, "So, Joe, what were you going to call me about?"

"A little Down syndrome girl named Angel, lives down toward West 25th at 3615 Divine," and Joe went on to tell her everything that happened that morning—from keeping his eyes wide open all the time, to praying for people living in every house he saw, to getting shoved by Gandy who thought he was a pervert and last, to how all that led to a middle-of-the-street prayer meeting.

Angel smiled at Joe's off-the-charts enthusiasm, and when he finally took a breath, she laughed and asked, "So? Besides that wonderful story, why was it you were going to call me?"

"Oh, yeah! I thought I could walk you down the street and we could introduce ourselves to little Angel and her parents, Gandy and Lydia. They could be your next Harbor and Divine Mission family, along with the Montoyas who got those beautiful bikes for their kids, Carlos and Carlita. You could start making a visiting list with notes about how you can help and how you see God at work. Interested?"

"Interested? More than that, Joe. I'm stoked! That's exciting! Let's go!"

Joe smiled at Angel's enthusiasm, and off they walked back around the corner and down Divine Street. "Just one thing, Angel. We've got to keep our eyes wide open all the time, so we don't miss God at work around us. I want to see it all."

"Yes, sir, boss! Eyes wide open all the time." If only Johnny Cash could see them now!

When Joe and Angel got maybe two houses away from Gandy and Lydia's place, Joe suddenly stopped, looked stricken like he forgot his name or something. "Angel," he said with some urgency, "I'm sorry, but I have never given one ounce of thought as to whether people in this neighborhood may be racist."

Angel laughed herself breathless. "*No ai problemo, Jose.* I've got this. We have that possibility with every breath we take, every step we make and every place we walk. You and I, we'll just trust that God's at work, and we'll follow His lead. Okay?"

"Whoa! Better than okay! You're an amazing young woman, Angel, and they are going to be blessed getting to know you."

"I hope so, I know I will be.

This the house? 3615?"
"That's it. Let's knock on the door."
And so they did.

Chapter 16

Two Angels

Angel knocked but no answer. Joe knocked with the same result.

Angel sighed, "I know people are in there — I can hear them talking."

"I've got an idea," Joe winked. With that he bellowed as loudly as he could, "Hey, Gandy, it's Joe!"

In two seconds the door flew open and a tall, dark-haired man with a grin on his face opened the door and said, "Joe! Good to see you again — already! And who's this beautiful young lady with you?"

"This is Angelina Anderson. Angel, meet Gandy Martin."

"Angel? Really? That's your name?"

Angelina smiled. "It sure is."

"That's my daughter's name."

"I heard." Her smile beamed.

Gandy couldn't help himself but to smile back.

Joe loved what he was watching, God working all the time, ALL the time. "Actually, Gandy, that's why I brought Angel— to meet your Angel. Angelina is the new community outreach worker for the Mission at Harbor and Divine. She's the "outreach" part. Her job is to connect with our neighbors and find ways we can help. So I immediately thought, when I found out your daughter's name, that these two Angels absolutely have got to meet, if you are willing, that is."

"Sounds intriguing. But, Angel, exactly what would you do?" Gandy asked Angelina.

"That's why we're here, to find out," Angelina explained. "Once Joe and I meet Angel and talk and pray together with you and her and your wife, we believe God will show all of us how we can best help."

Gandy balked, cocked his head sideways then said, "I'm not so sure there's any way you can help us. You see, our Angel is a Down syndrome little girl," he explained as if hearing the words 'Down syndrome' would scare Angelina away and that would be that. But Angelina surprised Gandy, when, not only did she not back off a lick, but she actually seemed even more interested in meeting Angel .

"Mr. Martin, Joe actually explained that to me before we got here. I had plenty of time to turn tail and run. But I agree with Joe that somehow God is working in this, and that we two Angels are just meant to get together."

"To do what?"

"Honestly, again I have to admit, I'm not yet sure, but I will be by the time we leave."

"I know it's cold out there, almost feeling like Christmas, but can you wait just a minute while I talk this over with Lydia and Angel? Not too long, I promise. I've left the door ajar so they both could hear what we were saying, because I had a hunch it might be about Angel, and Angel understands a lot.

"That's wonderful, Mr. Martin."

"Gandy, please?" he asked.

"Thank you, Gandy."

True to his word, Gandy was back in a short minute with a smile on his face.

"Here's the truth," Gandy began, and Angelina and Joe both braced for rejection as Gandy continued explaining. "I have never, ever seen Angel more excited to meet anybody, than she is right now to meet another Angel." He opened the door wide inviting Joe and Angelina, "Please come in."

The instant they walked in, Angel Martin jumped out of her chair, ran to Angelina, gave her a huge bear hug and said, "You're a Angel. I'm a Angel. I'm happy to meet you."

Angelina wept for joy as she hugged back and replied through her tears, "I'm happy to meet you too, Angel." Angelina knew that Down syndrome children are often very instantly affectionate and long-standing loyal. But for her to experience herself that affection so freely given in their very first meeting was a complete surprise as well as totally welcomed, joyful and exhilarating.

Gandy and Lydia said nothing; they just watched and smiled. They knew their daughter well and expected instant bonding with a 'sister Angel.'

Angel noticed Angelina's tears and said, "You're crying. Are you sad? Are you okay?"

"Yes, I'm okay." Angelina told her. "These are happy tears, because I'm so happy to meet you."

"I'm happy too,"

"Me too," Angelina intuitively replied to Angel in simple and straight-forward language, just like Angel had spoken to her. "Would you like to sit on the couch with me? Then we can all talk together. Okay?"

"Okay. Let's go here." Angel grabbed Angelina's hand and led her to the couch. "You sit here. And I sit here."

"Perfect."

"Perfect."

Transfixed by the little drama played out before him, Joe stood perfectly still and said absolutely nothing. After the two Angels sat he sat as well on a nearby chair.

Gandy and Lydia smiled like two kids at Christmas. Neither could imagine a more perfect Christmas gift for their daughter, for their whole family, than another Angel. Even though their Angel had attended a school for developmentally delayed children for the last five years, never had they seen her bond so quickly with an adult. Of course, the one big reason is that DD teachers, counselors and volunteers learn to divert a child's affections so as not to create inappropriately strong emotional bonds that could make a child vulnerable to emotional and/or physical abuse. All adult leaders are required to chronicle any physical interactions they may have with DD students. In fact, they can be held accountable for any inappropriate actions, words or instructions that may harm a student, even unintentionally. Adults, volunteers as well as staff, can be held accountable for any such inappropriate interactions.

Gandy and Lydia both welcomed such a friendship for Angel, but they also feared inappropriate behavior as well. They knew they would need to talk about such transference issues with Angelina if they should decide to continue to allow her to meet with their Angel.

Surprisingly for them, it was Angelina who opened that very conversation.

"I am wonderfully surprised at the joy I already feel getting to know Angel. However, I am also aware that I have much to learn about children with Down syndrome as well as your boundaries and whether you might be interested in my teaching art to Angel."

"Art!?" Gandy and Lydia both exclaimed. "For real? Art?"

Angelina couldn't tell if they were excitedly pleased or excitedly alarmed, so she just continued on. "Yes, for real," she said with a big smile. "I'm an artist and I'm now also affiliated with the Cleveland Museum of Art as their outreach worker at the Mission. I remember hearing that some developmentally delayed children actually have unexpectedly awesome eye-hand coordination, which makes their artistic, or even sports endeavors surprising successful. Maybe Angel is such a child." Angelina had glanced over at nine-year-old Angel several times and noted that she was paying close attention to everything Angelina said. Turning back to Gandy and Lydia, Angelina asked, "Have you noticed, over the years, if she is surprisingly good at playing with balls, singing songs, or drawing pictures?"

Animated and excited, Lydia's words tumbled out like water breaching a dam. "Yes! Yes! We have a piano in the other room, and Angel can actually pick out songs she learns at school, even in the right key. And, yes, she draws. She *loves* to draw, and actually it always looks like the something or the someone she is drawing. They spend some time at school encouraging her art, but they have too many children with such wide ranging needs, that there's not enough time in the day to focus on one girl to teach her how to draw. Besides, none of them are artists themselves. But you are, huh? That is really very, very exciting for us." She turned to Angel and asked, "Angel, honey, would you like Angel to draw with you?"

"Yes!" she beamed, looked straight at Angelina and said, "I love to draw with you. Mom, will you get us paper and chalk?"

"Please?"

"Please get us paper and chalk."

"I keep the paper and chalk put away, because if I don't she'd go through it all in a day."

"In a day?" Angelina asked surprised.

"She would draw and waste paper all day — and maybe all night."

"Can you bring out some of her drawings to show me?"

"How many do you want?"

"All of them."

Lydia laughed. "Okay. You asked for it."

Gandy laughed along, "Angelina, you just hit the jackpot. If I had any doubts about you and Angel spending time together, you have just dispelled them all. I can't wait to hear what you have to say about her drawings."

"Me too," said Angel.

"I can't wait either!" responded Angelina.

"You don't have to wait a second longer," said Lydia. "Here they are!" Lydia walked into the living room with her arms full of 11 by 17 inch works of art by this nine-year-old Down syndrome artist. Instantly, Gandy offered, "Let me get the card table. I'll put it right in front of Angelina."

After he unfolded and set up the card table, Lydia set down her huge stack of Angel art. Angelina opened her eyes really, really wide. She did not want to miss a thing.

"Wow!" said Joe, overwhelmed not only by the amount of paper, but also by the quality of the drawings that he could see. "Gandy, Lydia, this is amazing!"

Angelina motioned to Angel, "Angel, would you like to sit next to me and tell me all about your drawings and paintings?"

Angel rushed across the room and hugged Angelina again. She picked up the top picture, and said, "This picture is Mommy. I drawed it yesterday." Angelina did not need to be told who Angel's subject was. It looked exactly like Lydia. Worthy of framing.

"Angel, that is a beautiful picture of your mommy." Afraid Angel might misplace one of these treasures, Angelina asked, "Angel, from now on, could we always let Mommy be in charge of the pictures after you're finished drawing them? Okay?"

"Okay. Here, Mom. This is you."

"Thank you, Angel. It's beautiful." Then to Angelina Lydia said, "I do usually keep track of her pictures. We love them—all of them."

They spent the next hour and a half together looking at Angel's art.

First Angel would describe the picture like,

"This is the tree in the back yard."

And then Angelina would admire one aspect of that picture, such as, "Angel, the leaves on your tree are beautiful with wonderful colors. You did a very good job drawing this tree."

So with each succeeding picture Angel added more descriptive detail learning from what Angelina told her about the previous pictures.

"This is Marcie's house right there." She pointed out the window across the street. "I like the color of her red roof. It's smooth and has lines coming down."

"You did a great job drawing and painting that roof. That roof is made of metal. Metal is smooth and sometimes very shiny, like this roof in your picture. How did you make this roof look so shiny in your picture?"

"I mixed in a little white paint. There and there. See that?"

"I do. And that was a good thing you did to make it look shiny."

Lydia, Gandy and Joe watched in awe. Lydia and Gandy had never heard Angel talk about her pictures like that. They were all so impressed that within a short amount of instruction from Angelina, Angel more ably explained what she painted and why.

Two hours and 53 pictures later, Lydia thought Angel was getting tired and that Angelina could use a break as well, so she interrupted. "This is the last picture for today, Angel. Would you like to invite your new friend to come back tomorrow?"

Angel's face exploded in joy. "Will you come back tomorrow, Big Angel? Please?"

"Yes. I would be happy to. But before I go, maybe Joe, would you pray for us all before we leave? Is that okay with everybody?"

Gandy, Lydia, Angel and Joe all agreed. Joe prayed for everyone by name, especially giving thanks for Angel's beautiful pictures.

The instant they all said "Amen," Angel ran up to Angelina with one of her pictures in hand, "Angel, Big Angel, here's a picture for you. It's Marcie. She's my friend. Do you like this one?"

"I love this one! Thank you very, very much, Angel.

"You're welcome. I painted Marcie."

"She's very pretty. You used different colors in painting Marcie's beautiful face. Orange and yellow and white. Tell me, Angel, why did you use white?"

"Because that part of her face is shiny, just like the roof."

"Perfect. May I show Marcie's picture to my friends?"

"That's okay. Will they like her?"

"They will love her just like I do." Angelina smiled, and then said sweetly, "See you tomorrow."

Angel Martin gave Angelina a big boa constrictor hug and stage-whispered, "I love you, Big Angel."

"I love you too, Little Angel. And I love your Angel Art!"

As Joe and Angelina started to leave, Joe turned to Gandy, Lydia and Angel and said, "Thank you for inviting us into your house and showing us all those beautiful pictures. We loved getting to know you."

Gandy, face glowing with respect and appreciation for Joe and especially Angelina, responded, "Joe, thank you for knocking on our door and for shouting to tell me it was you knocking! This was incredible for all of us. Angelina, see you tomorrow morning? 11:00?"

"Absolutely. I'll be here. And, Gandy?

"Yes?"

"You and Lydia are such wonderful parents. I can already tell of your love for one another and for Angel. She is so blest that you are her parents. Thank you for welcoming us into your home."

"Into our family. You're family now, Angelina. Thank you for being our second Angel."

"It is my pleasure, Gandy, for sure. Bye."

And they all smiled at one another and waved good-bye.

As Joe and Angelina turned to walk up Divine Street toward the mission, they said absolutely nothing till they had gotten all the way to The Mission at Harbor and Divine. Just soaking it all in, they were.

Amazed, Joe broke the silence. "That was draining, wasn't it?"

"Yes, it was. But so sweet, as well as wonderful, exhilarating, lovely, intoxicating all at the same time!"

"Intoxicating?"

"Yeah, like I couldn't get enough, I hated to leave. Know what I mean? They are a wonderful family. And Angel is so precious!"

"I agree. And to think the day all started with Gandy shoving me in the shoulder. Hard! Well, not that hard."

"That's hilarious, Joe, simply hilarious. But, Joe?"

"Yeah?"

"You handled it perfectly. I'm not sure I know anyone else who, after getting shoved and shouted at like you did, could turn a violent confrontation into a prayer meeting, and then follow it up with the incredible house visit we just had."

"God leads. But thanks, Angel. You were awesome yourself. We made a good team today, didn't we?

"We sure did. Thanks for hiring me. Oh, and do you know what else, Joe?"

"No. What?"

"Thank you for how you are helping my mother and my father get together. I admire you for putting my mother and especially my father, whom you had never ever met before, ahead of your own sweet spot for my mom. You're a very special man, Joe Whitehorse, and I'm lucky to have two men like you and my father in my life."

Joe kept walking with his head down for a step or two, sizing it all up, thinking about what to say. In the end he just said, "You're welcome, Angel." And both of them stayed quiet until they got to Harbor Street and turned the corner.

All of a sudden Angelina got all animated and bubbled out, "Gary, Gary! Of course! Gary's home! Joe, let's show Gary Angel's picture of her best friend, Marcie! He'll want to know all about Angel and her art! Want to?"

"That sounds like a great idea. His car's there, which must also mean he's not staying at Annie's any more — which is good. I worry about Gary getting hooked up too soon, before he gets over his grief for Dianah and their daughter Lily. Not my business, but still I worry."

"They're both adults. Old, you know? They'll handle it."

"I guess you're right. I'll keep my nose out. Let's go knock on his door."

"Or ring the bell?"

"Sure, or ring the bell. I delivered newspapers door to door back in the day, The Columbus Dispatch. Once a week I had to go door to door and collect the week's payment. I could hear them moving around inside the house, like you heard Gandy and Lydia. And just like Gandy and Lydia, my customers wouldn't always answer the door bell either. True, sometimes the bell didn't work. So if I didn't hear it ringing, or if it rang and I didn't hear their footsteps coming to the door, I'd knock. The first time I knocked loud....the second time I knocked louder....the third time, if I had gloves on, I'd take them off and knock with bare knuckles as loud as I could so they'd think I was breaking the door down, and yell at the top of my lungs, 'Paper boy! Collecting!'"

Angelina laughed. "No, you didn't."

"Yes, I did. I wanted to make sure they knew I wasn't going away. Some of them were skinflints. Oh, yeah. And, sure enough, when I had rattled their house and shouted loud enough for the whole neighborhood to hear, they'd open the door and say, "Oh, it's you."

"Innocently I'd say, 'Collecting. A dollar twenty-five, please.' I'd say it nice and polite, because that was a real deal for seven newspapers. Good Lord, seven papers delivered to your door for a buck and a quarter?! Plus, sure, I expected a tip on top of it, because I never missed a paper."

"Did you get tips after all that house beating and yelling?"

"Most of the time, yeah. Some of them added a nickel a week, last of the big spenders. But lots of them threw in an extra quarter, and with 43 customers, those quarters added up, even the nickels. Sometimes those tips nearly doubled my weekly income. Anyhow, eventually I learned it was faster to bypass all the bell ringing and go straight to the door pounding. I got them trained pretty good."

"You're hilarious. And here we are, so pound away."

"Calling my bluff, huh?" They both laughed. So Joe pounded away.

Gary opened the door in a flash with an angry look on his face that melted away to a smile as soon as he saw their smiling, mischievous faces. "Joe, it's you! And Angelina! What are you two trying to do, wreck my house?"

Angelina answered laughing, "He was just showing off his paperboy prowess to me. And, I've got to admit, it worked like a charm. You got to the door in record time with a mean look on your face. And let me ask you, if he were your paperboy would you give him a tip after all that pounding?"

"A tip?" He took a breath, turned his frown upside down and said laughing, "Yeah, I would. After all it's Joe for crying out loud. I'd probably give him a nickel or two."

"See?" Joe interjected. "A nickel? Oy veh! Skin flint."

"Oh hush, or I won't even give you that."

And all three of them roiled with laughter.

Still laughing, Gary invited them in. "Have a seat, you two, and tell me what's happening."

Angelina grinned from ear to ear, thrust out her hand with Angel's portrait of Marcie and said, "This. This is what's happening. Take a look at this portrait done by a nine-year-old Down syndrome girl."

Gary took the picture, gasped and exclaimed, "What?! A nine-year-old Down syndrome girl painted this? This is miraculous!

Please come in, have a seat
and tell me all about her."

Chapter 17

Angel Art

Gary sat down, studied the portrait then asked, "What's her name — the artist?"

"Angel."

"What?! No way! Plus you found a little artist with your name?"

"Yep. Isn't that awesome?"

"Awesome, for sure," said Gary still studying the picture.

"You're going to have to go back to Angelina," Joe chipped in.

"I wouldn't mind that at all, one Angel is plenty. Besides, she's more of an Angel than I am, innocent, joyful, huggy."

Gary looked up from the picture to ask, "Is this the only one, or are there more? Pictures, I mean."

Joe jumped in with, "Tons more, Gar, a whole exhibition worth."

Angelina added, "We looked through 53 of them, and that was less than half the stack Lydia brought out to show us."

"Lydia?"

Joe answered, "Her mom, Gar. Lydia and Gandy are her parents, who are, from what I saw, doing a splendid job of raising that little girl, although I'm not sure I agree with her about rationing the paper."

"Seriously? She rations the paper?"

"I guess little kids are wasteful, so she doles it out. When Angel is finished with one picture, her mom gives her a new piece of paper."

Gary nodded and smiled in appreciation. "Actually, that's a great idea in training a creative mind that's prone to flit from idea to idea. It may also teach a budding artist to stay glued to the chair until something gets accomplished, increasing the artistic attention span. Hmmm," Gary thought for a long second then said, "From what little I know about Down syndrome, Mom's paper rationing may have done a lot to structure little Angel's artistic impulses."

"Gary, awesome point!" Angelina admired. "I may have to do some rationing on my self."

"Plus glue on your backside," Gary quipped.

"Right. That too," Angelina chuckled. "I have a lot to learn about teaching art if we're going to make this art outreach more than just scribble time for kids."

"Angelina, there's always more to learn, but don't diminish the value of good scribble time. Small, artistic sketches born of huge, expressive scribbles lead to artistic freedom that creates bold sketches, modern, non-representational art and expressive, beautiful washes. Besides, with scribbles, you can always fill up the paper, and then use the other side."

"Sounds like 'Readiness for Teaching Art 101.'"

"You've got it. And it sounds to me like you already have lesson plans cooking in that future-teacher's brain of yours. With that kind of creative thinking, I predict you'll be great as our CMA outreach worker, neighborhood organizer and art teacher. Besides, you also have Dr. Zurkos, a great artist and teacher, to learn from. She mentored me throughout my masters degree years, and I owe her a great deal of credit for getting me to complete "Old Tony" in Leonardo's classic style."

Gary paused to think and then said, "Like, 'Letting go and getting back. That's the rhythm of an artist,'" she told me. But it's neither circular nor linear, because when you come back to your work neither you nor your work exists in the same artistic plane as when you left it. Each time you return to your work your eyes see your art differently, because in the intervening time you have become deeper as a person and as an artist. That means every time you pick up your palette, you see things you never saw before. So the rhythm of an artist looks more like a descending spiral, getting deeper with each cycle of letting go and getting back. It's something young artists could easily learn. Not only does the art teacher ration the art paper, but the art teacher also rations the artistic effort spent one session at a time. Much of what I will teach in our Old Tony Studio grew from what I learned from Melanie Zurkos."

Gary's vision-casting was more akin to the work of a preacher or prophet painting with words the promise of a heavenly place where an artist can leap out of earthly restraints and freely fly. Fly and create, fly and create.

"I can teach you how to get 'from here to there' limited by what I have learned. But Dr. Zurkos, I don't know how she does it, she can teach you how to free yourself as an artist to move from the place where I might take you, throw off those shackles of trying to make art like mine or anyone else's and leap into not-yet-imagined flights of artistry determined by your own unique vision borne of your very own artistic soul. Really, very much like our little Angel paints–flights of artistry determined by her own unique vision of... what's her friend's name again?"

"Marcie," Angelina said.

"Marcie," he repeated. "Marcie. We have just got to make some prints of Marcie. A hundred of them. Numbered. Signed." Exhausted by his vision casting effort, Gary slumped into his chair to catch his breath, and think about whether he told any lies.

Joe quietly applauded with his finger tips. "Gary, I could just stand up and cheer. Your mentors would be totally proud."

"You're a good friend, Joe. But right now? Right now I want to frame this beautiful portrait, meet the artist and look at every single painting, drawing and charcoal she has ever done. I can't wait!"

"Well, then, how about tomorrow morning?" Angelina asked. "It's Saturday, so maybe their whole family will be free. I want you to meet Gandy and Lydia as well. Want me to call and set it up? I'm supposed to be there at 11:00 anyhow. I'll just add in Gary."

Gary nodded, "I'm free. How 'bout you, Joe?"

"I'll pass. You and Angel — oops — you and Angelina go without me. Even though I was married to an artist, I'm no artist, and I think this meeting should be more you two and the Martins figuring out what might be a good next step for Angel. Besides three more adults instead of two in that house would make quite a crowd. Are you two okay if I sit this one out?"

"Makes sense to me, Joe," agreed Gary.

"Me too," chimed in Angelina. "In fact, I'll call right now and just swap out Joe for Gary. One all-star for another," she winked impishly at the two men, as she swayed into the kitchen.

Joe and Gary ignored Angelina's flirtatious charm and jumped on the moment to check signals of their own, Gary first.

"Joe, between having Angelina in my Old Tony Studio and her working with Angel, I could probably use up a lot of her time. How much of her time each week do you want for community organizing for the mission? We should come up with job/time expectations for her so she feels she's meeting goals we have set for her."

"Good thinking, Gar. I have been asking myself those same questions ever since we talked with the Martins this morning. This is all new for me, so I may need a bit of help. Oh no!"

"What's up?"

"I told the Korvers, a volunteer couple, that I'd be working on bikes tomorrow morning. Hmmm. Actually, that might be more of an opportunity than a problem. Sandy Korver was a community organizer out of this very church back when you were here as a kid. Do you remember her at all? She said something about a Tot-a-Lot."

"Sandy... hmm... oh sure, Sandy. Not Korver. Matuski or something like that. She was a college student."

"Right. Korver is her married name," Joe agreed. "Thirty-five years married, I think. Oh, you've just *got to* be here too. I can move our bike repair time to eight o'clock. That way Sandy, her husband, Don, and I could chat about what Sandy's supervisors expected of her way back then. You want to join us before you and Angelina head down to the Martin's? In fact, I could invite Angelina to join us as well, cut out all the middle and let her go straight to the source. IN FACT, maybe the Korvers have an extra bed, and Angelina could stay at their house for the night! Hey, this is sounding better by the second, feeling like a good plan all the way around."

"Is that how preachers work?" asked Gary in sincere admiration.

"You mean, fly by the seat of our pants and invent as we go?"

"Yeah, I do. But I mean it as a compliment that you are flexible, adaptable, resourceful, creative and decisive," Gary said.

"Thank you, Gar. I like to think that sizing up a situation and pulling a good game plan out from it is actually a huge part of my job. So, what do you think? I mean, you're just across the street. How 'bout joining us at 8:00?"

"I'd love to, Joe. Can't resist being on the ground floor of a good plan, especially one so creatively fashioned by a man of the cloth!"

"All righty then! I'll call Sandy and Don right now and we'll be ready to go when Angelina returns. She already knows Sandy and Don."

As last minute plans sometimes do, this one worked to perfection. Don and Sandy were happy to be there by eight, delighted to invite Angelina to stay overnight and excited to help birth another outreach of the new Mission at Harbor and Divine.

When Angelina walked in, the guys were all abuzz, and she was excited that Gary's living room felt like mission control.

Once Joe got off the phone, he and Gary told her their ideas about the overnight, working together in the morning and Gary joining in on her trip back to Angel's house which got Angelina way fired up. "And I get to spend the night at Sandy and Don's? Cool! That sounds fun — like an old fashioned overnight with church friends that my mother used to tell me about. And it's the perfect time to get to know Don and Sandy better and pick their brains about what happened back in the day. Hey, you know what? You guys are fun to work with, you know that?"

"Thanks," they said laughing.

"You're pretty cool too," Gary told her. "Plus with Don and Sandy, the Martin family, Melanie Zurkos and her staff we're growing ourselves into a dynamite team, don't you think?"

Joe nodded his head and smiled saying, "I agree. This is already fun. Warm fuzzies all around. Plans we agree on. This feels good. Really good!"

Two voices concurred, "Amen!"

Chapter 18

Plan the Work, Work the Plan

Joe and Angelina left Gary's house and walked around the corner to Dr. Don and Sandy's home. Joe wanted to be sure there were no glitches yet to be worked out. But when they knocked at the front door and Don invited them in, Joe discovered he had absolutely nothing to worry about. Sandy had already prepared the spare bedroom for Angelina with clean sheets, fresh towels and toiletries. Plus she even offered to loan Angelina a pair of Sandy's freshly laundered pajamas. The two women got along so famously that Joe soon felt like a fifth wheel. So he excused himself, left the ladies to their happy talk and went looking for Don, whom he found in a flash.

"Oh, Don, there you are."

"Hey, Joe! Did the ladies release you on good behavior?"

"Sorta. I think they actually forgot I was even there."

"The plight of a man."

"I guess. It's been so long since Val died that I have forgotten a thing or two about living with a woman."

"I'm so sorry. But you are welcome to visit with me for a night if you think you need a refresher. In fact, why don't you just hang with me now while Sandy helps Angelina get settled for the night, and this will be your re-introductory class to 'Living with a Woman 401,' for advanced students." They both laughed.

As tired as he felt from his busy day, Joe surprised himself and accepted Don's invitation. "Thanks, Don, I'd love to — but just for a little while. It's been a wonderful but exhausting day."

"Great! Come on into the kitchen and I'll find us something to drink. Cup of coffee, tea, decaf, lemonade — no beer or sodas, I'm afraid. Serving yourself is lesson number one."

"Thank you, Don. A cup of hot tea sounds great."

Don passed Joe a small basket of tea varieties.

"Here you go. While you find a tea you like, I'll put a log on the fire and heat up the water."

"Say what?"

"Just kidding. Wanted to see if you're still awake."

"Just barely, but obviously not enough to get the joke."

"Obviously. Even at our age, Sandy and I are still twenty-first century Americans, so I'm going to nuke your water. It'll be ready in a jiffy."

Joe grinned and yawned. "Thanks, Don."

"Oh, yeah, I just remembered that you like to walk your way here from your apartment on West 25th, so how about I give you a lift home in a bit?"

"Thanks, Don! I accept. You're a life-saver."

"My pleasure." The microwave timer dinged, Don passed a cup of hot water to Joe and cautioned, "Careful. It's *really* hot."

"Thanks," Joe said as he plopped in his tea bag. Don made a cup of tea for himself and sat down at the kitchen table with

Joe like the manly men they were — or, at least, imagined they were.

"So tell me, Joe, how are you doing starting up a brand new mission there at Harbor and Divine?"

"Great, I think. Way better than I deserve. In fact, as Elizabeth Barrett Browning might say, 'Let me count the ways.'" And he did. He counted, from the moment he left on his walk, all the good things that had happened to him just that very day including getting smacked by Gandy, bumping into Don on his midday walk and now this very minute Don inviting him to tea and chit-chat.

"Sounds like it's been a wonderful day for you, my friend."

"You're right, Don, it has been. But, I've got to tell you, I am exhausted and ready to get home. Wow," Joe yawned, "In fact, I guess I'm ready any time you are."

Don chuckled as he looked at Joe's nearly sleep-closed eyes, "I'll say! Let me tell Sandy first."

But she and Angelina beat him to the punch. When they came down to say goodnight, Don joked about the old man helping the young buck walk to the car. He had truly enjoyed the company! He opened his car door for Joe, hopped behind the wheel and six minutes later he dropped Joe off in front of *La Cocina* twenty feet from the street level door up to his West 25th Street apartment.

"Don, thank you so much. I owe you, my brother."

"*De nada.*" Don replied. "It's nothing."

"What? *Habla Espanol?*" Joe asked surprised.

"Joe, anybody who lives here has got to speak at least a little Spanish. Do you?"

"Yes, I sure do. I grew up speaking Spanish. I'll tell you about it sometime, but not now. I'm exhausted. Thanks again. Good night."

"Good night, Joe."

Joe fumbled through his keys — one for the street door, one for the hall door and one for his apartment 2B. He opened up his apartment, said, "Good night, Frank" to his St. Francis statue in the entry, plopped his weary frame into bed and fell straight to sleep until morning with his shoes still on.

Chapter 19

The Champs of Bicycle Rehab

By 8:00 the next morning the sun was bright, the December sky was clear, the temperature was already over 40 degrees F, and the champions of bicycle rehab were ready to rock'n'roll. They decided to do the degreasing, sanding and washing outdoors in the sunshine and make all the mechanical repairs indoors in the basement of the church building where they kept the tools — and it was warmer. Joe was late, so Gary, who also had a church key, unlocked the door so he and Don could head down the basement steps to bring up four bikes that needed cleaning. Angelina and Sandy followed them down to find cleaning rags, soap and solvent, fill buckets with warm water and carry everything up the stairs and outside. In no time at all, the bicycle rehab champs were busy degreasing chains, wheels and sprockets; washing and polishing frames and wheels; and running the cleaned parts and frames down for the mechanical team to reassemble. As a 9:00 surprise, Gandy, Lydia and Angel arrived to pitch in — Gandy wrenching with the guys, Lydia and Angel degreasing and cleaning with the ladies. They chatted, laughed and even sang "If You're Happy and You Know It," much to Gary's delight. By 9:15 even Annie bopped in to lend a hand — again, much to Gary's delight — in the basement reassembling the bikes. Evidently, somehow, the word had spread, and good people came to help. With Christmas just around the corner, it was like Santa's elves gathering for a work day in Santa's bicycle department. Still no Joe, though, so Don called his cell.

By 10:00 four finished bikes stood in the mission yard with 'For Sale' signs and prices, causing Don to crow, "This is the best bicycle work day ever!" Never mind that it was only the second one ever, it was still something to celebrate. One of the bikes was a 20" girls bike with training wheels, just right for Angel, Gandy and Lydia noted. Angel thought so too, and in a flash, to everyone's delight, Angel hopped on that bike and started tooling down the sidewalk, around the corner and out of sight.

Both laughing, Gandy and Lydia ran after their suddenly mobile daughter calling, "Angel, Angel, wait for us!" while everyone else cheered. Lydia was gaining on Angel quite impressively, so Gandy stopped, turned to the cheering group and called, "I guess we'll buy that one!" causing everyone to cheer and laugh even louder. "I'll be right back with the cash." And off he ran.

All the loud happiness along with the beautiful bicycles drew another family to cross Harbor Street, smiles on their faces, to see what was going on. At that moment Joe finally arrived just in time to use his rusty Spanish.

"Buen dia!" greeted the man.

Joe jumped into action, eager to respond to what he thought was an idiomatic "Good morning" from Mexico.

"Buen dia!" he responded. "Que tal?"

Surprised and delighted with Joe's Spanish, the man went on to introduce himself, Miguel Hernandez, his wife, Gabriela, and their children, Tomas, 10 and Ana, 8. Joe began translating for everyone else, though Angelina spoke Spanish even better than Joe. So, rather than translate, she dove right into the conversation introducing herself to Gabriela and the children in Spanish.

Don, who knew a little Spanish from his days as an ER doctor at Cleveland's Metro General Hospital there on the West Side, enjoyed listening to the chatter. Even though he was now retired, Don occasionally still took a shift at Metro General's ER to help out the overworked weekend staff. Most of them knew him very well from his doctor days and loved it when he filled in. Since the hospital was only a couple miles south on West 25th Street, Don was happy to oblige. "I'll never stop being a doctor," he often said to his wife Sandy, "because I'll never stop wanting to help people whenever I can."

As they were all talking, Miguel scanned the faces in the group to find someone he might know, and he did, Dr. Korver! In Spanish, Miguel asked Don, "Are you an ER doctor at Metro General?"

"Yes, sometimes."

"You treated Tomas when he broke his arm last summer."

"Oh, yes. I remember Tomas." Then turning to the boy, he asked in Spanish, "How is your arm today, Tomas?"

"Very good, thank you," he politely replied.

"Excellent. That makes me happy."

By this time Angelina had picked up the general translating instead of Joe, while Joe stood by admiring her as he said to Gary, "She sure is a wonderful find for us, isn't she?"

"A godsend for sure!" Of the three bicycles left, two were 24 and 26 inch girls bikes, both too big for Ana. But the third bike was a flashy metallic red and gold 20 inch boys beauty, and Tomas stared at it with a big grin on his face.

Miguel smiled at his son and asked, "Tomas, do you like that fancy bike?"

Tomas laughed and said, "Very much, Papi. It's beautiful!"

Miguel turned to Joe, "How much for that one?"

"Eight dollars."

Amazed, Miguel asked, "That's all?"

"Yes. We're not here to make money, we're here to help folks out and lead people to Jesus. You want to buy it?"

"Absolutely!" Miguel responded, as he dug into his pockets to pull out two crumpled up five dollar bills handing them to Joe. "Thank you very much. No change. You keep it to help somebody else."

"You're welcome, and thank you very much. Enjoy your new bicycle, Tomas!"

"Thank you! Thank you, Papi!" he crowed as he hopped on his flashy new bike and rode down the sidewalk around the corner and out of sight. Miguel and Gabriela laughed and said together, "He'll be back!"

But he wasn't.

Instead, from down the street where Tomas rode, came a violent crashing of steel, the squeal of car brakes, men yelling and women screaming.

Miguel jumped up in high alert, shouting, "Tomas! Tomas! *Dios mio! Madre mia!*" and ran down the street. Joe and Gary ran closely behind followed by Dr. Don, Annie, Gabriela, Ana, Angelina and Sandy in a posse of love.

Sirens had already started to wail as the crash scene came into focus for the posse. A pick up truck had crashed into and rolled over a parked car landing upside-down on the sidewalk knocking Tomas off his shiny new bike. There lay the motionless Tomas between the steaming pick-up and his shiny new bicycle, with its wheels still spinning. Tomas was motionless when helpers rushed in to give aid, led by Dr. Don kneeling by Tomas's side and Miguel speaking tenderly to Tomas in Spanish.

"Oh, my little boy! Tomas!"

"Papi, Papi, it hurts. Papi, it hurts very much."

Miguel comforted his son, and told him, "Dr. Don is right here. He will help you."

Dr. Don's Spanish suddenly flooded out like a native born Latino, asking Tomas to point where it hurt. Tomas began to cry as he pointed and said, "Aqui, aqui, aqui, y aqui," as he pointed to his hip, his leg, his head and his arm, the same arm he broke last summer. "Dr. Don it hurts so much." Don looked into Tomas's eyes and asked him to move his eyes up and down first and then side to side.

A police officer ran up and asked, "Is the boy hurt?"

Dr. Don answered, "He's hurt in several places. I'm Dr. Don Korver, ER doc at Metro General. This is Tomas and his father, Miguel Hernandez. We need to wait on the EMTs to make an assessment before we move him at all. But Tomas seems quite stable at the moment."

"Good. I called for two squads, one for the pickup driver who is still not conscious, and one for the boy. As you can hear, they're on the way." He knelt down beside Tomas. "Hi Tomas, I'm Sergeant Rossi. How do you feel now, son?"

"It hurts a lot, sir."

"I'm sorry. Will you be okay until the EMTs get here? If you listen, can you hear them coming right now to help you?"

"Yes, sir."

"Good. You're a brave young man, Tomas. Here they are now."

As the EMT's arrived, the paramedic in charge approached Sergeant Rossi. "I'm Paramedic in Charge, Esther Williamson. Looks like we have a young man down?"

"Yes, we do," Rossi said. "I'm Sergeant Angelo Rossi, and this fine young man is Tomas. He told me it hurts a lot, so please take good care of him. This is Dr. Korver out of Metro General and Tomas's father, Miguel Hernandez. I'll be right over there if you need me," he said pointing to the overturned pickup as he spun a nifty 180 and quickly walked away.

After Paramedic Williamson checked Tomas's vitals, the EMT's gently placed him on the spinal board, strapped him in, strapped him to the gurney and loaded him into the EMV inviting Miguel to ride along.

Miguel smiled, said, "Gracias," stepped up into the vehicle where an EMT strapped him to a jump seat along side of Tomas as they soon took off to Metro General Hospital, sirens blaring. With his Papi sitting next to him, Tomas was brave, calm and actually enjoyed the ride.

Miguel smiled at Tomas. "How're you doing, *muchacho mio?*" he asked.

"Much better, Papi, with you here. But the bumps really hurt."

Miguel chuckled, "We'll be there soon, Tomas."

"It's really cool riding inside an EMV. Is that what you call them?"

Miguel shrugged, *"Yo no se."*

"No problemmo, Papi," Tomas said. "The kids at school will be so jealous when I tell them no matter what I say it is!"

Miguel laughed and went to muss Tomas' hair like he always did when he was proud of his son. But he remembered Tomas said his head really hurt in that one place, so he pulled back his hand and kissed Tomas on his forehead instead, saying,

"You make me proud, my son!" as a tear slid quietly down his cheek. The attending EMT smiled at them wishing that he and his father had had such a loving relationship when he was growing up.

Back at the scene of the accident, Sergeant Rossi returned to get information from Gabriela about Tomas and then to interview bystanders concerning the accident. In the meantime EMTs had loaded the still unconscious pickup driver into the second EMV and drove off to Metro General as well, siren wailing. When Rossi and other officers had completed their interviews, they thanked the bystanders and dispersed the crowd.

Joe, Gary, Angelina and the others walked back to the mission abuzz with observations and stories about the accident while assuring Gabriela and Ana that Tomas would be well cared for at Metro General, especially with his papi at his side. They told her that Dr. Korver had walked home ahead of them so he could drive his car to the ER and offer to help with Tomas.

"Dr. Korver, he is a good man, don't you think?" asked Gabriela.

They all agreed, saying, "He sure is!"

Joe asked the rest of the "posse," minus Dr. Don, to finish up the bikes they had been working on and then clean up for the day. Everyone agreed they had had enough excitement for one day. After cleaning up, Angelina walked Gabriela and Ana to their home, while Joe walked to the mission offices to call DJ and brief him on the morning's events. Gary and Annie walked across the street to Gary's house for a bite of lunch and some chat time. They didn't talk long, because Annie was pretty well exhausted from a very busy morning added to her need for recovery time from her own all too recent accident.

She stood up to get her coat to leave with Gary at her side, when timidly Gary said, "Annie, before you leave, I've got one thing for you to think about."

Annie turned to Gary with a soft smile and tilted head just right for kissing, so Gary obliged with a tender kiss that melted their two hearts into one. "Oh, my," he said, "that was way better than what I was going to say."

"Unless," Annie said with a mischievous grin, "unless you were going to ask me to elope with you..."

Gary burst out laughing. "I'm getting more and more used to the idea every day. Maybe tomorrow."

"Elope?"

"No, silly girl. Tomorrow I'll tell you what I was going to say, if that's okay with you."

She smiled that killer smile that made his knees wobble, touched his cheek and said, "At least the idea is on the table."

Annie kissed his cheek, leaving Gary wanting more. "Some day," he said quietly to himself as she walked out the door.

"I heard that!" she said.
And they both laughed.
Sorta.

Chapter 20

Melvin and Carmela

A t last! This was the day. Saturday! After ten years of separation Melvin and Carmela had finally agreed to talk. Well, more than just talk. Decide. Melvin had moved out, left his wife Carmela and their then nine-year-old daughter Angelina because he felt he couldn't be the man Carmela deserved. After three tours of combat duty in the Middle East Melvin became, what he described, 'a whimpering, cowering shell of man not fit to be Carmela's husband or Angelina's father.' Of course, neither of them agreed with that assessment. Yes, it was true he did have night terrors with violent shouting, cursing and ordering unseen soldiers in his command to their posts. Yes, he often responded to loud, crashing sounds by diving for cover, shaking with uncontrollable sobbing. Yes, he sometimes clutched Carmela with vice-like embraces sobbing quietly, "I'm sorry, Carmela. I'm so sorry," until she kissed away his demons assuring him "Everything's all right, Melvin. Everything's safe here."

Those episodes weren't every day occurrences. True. But when, at a U-10 junior track meet with Angelina in the ready, set position for the girls 60 meter dash the starter's pistol sent him diving for cover, he knew it was time. He had embarrassed his nine-year old daughter, her track team and her school as well as himself and his wife in public.

He left the next day.

Carmela pleaded with him to stay. "Melvin, you're a good, good man. You gave your life for your country. I'm so proud of you. Please stay."

Angel had no words. She just cried and clung to her father. Finally she choked out, "Daddy, please don't go." But even that did not alter his resolve.

With tears streaming down his stone-set face, Melvin climbed into his old beater work car and drove off. No good-byes. No waves. Just tears. Melvin was a good, good man. Yes, he was. Yet he still abandoned his wife and daughter. Had to. Just had to.

After staying with a friend for a couple of weeks Melvin found an inexpensive rental in Lakewood's Birdtown neighborhood, never telling Carmela its location. He kept his job, paid all their bills, lost a lot of weight and kept his appointments at the VA. Miraculously, after three short months the night terrors vanished, and loud sounds no longer instantly catapulted him back into war. He and his VA counselor decided that the added stress of protecting his family had made Melvin's PTSD demons impossible for him to cast out. But now, strangely enough, without the two people he loved the most, he was able to effectively cast out those demons and reclaim his stature of being the man his family deserved. Unfortunately, the three times he convinced himself to reconnect with Carmela pulled him right back into the darkness before he ever made the connection. He felt defeated, demoralized and useless as a man. Funny though, when he went to Angel's track meets to watch from a distance, he felt just fine. Proud of his little girl. Not afraid. Not even the starter's pistol shots cowered him any more. So he kept attending Angel's away meets figuring Carmela would probably go to her home meets.

It worked well until one day at an away track meet Angelina spotted him near the finish line of her 100m race. She was ten now, and no longer ran 60m races. Even though she won the race, rather than go celebrate with her teammates, she ran straight to Melvin.

"Daddy? Daddy?" she asked from a distance, uncertain it was really him, what with how skinny he was and how unexpected his appearance was. "Is that you?"

Melvin, unsure about breaking protocol, finally gave a slight nod to his beautiful little girl, and she flew into his arms.

"Daddy, Daddy! It's so good to see you!" she sobbed with joyful tears streaming down her face.

"It's good to see you too, my Angel."

"Do we get to see each other now?"

"How about at away track meets. Just me from a distance."

"Why not Mommy? She misses you. She still cries a lot."

Melvin didn't answer his daughter—just couldn't.

Over the next eight years Melvin attended every one of Angelina's away track and cross country meets, and Carmela's weeping jags fell from three or four times a day to three or four times a week, but neither one of them ever gave up yearning to be husband and wife together again. It's just that they never did anything about it. They never got divorced, yet they never reconciled either. Never even talked. Never. Not in ten years.

Until Joe Whitehorse showed up, that is. In hero fashion Joe somehow convinced them both that it was time to talk face to face. Part of that *somehow* was that Joe and Carmela were falling in love, but she was still holding back for Melvin.

And now this was the day. Melvin had called Carmela.

"So how 'bout I drive to your place this Saturday, and we can finally talk?"

"You sure?"

"No. I'm not sure at all."

"Then why, after all these years?"

"Two reasons. The first one is I still love you. The second one is I always have and I always will."

"Me too, Melvin. I can't stop loving you."

"Well, check that off the list. Now I know. And I'm glad."

"Hearing it said out loud, you mean? That I love you still?"

"Yeah. Makes me want to sit near you again, inhale your beauty, hold your hand, wrap you in my arms, kiss your lips."

"Me too, Melvin. But we could have been doing that for the last ten years." Carmela paused. She took a breath, and decided to take a chance. "After all these years, what convinced you to take a chance. To risk those demons taking over again?" She paused, bit her lip. Then she took a chance and asked, "Was it Joe?"

Melvin laughed. "One hundred per cent it was Joe. But how 'bout I tell you all about it when we talk. Say, 2:00 Saturday afternoon?"

"I say yes. You've got me hooked Melvin Anderson. Again."

"And you've got me goin', girl. Always have."

"Saturday, then."

"Two o'clock. I'll be there."

"I can hardly wait."

Melvin left Birdtown at 1:00—he did not want to be late. Nervous he was, like a teenager on his first date with his dream girl. But Saturday traffic to the East Side was so light that when he got near his old house where Carmela and Angelina still lived he was half an hour early. "Can't be that early. No, no, no. Not manly," he told himself. But then he had a brainstorm, and almost shouted, "Ooh! I've got time to get her some flowers!" And off he drove.

The neighborhood had changed some. Mostly a lot of drug houses had been demolished. "Good riddance," he said spying a vacant lot that once had a house with so many drug busts that the neighborhood kids started calling it "The Drug Store." He said it out loud, laughing at the memory. And he still remembered that just down the street there used to be a corner IGA grocery store that sold small bouquets for occasions just like this one. He made the turn and there was the store. "Perfect!" he celebrated clapping his hands. "Now if only they still sell those flowers."

He unfolded himself to step out of his Honda Civic. "Just like Joe," he chuckled. "An SUV next time. Oh, yeah." When finally disgorged, Melvin stretched, cracked his back and walked toward the steel-barred front entry, sighing at the sight that he never saw in Lakewood. "Not even in Birdtown," he said out loud shaking his head in dismay, but forgetting that there were barred stores on West 118th Street just a half mile from his Birdtown home, although that was actually in Cleveland and not Lakewood. Nevertheless, he walked through the door, eyes to the left, and there they were, Bouquets exactly where they used to be back in the day. He walked over, picked up a bunch of every-color-in-the-rainbow flowers, paid, strutted out the door and proudly said aloud, "I've got beautiful flowers for my beautiful wife. Hmm. Wife? I guess we'll see about that real soon."

He folded himself back into his Honda, placed the flowers on the passenger seat and started whistling. "Whistling?" he questioned himself. "Really?" He shook his head and checked the time. One forty-five. "Perfect," he announced to himself. "My-oh-my will she be surprised! On time, whistling and with flowers." He laughed, "Lawd have mercy!"

Ten minutes later he parked in front the house that had been home for him, Carmela and Angelina until he just walked away ten years ago. He stared at the house and remembered the deep love he always had for Carmela and their home together. Without warning, emotion started swelling in him like a big old pipe organ. "Nope! Nope! Don't you dare start bawling, Melvin Anderson! Cut it out right now!" Too late. Tears flooded like water from the rock down his face, and the old Marine Corps Sergeant began to sob. Overwhelmed, "Sheeeeeeet," was all he could say as his chest heaved driven by regret, guilt, sadness, love, anger and hope.

Just as he picked up an old McDonald's napkin to dry his face, he saw the front door open and there stood Carmela. Through the clear, cold, early winter air she could plainly see Melvin's tear-drenched eyes. With any pretense of Marine toughness vanishing, their eyes of love connected and Carmela stepped out the door onto the stoop with tears of her own streaking down her cheeks. She tilted her head, smiled at her good, good man and opened wide her arms to welcome her prodigal lover back into her heart—no words needed. None.

Melvin's heart raced at her invitation. He grabbed the flowers, flew out of the car and bolted up the walkway straight into her open arms. They kissed with a ten year hunger for the love they had never lost for one another. Gently they eased their embrace to gaze into each other's tear soaked eyes.

"I love you, Melvin Anderson. Always have."

"I love you, Carmela. Always will. Flowers?" he offered.

She took them. Smiled. "Thank you. They're beautiful."

More tears. More impassioned kisses. More healing embraces.

"It's cold out here. Want to come in?" she invited.

"Yes!" he answered excitedly, and he scooped her up into his arms and carried her over the threshold. Again. After twenty years, Carmela remembered how much she loved the feel of his strong arms carrying her into their honeymoon home, this very house. They both knew what he was doing, and she loved it, every bit. It was a new beginning. No words said. No words needed. Just love locked in their hearts for ten years exploding the chains of exile.

Once inside Carmela whispered alluringly, "No one else is here."

Melvin grinned, drew her face to his, and they kissed all over again never stopping as Melvin carried his beloved to the bed they hadn't shared for ten years, into the room Carmela had beautifully prepared — just in case.

After their magical reunion, Carmela cut right through all the fear, all the doubt, all the regret — right though it all. She hadn't been exactly certain how things would play out between them, so she had prepared fried chicken that morning to go along with freshly trimmed collards and white rice that they could eat while they discussed the possibilities of getting back together. But, well, now they would still eat that delicious food, but she felt they could probably reduce their discussion to six words, five for her, one for him. So on a hunch Carmela smiled at her good, good man and softly asked, "Would you like to stay?"

Before Melvin could even say his one word reply, his huge grin gave away his answer, caused her to giggle like a teenage girl and roll back into his arms. He laughed. He embraced her. He answered. "Yes," he told her, rejoicing that she had asked. "For ten years I hoped for this moment. Yes, I say. Yes! Yes! Yes!" She smothered his fourth "yes" with ferocious kisses.

The fried chicken could wait.

Chapter 21

Prayers Answered

Now it was 9:00 am, and Joe had been up since 5:00 fretting about whether God would answer his prayers to bless Melvin and Carmela with a renewed marriage. He tossed and turned all night hoping that God would honor his prayer and hoping He wouldn't. Joe was 60-40 in favor of their reconciliation because it was the *right* outcome for him to root for, at least for Melvin and Carmela. All right, and, yes, for God. Joe had trouble praying for himself. Selfish it seemed. But he couldn't one hundred per cent stop the selfish Joe from wanting Carmela for himself. Finally the 60% in favor of their marriage won out over his selfish 40%. After all, as DJ told him, Carmela is another man's wife. And Jesus even said that it is adultery just to lust after another man's wife. And lust he did. Not any more. Well, that's not true, but he had tamped it down by 90%. Joe had thoroughly reconciled himself to accept that Carmela and Melvin were, at least legally after ten years, still married.

Joe finally capitulated to "yet not my will, but thy will be done," like Jesus in the garden the night before they crucified him. Blood, sweat and tears led Jesus to sacrifice himself for the good of others, even though he too wasn't exactly thrilled about the prospects.

That Saturday, that's exactly how Joe felt, and embarrassed that, for the first time in his life, he was worried that God would actually affirm one of his prayers, bind Melvin and Carmela together in renewed love, and break Joe's heart. "Thy will be done," he said again *sotto voce*. And then even softer, "My, oh my. I believe it's done."

He went to the front door of his apartment, sat on the floor near his statue of St. Francis and sought counsel. St. Francis of Assisi was his number one spiritual hero, next to Jesus, of course. Somehow St. Francis seemed more approachable than Jesus, probably because Francis was not sinless like Jesus was.

"Frank, what would you do?" he said aloud.

"Exactly what you're doing, Joseph," he heard in his mind's heart. Frank would always call him Joseph when they had these talks. Somehow it seemed more intimate, transparent, official. And in this case Joe knew that Frank absolutely understood what Joe was talking about. Oh yeah, Frank had lots of experience. When he was a young hotshot before he got holy, he was quite a playboy, serenading the young ladies with his guitar beneath their windows there in Assisi, Italy. A regular Don Juan he was—no saint for sure. Then when God surprised Francis and called him to build His church, Francis chose God. God's will over his father's lucrative cloth merchant business. God's will over the swooning young ladies who were captivated by his sensual, invitational songs. God's will. Francis gave up being a playboy to follow God. Not Frank's will, but God's. Like Jesus. He even gave up the foppish clothes the ladies loved, which, of course, his father's wealth had bought him. Not Francis's will, but God's. That's when the 'opposition' brought in the heavy hitters—his father and the bishop. His father shouted that he would disinherit Francis, take away his fine clothes, kick him out of their beautiful *villa* with no food and no shelter. He and the bishop became a spiritual tag team telling Francis, of course that's not God talking to him, and Francis's plan to become a mendicant friar was pure foolishness, not godly holiness. Francis responded by, right in front of them, stripping off every stitch of fancy clothing and throwing every foppish bit on the floor at their feet. Then, stark naked right in front of them both, he testified, "God indeed has spoken to me, and He said these are filthy rags in His sight." Turning on his bare heels, Francis then stalked out the door bare-butt naked into the town square, to shouts, cat-calls, derisive laughter and loud insults from his carousing pals and the very same young ladies he had once lusted over, thus, like Paul, becoming one more fool for Christ.

Yes, St. Francis truly knew what it was to give up worldly pleasures to follow the will of God.

So Frank's answer to Joe's question was simple: "What would I do, you ask? Exactly what you're doing, Joseph. Not my will, but God's will be done." Joe chuckled at the realization that he was preaching to himself again, saying aloud, "If you're not preaching to yourself, you might as well sit down and shut up, because your words are empty, hollow, meaningless and inauthentic. 'Like a noisy gong, or a clanging cymbal,' as Paul said."

Worn out by all that inner turmoil Joe took a deep breath and sat back against the door so he and Frank could smile at each other—well, however it is a statue smiles. Then a peace came over Joe, God's peace, he was certain. So he just sat there in his crossed-legged prayer position enjoying God for a good hour saying absolutely nothing—just listening. Similar it was to walking up Divine Street with his eyes wide open, listening, just listening, opening up his ears, his mind and heart to the things of God that he wouldn't otherwise hear in the noisy world.

He ended his listening prayer with a dozen thank you's to God, saying the 23rd Psalm, then the Lord's Prayer. In the end, when he stood up, he felt as rested as if he had slept the whole night through. "Rest in the Lord is better than sleep," he said with a smile.

He decided to walk toward the mission. Then it hit him: "Oh, man! The mission!" he shouted as he smacked his forehead. "I was supposed to be there to fix bikes hours ago!"

At that second his phone rang. "Hi, Joe here."

"Joe, this is Don at the Mission at Harbor and Divine. Remember us? Repairing bikes for kids? Saturday morning?"

"I'm so sorry, Don. I've been so wrapped up in a personal problem I totally forgot."

"Let me guess. Carmela?"

"Yeah. Good guess. But it's okay now. God and Frank and I worked it out."

"You all met today? God and Frank and you, huh? How about Carmela and Melvin?"

"Hah-hah! Actually yes to both, God and Frank and I met already, and Melvin and Carmela will meet in about an hour. I'm pretty sure they're going to get back together. And I'm good with that. More than good. I'm happy for both of them. As well as for me, you know, because I'm doing the right thing. Not my will, but God's. Even in my warped, messed up mind, I know that's best for all of us."

"You sure?" Don asked.

"I am. I wasn't sure at all last night. But I am now. You know, 'Twas blind, but now I see'?"

"Good for you, Joe. I admire you. You're walkin' the talk."

"Eventually I will, I guess. But thanks for calling, Don. I'll be right there. I'll drive. Then you can admire me close up."

Don laughed and said, "It's a deal. See you soon."

"Oh, Don, I forgot to ask you before this. How is Tomas?"

"Oh, he's doing splendidly. Nothing broken. No internal injuries save for a mild concussion. So we tended to the bumps and bruises and let his family take him home. He was quite a trooper, and nice and polite to boot. How's the bike?"

"Great. We gave it a once over in our shop at the mission, cleaned it up a bit then took it to his home. Sounds like a happy ending all the way around, don't you think?"

"I sure do. And, Joe?

"Yeah?"

"We make a good team, don't we?"

"Sure do. See you soon."

Chapter 22

Jose, Maria and Hay-soos on the Run

B y the time Joe got to The Mission at Harbor and Divine, Gary, Annie, Sandy, Gandy, Lydia, Angel and Angelina were all there working and waiting for him. Plus there was another family Joe had never seen before crossing the street right in front of him to meet the group. Funny, Joe thought, it was the very same spot Gary had gone catatonic crossing the street with DJ a while back. Crazy how it is when you keep your eyes wide open all the time. People keep showing up right in your path. People show up, things happen and then you can't help but notice that everything fits, like that's the way it's supposed to be: the people, their spot in the road, their gifts, their needs, your gifts, your needs, all the helpers you could ever ask for, and a plan that fits it all together. Like when Gandy shoved Joe in the arm, and it ended up being a prayer meeting in the middle of Divine Street. Crazy. But when you've got your eyes wide open, sometimes you can see it happening even before it happens.

And at that moment Joe actually could see and even *smell* that something was about to happen. Yessiree, God was up to something.

So he said a little too loudly, "I smell something brewing," Angelina heard him. "*Que?*" "What?"

"Oh. It's just that with all of us here, and now these new folks, it's like *something* is about to happen."

"Never know," Angelina said with a smile. "We'll just keep our eyes wide open, right? After all it is almost Christmas."

They both made googley wide eyes and laughed.

"True that," Joe said. Angelina continually amazed Joe with her instant awareness of a situation pregnant with spiritual possibility.

That's when Joe turned to the stranger, thrust out his hand and said, "Hi, I'm Joe."

"Me too!" the stranger said laughing.

"No, you're not," Joe said with a six-foot smile.

The stranger didn't miss a beat. "Am too. Except my real name is Jose." His accent was just barely perceptible.

"Me too!" laughed Joe. "My parents are — were — Navajo-Latino, so I was Jose, but now I'm Joe. Nice to meet you, Joe."

"I'm still Jose. I haven't become an American yet."

"Soon?"

"Very soon!"

"And who's the lovely *senorita* with you?"

"This is my almost wife, Maria."

Joe's eyes went ballistically large. "Really? You guys have a bunch of 'almosts' on your plate, don't you?"

"Yes. And this is my almost son," he said proudly pointing to a toddler standing between him and Maria.

"Don't tell me. Jesus?"

"Si. Hay-sooos," he said Latino style.

"Oh, for evermore!" Joe wasn't sure whether to laugh or cry or run for the hills. He did none of those, although later that day he would wish he had run for the hills. For now he just listened as Jose talked.

"Actually, his parents were murdered by drug lords of *la banda de canon cobra,* the Copper Canyon Cartel, in Ciudad Juarez, two years ago right near the orphanage where Maria and I were working. He was just a baby, but that particular drug cartel has a reputation for murdering young parents, stealing their children and training them to be innocent drug couriers. Well, we knew the baby was not with any of his extended family, because he was with us in the orphanage, meaning that the murderers wouldn't know where to find him. So, we kept him. We kept him for two years.

"But then two weeks ago those creeps came back, looking for the kid. So that night, after telling the director we were going 'on a holiday with Maria's parents' (wink, wink), Maria and I snatched up the toddler, and crossed the border in a secluded spot only some of us know. Once we crossed the river and backtracked to El Paso we took him to a doctor we know who, we were certain, would help us. We explained the situation, and the doc was all in with us despite the danger of a trip all the way up to Canada. He gave Jesus a physical and then made a birth certificate with all our Christmas names. Maria and I already had papers for ourselves, but it never hurts to have spares."

Joe looked like he was about to have a cow. "Whoa, whoa, whoa. Whoa, whoa, WHOA! Angelina, let's go in the mission with these folks." He turned to Don and said, "Don, we're going into the church with our new friends. This could be a lot of trouble."

"Joe, I heard a little of it, and I agree it sounds like trouble. And, Joe?"

"Yeah?"

"It is not your job to save them. Counsel them, yes. Save them, no. You grew up in the southwest close enough to Juarez that you should know that if you get involved in this you will put our whole mission in jeopardy." Don studied Joe's face, then he offered, "Since DJ's not here, I'd like to sit in on this conversation with you and your new friends to provide you with some honest feedback from someone who's been around the block a time or two."

"Thank you, Doc." Joe took a short minute, begged God for direction then said, "I'd like that."

"Good. I'll ask Sandy to keep the bike rehab going for a while."

"Great idea. Tell her we'll join them as soon as were done here."

As Don left, Joe turned to Jose, Maria, Jesus and Angelina and was just about to say something like, "Let's go inside," when Maria cut in with a flood of Mexican Spanish. She took Joe by such total surprise, that the only thing Joe comprehended was, *"Juarez?"* If she were testing Joe's Spanish speaking credentials he would have definitely failed the test by virtue of his astonishment. Fortunately, he recouped enough to reply fluently that, yes, he grew up near the little town of Truth or Consequences, New Mexico, on the shore of the Caballo Reservoir north of El Paso and Juarez until his family moved up near his grandparent's home in Farmington. Occasionally Joe and his family took trips down to Juarez to visit family and friends still living there. Joe said he only had a five-year-old's memory of the orphanage, vaguely remembered Maria's family including hearing about Carmela's uncle being gunned down on the street in front of his own house under the cover of night.

Maria was so flabbergasted all she could say was *"Dios mio..."* before she swooned into Jose's arms in woeful weeping.

Dr. Don rushed in, incredulously asking, "What's happening Joe? What did I miss?"

"Maria, or whatever her name is, heard us talking about my living near Juarez and El Paso as a small child, so I told her I remember a little about her family and the orphanage, including Carmela's murdered uncle." He then turned his attention back to Jose and a recovered Maria, "But my friends, there is no hiding, not from the cartel. We in the mission must not, and we will not help to keep you hidden. Let's take our show inside and talk."

Once they were inside sitting together in one of the offices with the door closed, Joe put his head in his hands, groaned and started praying. "Holy Father God, I had a hunch you were up to something today, but this is absolutely crazy. And it's way beyond my pay grade to deal with. Yet, you have seen fit to give Angelina and me and Dr. Don this off-the-charts, intense, holy and very illegal assignment. If, Lord, you want us to help these people, then, like Moses prevailed upon you, we beg of you, you must go with us. We can't do this without you. Without you we are lost, sheep without a shepherd, criminals without a prayer. Send us your helpers, angels and guardians to keep us safe and do your will. Come, Lord Jesus, be our Way, be our Truth and be our Life. Amen." Joe hadn't prayed with such angst since Afghanistan; since his wife, Val, lay dying of cancer; since — nuts — since who knows when else. He'd never in his life been faced with jail time for doing good. Never. This was just crazy.

The others felt his desperation, and his fear, fueled by his desire to follow God's lead. So Joe said, "This is when a man or a woman shows his or her metal and lives their faith in God. This is when, like that congressman from Georgia, John Lewis, would say about standing against injustice—this is my take on what he said—when you are fighting for justice and mercy, and there is no way around getting into trouble for doing the good that needs to be done, then just stand tall, do what needs to be done and risk getting into 'good trouble.'" Joe thought to himself, then said, "However, even good trouble can still land you in jail, get you fire hosed and even get you killed." Then he looked straight at Angelina. "So, Angelina, we can get into some very serious trouble here that could lead to prison or even being murdered. For those reasons, I want you to leave right now. I will never implicate you in anything that Jose and Maria and Don and I decide. But you are just too young to risk even jail time."

"No," she resisted, "Joe, like you and like my father, I have enough steel in my spine to see this through. I'm with you 100%. We may get into trouble, but you're right, this is good trouble. It's worth the risk."

"Angelina, I am so proud of you I could shout for joy. And I'm sure that Melvin and Carmela would feel the same way. But I don't want to be the one who takes you away from them. Please. Please leave, and don't say a word of this to anyone."

Angelina balked, already knowing she would tell her father. Once again Joe urged her, "Go on, now." Slowly she got up teary-eyed, slowly she turned to Mary, Jose and Jesus and told them, "I admire your courage to do the right thing. But please be careful and stay safe. The cartel has ways of tracking people to get what they want. If they would kill his mother and father in broad daylight, they won't hesitate a second to kill you as well. You too, Joe. You too, Dr. Don. Joe, please be as wily as a serpent, you good, good man." And with that she turned and walked out the door.

Joe got up, clicked the door shut and gave a sigh of relief, even though his eyes were full of stress and fear. Joe, Jose, Maria and Dr. Don all knew Angelina was 100% right: those cartel thugs wouldn't hesitate a second to kill them all to take the boy and to leave an ominous warning to anyone else would double cross the Copper Canyon Cartel.

Chapter 23

A Latino Underground Railroad?

After leaving the mission, and driving through downtown to Cleveland's East Side, Angelina turned the corner off Quincy Road and drove down the street to her house and immediately she saw her father's old, beat up Honda. "He's really here!" she marveled to herself pulling her car over to the curb to reconsider her plan. If things were going well, then probably she was interrupting some intimacy in there. "Hmpf!" she snorted. "Need a new plan, Big Angel." She had taken to calling herself Big Angel ever since she had met Angel Martin, now 'Little Angel.' Beside that, she had also actually come *to think of herself* as a Big Angel sent from God—a real flesh and blood angel. 'Yeah, maybe it is goofy,' she thought. 'In fact, it's probably even worthy of getting me institutionalized, but that's how I roll these days — God's Angel sent to help people in need and get into Good Trouble.'

Then she said out loud, "Really, if Old Tony's face could be carved by the Hand of God, like Gary says, then surely

Angelina could be a Big Angel sent by God first to Little Angel Martin, and now...now to Joseph, Mary and Jesus." She crossed herself as she said their names. "Oh, come on, girl! You're not even Catholic," she chided herself aloud. "And, besides, they're aliases, for crying out loud! But still, you never know how God works." So she grinned and crossed herself again. "Thank you, Lord."

She parked her car down the street from their house and just sat for a while, sort of thinking, sort of praying, sort of talking to herself. "Joe was right about one thing," she said out loud, "this is way above our pay grade. And if it's not God leading, then we are in deep doo-doo and it's not *good* trouble. If God's not orchestrating this, then it's Bad Trouble with a capital 'B' that rhymes with 'P' and that stands for–oy–Prison." She kept talking to herself in the car, periodically glancing outside in case somebody was watching her, thinking she was going crazy.

"Oh, who cares, Big Angel?! This is not like jumping into a pick-up three on three game with the guys at the Willow Park Courts. This is like running with the gangs — guns and knives and dumb stuff." That's when the tears came. She dried her cheeks with the back of her hand, took a breath and decided. "Time to tell Dad." Sliding out of her car she walked to the house, her house, for crying out loud, yet she felt like an intruder, maybe even unwelcome. "Just do it, Angel," she admonished herself as she pounded on the door remembering what Joe had told here about his paper boy days. "Right. You never know what they're doing that you have to pull them away from. Oy." She shuddered at the thought and pounded all the harder. "That ought to get them." Indeed. From inside the house she heard her father's agitated "Hold your pants on!" Angel giggled and mused, "He might be talking to himself!"

The door opened, and Angel and Dad just stood staring at each other with love grins on each face a mile wide.

"Angel!" Melvin shouted opening the door to bear hug his little girl. "So good to see you especially right here in *our* house." Hugs and tears sealed the love. "It's your house, you know. You coulda just... walked... well, maybe not. Good choice, girl." They both snickered knowing giggles. "You're a grown-up now, so," he paused, then said, "Come on in. Carmela, it's Angel!"

"I'll be right there," came a slightly frenzied response.

Angel's face tightened up, her eyes still wet, and Melvin noticed. "What's up, little girl? You look like you just ate a batch of sour grits. Mmm-mmm. Come on now, tell me."

"Well, I did want to know how it's going with you and Mom."

"Great," Carmela answered walking over to put her arm around her good, good man. "It's going really, really good, wouldn't you say, Melvin?"

"I sure would! But, Carmela, look at that face. There's something else going on here, don't you think?"

"Looks like a troubled face, for sure. A sad face. Looks like a let's-sit-down-at-the-table-and-have-us-a-talk face. That right, Angel?"

Angel nodded, not feeling much like a Big Angel at the moment. The diminutive "Angelina" felt much more like an appropriate name at that moment as she looked at her parents sitting together in the dining room for the very first time in ten years. She couldn't stop the tears. "So, are you two getting back together?"

Carmela smiled at Melvin who smiled right back. They both nodded and together said, "Yes!"

"We sure are," said Carmela. "And we are both as happy as can be about it, aren't we, Melvin?"

"We belong together. Always have. But, Angel, you don't look happy about it."

"Oh, I am. Very happy. I'm stressed about something else, but not about you guys. I've been praying for this moment for the last ten years, and here it is. I love you both, and I'm really glad to have my mom and my dad back together."

"But?" Melvin asked.

"But there's these three people from *Casa de Juventud.*"

"What?" exploded her mother in instant worry. "Friends or not?"

"Friends, I'm pretty sure, Mama. Maybe you even know one of them. But, anyhow, they are running from enemies, and they need our help. Joe is talking with them as we speak, but he needs our help. He told me to go away, to leave, to keep me safe so I wouldn't know any more than I do. But I already know too much to run away from helping those poor people. Joe told me not to tell anybody, but I just have to tell you, especially since that's your home, Mama."

"Is this illegal?" Melvin asked.

"Yes,"

"Are the drug lords involved?" asked Carmela.

"Yes."

"Then," Melvin said, "you already know enough to be in grave danger. Maybe you need to take a deep breath and tell us everything you know, and we can figure out how to help those poor people and that good, good man Joe, and keep everyone safe at the same time."

"Thank you, Papa. So… okay?… ready?"

"Ready."

"Here's what I know about Joseph, Maria and Jesus…." And she told them the whole story as she knew it.

After nearly an hour of Angelina's tale and questions from Melvin and Carmela, Melvin said, "Carmela, I think we need to help. What about you?"

"Melvin, I'm with you all the way. Till death us do part. Besides I know there still is a Latino underground railway from Mexico all the way into Canada."

"Whoa!" he exclaimed. "How do you know that?"

"Remember my uncle who got killed in Juarez?" Carmela asked.

"Yeah."

"He knew how to get kids into Canada. That's why they killed him. I mean, this is serious stuff."

"So you think we should back off?"

"Back off? No, I absolutely think we should help somehow. And this Maria, I might know her. But those cartel guys are murderers, so we just *really* need to be hyper-vigilant and very careful."

Melvin grinned at his wife, "That's the woman I married!" Then turning to Angelina he said, "Angel, I think that means we're in. Let's drive to the mission, meet this Joseph, Mary and Jesus and find out how we can help. Okay with you?"

"Well, Joe's going to be ticked off at me for telling you," she said with a worried frown. "But," she brightened up, "when he sees you two together again plus signing on to help, I think he'll be okay. And, remember, he already told them that the mission will not hide them."

"That's all right. That's good. He's got the mission and the whole neighborhood to think about. But I'm sure there is something we can do to help," declared Carmela. "Let's go, talk to our good friend Joe and find out how we can lend a hand."

So out the door they went, climbed into Melvin's beater, got buckled in and Angelina said, "Papa, Mama, just so you know, I'm ready to sign on for whatever I can to do help Maria, Joseph and Jesus. After all," she added, "it *is* Christmas!"

Melvin and Carmela smiled and muttered, "Maria, Joseph and Jesus. Good grief!"

Half an hour later, they got to the mission. Melvin parked the car on Harbor Street at the curb right in front of the bicycle rehab work with Joe back outside helping and lots of people Melvin didn't know. Still, he just started grinning. Then deep roiling laughter started deep in his belly, and he couldn't stop it. Nope. He tried, but he couldn't stop it! And that laugh just rolled out of his belly, up his throat and out of his mouth, making him laugh and grin from ear to ear, as he shook his head and said like a preacher on Sunday morning, **"Mercy, mercy, dear Lawd Gawd, have mercy!"**

"What?" Carmela asked in confusion. "What's with the grinning, the laughing and the 'mercy, mercy?' This is serious stuff, Mr. Anderson!"

"True enough, but there's my man. And he's large and in charge. And the Lord God is in charge of him. I know that for a fact! So, I'm telling you right now, I don't have a worry in the world about how this is all going to work out!"

Carmela couldn't help smiling right along with him. "I'm so proud of you," she told her husband, "and happy we're in this together."

Even Angelina broke into a victory smile, as if she already knew the end of the story. In fact she told them so, "You know that I already know the end of this story, don't you?"

"You do?" asked Melvin. "And how's that?"

"Sure I do," she answered, pleasantly defensive.

"Well, do tell. Do tell," Melvin egged her on doubting she actually *knew* anything of the sort. "What? Do they all hop on the Underground Railroad and ride, sister, ride?" At that he started singing, "Ride, Sister, Ride!" And dancing with his fanny while they still sat in the car.

"Of course they do!" Angelina laughed at Melvin's bad singing and car-rocking fanny-dancing. "It's in the Bible, father of mine. Jesus, Joseph and Mary make it safely to Egypt, and King Herod loses." She raised her eyebrows over her victory smile, and added. "And that's exactly what's going to happen for our Maria, Jose y Hay-soos.

"After all, you know, this is Christmas.
This is Christmas."

Chapter 24

"All Aboard for the Glory Train!?"

W hat in the world?" Joe gasped when Melvin pulled up in front of the Mission at Harbor and Divine. Then he watched as the car bounced around, the doors opened and Melvin, Carmela and Angelina, grinning and laughing, piled out two feet from where Joe stood totally amazed. Slowly things dawned for Joe. Melvin just grinned.

"Yeah, but what're you *saying*?" Joe asked the grin.

"Three passengers bound for the Glory Train!" Melvin announced with a flourish.

"Exactly what *are* you saying?"

"First off, we're a family of three again, Joe, thanks to you and the Lord God."

"Wahoo! And Praise God! Congratulations!"

"All thanks to you, my brother. But second, Angelina told us what you are doing for Maria, Joseph and Jesus, so we're enlisting!"

"Whoa, whoa, whoa! Melvin, no congrats there. I'm not doing anything. Really. Absolutely nothing."

Melvin looked sideways at Joe. "Hmmm. From what Angel told us, the kid is from Carmela's home, her father's orphanage, and Carmela used to know all about the Latino Underground Railroad. In fact, she used to know the way, because she helped her uncle sneak kids out when she was a teenager."

Breathless, Joe said, "Holy cow! I mean, HOLY COW!"

He paused to catch his breath, corral his fear and reclaim his temper. It just was all too, too much for Joe to take in at once. First, right there in front of him were Melvin and Carmela acting like they'd actually been married 20 years and not living apart for the last ten. Like they actually loved each other. Like they're a team. Holy cow! That by itself was enough to make Joe swoon, as in faint out cold from distress. But wait! That's not all! Secondly, they may already know all about Maria, Joseph and Jesus. Holy cow! Plus third they want to help. Help, nothing: Give their lives, or whatever! Holy cow! And fourth, they want to offer the key piece to the whole puzzle about getting those three refugees safely out of the grasp of the drug lords and into some kind of safe house some-where—who knows where. And, that wasn't all. Fifth, it seems Carmela once knew the how's and the where's of this supposed Underground Railroad. He doubted it, but that's what he heard through his tormented ears. Holy cow! Holy cow! Holy cow!

Joe's head, heart, body were all throbbing. This is the kind of over-the-top stressful time he used to run from back in his bad old days. He would run into *la Cocina,* sit at the bar, talk Spanish, drink margaritas until he got *borracho de poder,* stumble out to the street and then crawl up to his 2B apart-ment past Frank and into the bathroom before it was too late. Sometimes it was too late, and he'd soil himself, crumple to the floor, pass out and land in his own vomit. The bad old days, yessiree.

And then to top it off, at that very second, Maria came running, screaming, weeping, "Carmela! Carmela!" She knew Carmela for crying out loud! And she nearly knocked the poor woman off her feet with a passionate love tackle. "I am so happy to see you!" she screamed. "You are a life saver. You know that, don't you? You're an angel sent by God, for sure!"

"Whoa, whoa, whoa!" Joe shouted with hands outstretched like a football referee trying to stop a brawl on the 28 yard line. He was totally on overload. "First off," he was inflamed, "I already said we are NOT hiding you! Secondly, do you know each other?"

"Carmela? Of course, I know Carmela. I grew up in her father's orphanage in Ciudad Juarez where my mother was the cook. Carmela used to baby sit me so my mother could do her job and not have to worry so much about me. Carmela's like my second mother. Right?" she asked turning to Carmela.

"All true, Joe. How old are you, Cristina?"

"Thirty-six."

"I have known Cristina... ."

"Wait, wait. You said your name is Maria," Joe said looking too much like the befuddled middle aged guy he actually was at that very moment.

Maria laughed. "Cristina Maria Panchita Oswego. I am both Cristina AND Maria."

"Oh, I get it. Maria is your stage name," he said none too happy.

"Si. With Joseph and Jesus we make a great Christmas family on the way to Egypt, no?"

"Yes. Very clever. But what does Carmela have to do with it?"

"She used to be one of the stops on the Underground Railroad Latino-Americano Style."

"What?!!! You all are giving me brain cramps. So you are here because of Carmela?"

"*Si*. And Melvin. We know they will help us, because they love us! We are like family after all these years. Right, Mama Carmela?"

"Not exactly," answered Carmela, a little befuddled herself.

"What do you mean, *mamita mia*?"

"Of course we love you! And we are like family for more than thirty years."

"Oh good. So then you will help."

"However, Cristina, we are not a stop along the Latino/Americano Underground Railroad from Mexico to Canada. We are a mission helping people in need, but not hiding people, not even you, from gangsters or from the immigration authorities. That's why, as Joe told you, we cannot hide you. We cannot allow The Mission at Harbor and Divine to break immigration laws or become targets of the Copper Canyon Cartel."

"*O que lastima!*" cried Cristina Maria as she burst into tears. Caramel put her arm around her and dried her tears.

"However, Joe," Melvin said, slowly shaking his head in concern for his new friend as well as for his wife's family, "because *they are here*, because they have told you who they are and what they're doing, you know you are already complicit in this."

"And," added Angelina, "I'm sorry to say, so is our mission."

"Whether I like it or not. Huh?" Joe snarled.

Melvin answered, "Afraid so, my friend. We all need to have some more serious talks like you already had with Angelina."

"But you're really not underground conductors smuggling kids from Mexico to wherever? Right?" Joe asked.

"Right, we are not," Angelina said.

181

"Oh, praise God!"

"But there is one—an underground railroad Latino/ Americano style. Just not us. Still, we are definitely not a stop on it."

"But, Carmela, Cristina Maria came seeking your help in particular," Joe restated, as he began to understand more of what as happening.

"Yes, that is true, because she is like a daughter to me. And I find it very difficult to turn my back on her, Joe."

Joe was feeling the pressure. "Where in Canada?" he asked.

"Makes no difference, Joe," Angelina jumped in. "We're not part of it. But the unfortunate thing that really matters is that you already know enough to get all of us killed, including yourself and little Jesus. We trust you, but we didn't want to put your life in such danger. I'm sorry, Joe. We all are."

"And besides," Carmela added, "to answer your question, I don't really know where in Canada. It changes all the time anyhow."

"Actually, my brother," Melvin interjected, "you got to be quite a complication after Carmela and Angelina began to call you a "good, good" man — our code words back in the day for someone worthy of clandestine trust. It was confusing for me."

Jose jumped in, "And that's exactly what we heard, through the grapevine, that you were a 'good, good man.' Our seeking you out, you in particular, Joe, was, in fact, part of our plan, because we heard you had proven yourself to Carmela, Melvin and Angelina to be a man of high character and trustworthiness. We knew about you before we met you this morning."

"Plus," Maria added, "on line we found out about your steadfast loyalty and bravery as a soldier in combat under live fire in battle, and we just knew you were a man we could count on."

Joe felt the squeeze. "This is way too crazy, you guys."

"So, Joe, tell me, how are you doing with all of this info, my brother-who-is-just-like-me?" asked Melvin smiling rather slyly.

"For real? To be honest, Melvin? Not so good—in fact, terrible! First off, it's overwhelming. Second off, I feel like I've been sold a bill of goods, wrapped up in Christmas paper but filled with darkness and trouble. And third, it's *immediate*. It's right this cotton-pickin' minute. Were we to help, we'd need a plan right now, this second, because lives could be in jeopardy with drug cartel thugs breathing down their necks—maybe even as we speak even if we don't help. Those thugs could already be tracing these three to right here to The Mission at Harbor and Divine putting every single one of us in jeopardy. We might not have a choice, and that scares the sand out of me."

Melvin shook his head slowly saying, "Joe, I'm truly sorry, I am. But things happened so fast with you and me and Carmela, and I had no clue about Mary, Joseph and Jesus coming here. I'm sorry we blind-sided you. That's no way to start a friendship."

"No. But thank you for your apology. I forgive you. And honestly, I've got to tell you, I'm also really proud of you. All of you. I feel as though I really am standing with a band of angels, you know like in "Swing Low, Sweet Chariot." In fact, in some ways, good ways, I feel like I'm back with my squad in Afghanistan, with my most trusted comrades, some of whom actually ended up dying to save my life. In the same way, at one time you were all willing to give your lives for one another and for the lives of children, like this little Jesus. And, I'll tell you," Joe choked up a little, "I am proud to stand with you. Very proud. But at the same time, I'm totally scared to pieces, because I know about the jobs battle squads do. Lives risked sometimes lead to lives lost, even innocent lives. Team members pledge their lives to one another and to those they are called to save. Carmela, I feel you once made that pledge, a love pledge to Cristina Maria as her second mother. And I'm proud of you for wanting to take risks for her. But here's the truth: I have not made that pledge. And I surely haven't made that pledge on behalf of The Mission at Harbor and Divine."

"You're right, Joe" said Melvin, "Carmela has a pledge of love to Cristina Maria, but also, and hear this loud and clear, we're really not the freedom train conductors we occasionally were twenty years ago. Yet, Joe, the reality still remains that Christina, Jose and Jesus are here."

"You're right, Melvin." He took a beat to think. "So then tell me, Sarge, what do we do now? What's going to happen? We are already at risk. Cristina Maria and Jose have already put us all in jeopardy, including the mission. Now what?"

"Honestly, Joe, I don't know, except to call the FBI and the DEA."

"Noooooooo!" howled Cristina Maria.

Chapter 25

Meanwhile... The Siciliano

H ey, Annie!" Gary chortled as he walked into Annie's office. "Hi, Gar. What brings you out from the mission on such a gorgeous winter day all the way to Dunlop Realty?"

"You," he answered with a flirtatious grin on his face.

"Awwww. You're so sweet." Annie smiled and reached out to give Gary's hand a gentle squeeze. "But, really, you usually don't stop in the office on a work day just to say, 'Hi.' True?"

"True enough," Gary admitted. "Everybody else–you know, Joe, Angelina, Carmela and now Melvin–they all seem to be caught up with who Carmela is going to choose, Joe or her estranged husband. I care about it–I care about them, but, still, it's all kinda goofy. Plus, something else is going on. I don't know what, and I don't want to know. So I thought I'd stop by for a midday visit with you. Besides, I have something I want to share with you."

"Oh? Cool." Annie suddenly perked up and leaned toward Gary with a flirty smile on her face which she moved to just four inches away from Gary's. "What's up?"

"Well," Gary paused to catch his breath that Annie's flirty smile four inches away sucked right out of him. After he got himself gathered — Annie sure knew what she could do to him—he smiled back.

"Sorry," she said, confessing with a grin every bit as devastating to Gary as that flirty smile close enough to smell the love.

"Annie, you sure can turn me inside out in a hurry."

"Not sorry. I hope I never lose the touch. And I hope you never stop falling for it. But, really, what is it you wanted to share with me — other than flirting, that is?"

Gary chuckled, "I too hope you never lose the touch. And I'm pretty sure I'll never stop falling for it."

"Good. But, for real, tell me."

Gary took another deep breath, only halfway wanting to get over her grip on his heart. Halfway turned out to be enough for him to get back to what he wanted to share. "Okay." Breathe. "So a while back I took one of those DNA tests to tell me about my ancestry. My mom and dad could only tell me so much, and I wanted to know more about my last name, especially since moving back to Cleveland. You know, part of it is the usual curiosity. Did we really originate in Sicily? When? Any skeletons in the closet. In fact, Mom and Dad went in on it too."

"Oh? Hmm. You never told me you were doing that."

"No. That's true. I guess you and I weren't all that close back when I sent it in. Actually. it was right around the time you first showed us the parish house for me to buy."

"Well, as far as not being close at the time, that's true. But to be totally honest, you had me hooked that very first day with your story, your tenderness and your vulnerability. But, you're right, things sure have changed for us since then, and fast. I mean, in a hurry.

"Is that still all good?" she asked with uncertain flirty undertones.

"Oh, heavens to Betsy," Gary laughed embarrassed that he was such gooey putty in her hands. "Absolutely!" he confessed. "As you can surely tell, by the way you captivate me, things are very good."

"Phew! I'm glad of that," she smirked.

Gary grinned back. "You have a way, you know."

"I know." She put on a pretend, serious air and directed, "But, Gar, get to the point. I'm just still not sure where you're headed with all this." She paused, wiped the rest of the smirk off her face in a cartoonish, back-of-her-hand manner, and said seriously — sort of, "Just where are you headed?"

"Well... I got the results back in the mail this morning, and I just had to tell you first."

"Oh, cool! So what does it say? Are we meant for each other?"

"Stop."

"Okay." And she did. Didn't want to. But she did. She let him breathe.

And he did, breathe, that is. "Thank you. Not that I don't love it. But, still, thank you." Another breath. "So... so they do two different searches. The first one, of course, is the biological DNA search, and it does show that our racial mix indicates we could well have originated in Sicily."

"That's good, right? Makes sense, with Siciliano and all."

"Right." They both laughed at her sarcasm. "But here's the catch: they also do a name search. In its basic interpretation, the name Siciliano simply means 'that guy from Sicily.' But the name search explores legal documents, property ownership, wills and such that identify people by proper name as well as identifiers like 'that guy from Sicily.' As you might expect, the older the documents are, the more vague and uncertain the search. But they can still be very interesting.

"Here's the case in point: among the oldest findings of the actual name Siciliano, rather than it just being an ethnic reference, was one they found in France, not Italy. And get this: they found the name in what is now southeastern France in, of all places, the Chateau de Cloux."

"Of all places! Of course, the Chateau de Cloux. Of ALL places!" Her sweet sarcasm was over-the-top silly, and once again she had Gary wrapped around her little finger.

"Annie!" He got up walked over to her, gently sandwiched her face between his two strong hands, brought her face to his and kissed her so ferociously her face turned bright red and she totally could not breathe. They both loved it, but after that kiss Annie could not even stand up straight. She fell back down into her desk chair, fanned her face with both hands, stared at Gary with a "Who ARE you?" look and gasped, "WOW! And now you expect me to have a serious conversation about the Chateau of Clouds, or whatever. Holy cow, mister, if that's what happens because of all my silly Mae West flirting, I'm doing it all over again! ... As soon as I can catch my breath."

Gary laughed, and kissed her again, but this time way more tenderly, and Annie, she swooned into his arms.

"Had enough?" he asked.

"Not nearly enough, cowboy. But you should save some of that for me to look forward to next time." She gathered herself. "It's going to take me a day and a half to get back to breathing again. Now what's this about the Siciliano?"

"I'm so glad you asked," Gary teased, his smile totally betraying his growing love for Annie. Needless to say, Annie loved it.

188

"The Chateau de Cloux was the last place Leonardo da Vinci lived. He died there. And, in fact, there was young man, a teenage boy named Dario, from Sicily who helped nurse Leonardo as he lay dying. That kid was actually named in Leonardo's will: Not Dario from Sicily, nor Dario the Siciliano, but Dario Siciliano!"

Annie came back to life. "Holy mackerel, Gary. Is there proof that he is your true ancestor?"

"That's another question. Maybe, maybe not. You never know. But there is still more intrigue surrounding this Dario. For example, it's been said that Dario actually helped Leonardo put the final *sfumato* touches on the Mona Lisa while Leonardo lay on his death bed telling him how and where to paint, including, perhaps, instructing Dario to paint with his fingertips, just how Leonardo often applied his glazed sfumato layers."

"His fingertips as in finger painting?" asked Annie suddenly very interested.

"His fingertips," smiled Gary, pleased with Annie's excitement.

"Then you're saying that the real Mona Lisa actually has Leonardo da Vinci's fingerprints all over it? Is that right?"

"Bingo, Annie! And maybe, just maybe..."

Annie interrupted jumping up and down, excitedly shouting loud enough to crack plaster, "Dario's fingerprints as well?! Oops." She dialed it down. "Sorry. A little loud."

Gary laughed, shook his head saying, "It's your office, lady. Nobody else is here to care. And, Annie, I love it."

Annie's jaw dropped, eyebrows popped up. She said nothing, but she realized in that moment just how much in love she was with this Leonardo Siciliano, and how much, it seemed, he was in love with her. She cocked her head, smiled and just let her smile do the talking.

Gary got the message, smiled back, paused, but still went on to finish his conclusions, temporarily choosing art over the girl. Temporarily! Oh my, how he loved being with her.

"But the clincher for me is this: in his will Leonardo left Dario an 'unnamed painting' which may or may not have been an actual, original Mona Lisa. The Mona Lisa Society has long maintained that the Mona Lisa that hangs in the Louvre may not be the original, or at least not the *only* original. It could be a marvelous copy, perhaps by one of Leonardo's students, or, maybe, and even more likely, a second rendition by Leonardo himself. Some contend that the authentic Leonardo painting that he carried with him for nearly 20 years of moving from patron to patron has never been found. They contend that conservationists at the Louvre are covering up that they are convinced Leonardo's original painting has a sister painting, perhaps titled with a different name, but actually painted by Leonardo for another patron, like the Isleworth Gioconda which is housed in Great Britain.

"Plus, perhaps there is even a third Mona Lisa painting testified to in eyewitness accounts, but which has totally vanished from public view."

Annie's eyes were glazing over with too much information. Gary noticed. "Sorry. TMI," he said. "I'm done."

Annie was still fascinated enough to ask, "So you think that third Mona Lisa was the gift, the bequest, to Dario from Leonardo?"

Gary grinned a replica of Mona Lisa's enigmatic smile and said simply, "Yes, I do."

"Whoa!" gasped Annie, followed by a soft spoken, "I hope you're practicing those words." And then she shouted, "So then, that Mona Lisa belongs to you? Gary the Siciliano!"

"Maybe. But first somebody like the Mona Lisa Foundation is going to have to find it and authenticate it. And that authentication process could take, who knows, years after they find it to track its provenance and then more years to authenticate the painting style. Plus add even more years to prove that I am actually the heir — along with 500 other claimants named Siciliano who want a piece of the pie."

"Yeah, but *maybe*," she smiled that killer smile.

"Yeah," he answered smiling back. "Maybe. But even if I am the heir, that painting still belongs in a museum. Besides, you know what?"

"No. What?" They both laughed at the silliness.

"I'd rather paint my own version. Wouldn't that be fun!?"

"Huh? Ohhhhh," Annie said dreamily, "Leonardo Siciliano. Imagine that. It has a ring to it. And it does sound like fun!"

"I'm calling Dr. Zurkos right now! Right here!" Gary declared totally pumped up with a great idea.

"Right now? Right here in my office?" Annie asked. "Could you use that office over there? Would that be all right?"

"Oh, I'm sorry. You probably have some work to do."

"Yeah, a little. I'm still interested though. But for now I'm one-office-away interested. Gotta sell some houses, Gar."

"Okey dokey. That office would be great. And I won't even use your phone. Promise. Got my own, you know." He held it up. "Phone?"

Annie laughed at Gary's supercharged excitement. "Got it. Tell Mel 'Hi' for me."

"Will do. Wow! Leonardo Siciliano! Annie, I love it!"

"Go get 'em, Tiger," Annie chuckled as Gary walked out the door and then said to herself, "I'm loving that man more every day."

Gary stuck his head back in her door, "Did you say something?"

"No, no. Just talking to myself."

"Okay. See you in a few."
He blew Annie a two-finger kiss.
"And, Annie? You're the best!"

Chapter 26

Leonardo Siciliano

Gary loved the new idea of painting a copy of the Mona Lisa so much that he just wanted to scrap the notion of repainting Old Tony *sfumato* style. Now he wanted to paint Old Tony only in French impressionism like he always intended with the blank canvas he had carried with him for years, and paint the new Mona Lisa in *sfumato* on wood *ala* Leonardo. That way in the Old Tony Studio Leonardo's work on the Mona Lisa would be the true teacher along with CMA *sfumato* expert Paulo Ringetti. Then Gary's French colleagues would be the master teachers for his impressionistic Old Tony. "Yes!" he shouted.

"Hey, quiet in there!" came the realty boss's voice.

"Yes, ma'am! Sorry."

"No problem. I wish I had that kind of enthusiasm around here for selling houses!" They both laughed.

"Well, just don't flirt with them like you do with me! Because, honestly, lady, you, and you alone, are where I get my enthusiasm."

"Oh, Gary! Never!" And then she turned it on with a hip swing-stroll out of her office and into his, put her fingers through his hair and said with panache, "You're my one and only, big guy," giving his hair one last twirl, asking, "you mean like that?"

"Holy cow, Annie!" Gary stumbled over his words. "Exactly. Like that. Don't do that—except to me."

Annie turned, walked away still swaying and said over her shoulder, "Just wanted to be sure I got your drift, cowboy. How'd I do?"

Gary laughed a happy, thrilled, knee-wobbling laugh saying, "You did great Annie. Grade 'A.' You're the best."

"Good! I just want to keep my "A" rating." She sat down at her desk and went back to work with a very, very satisfied smile on her face.

Gary stared at her walking away and then at her beautiful face and said, "A-Plus, ma'am, A-Plus."

Still chuckling Annie got back to work and Gary punched in the number of Dr. Melanie Zurkos's office at the Cleveland Museum of Art.

"Hello, Greater Cleveland United Methodist Church, this is Clara. How may I help you?"

"Oops!"

"Gary?"

"Wow! Clara, you've still got it! You've got the gift, lady!"

"And you still know how to schmooze a girl!"

"I take it you mean that as a critique and not as a compliment."

"Bingo!"

"Clara, you sure know how to put a guy in his place."

"Got to. In this office we deal with headstrong, arrogant pastors all the time. You don't quite fit the calling, but you sure match the mold."

"Clara, Clara! When you answered the phone, I thought I had dialed the wrong number, but I was wrong! I guess I needed my semi-weekly dress down."

"Glad to oblige. Annie can thank me later."

Gary laughed. "Yeah, but she started it!"

"Oh, right."

"It's true!" he defended. "But that's not why I called."

"Oh? Did you want to talk with the Rev. Dr. DJ, the DS?"

"Well, no, not really. I actually wanted to talk with Dr. Melanie Zurkos at the art museum."

"Well, she's not there."

"How do you know that?"

"Clara knows all."

"Oh, come on. How do you know Mel is not in her office?"

"Because, Mr. Arteest, she's here in DJ's office. Want to talk with her? I'll get her. I'm magic. And, actually, they might be chatting about you anyhow, since they both supervise part of your life."

"Hmmm. True that," Gary laughed. "Sure, I'd love to talk with her — with them. Maybe they can put me on speaker phone. I mean, come to think of it, what a great coincidence!"

"Come on, Gar, don't you know with God there are no such things as coincidences? Let's see what God has in mind. Right?"

"Right. Okay then, let's see. And, Clara?"

"Yes?"

"I'm glad you agreed with DJ to help us out part time at the mission."

195

"Me too, Gar. And no smart mouth about it. I just know I will enjoy working with your team in a neighborhood with lots of needs. Let me connect you with DJ. Hang on."

Click, click. Rev. Dr. DJ Scott, district superintendent, picked up the phone. "Hey, Gary, great to hear from you! How are you doing and how can I help you?"

"Hey, DJ. Great to talk with you too. Actually, though, I thought I had dialed the art museum for Mel, but I got Clara instead, and she said Mel is with you. And I said, what a coincidence, and she said — oh forget it. Why don't you put me on speaker phone, and I can talk with you both at the same time."

"Already done, my friend."

"Hi, Gary!" came Melanie's cheery voice. "How can we help you?"

"Hi, Mel." And Gary told her and DJ the whole scoop from Dario Siciliano up until that very moment. "So, what do you think about me painting in public view a *sfumato* copy of the Mona Lisa along side an impressionist painting of Laughing Old Tony and have Paulo supervise the *sfumato* Old Tony for my studio?"

"Well, it sounds creative, fun, ambitious and awesome!" Mel excitedly replied. "But, Gar, I think we need to talk face to face about this. Could you drive in and meet us here in DJ's office so we can all talk together face to face?"

"Great idea, Mel. I'm at Dunlop Realty, so I'll be there in about 45 minutes or so."

"All righty then. See you soon, Gar."

Forty minutes later Gary parked his SUV in the church parking lot and made his way to DJ's office. DJ had his single cup coffee maker fired up and he and Mel were already sipping their joe and chatting when Gary walked into Clara's outer office.

"Hi, Clara."

"Hi, Gary," Clara greeted him while pointing to the partially open door to DJ's office. "They're in there, and they–are–pretty–charged–up. You going to be okay in there?" Clara asked with a smile.

"I think so."

"Just in case, help yourself to a cup of coffee just so you can keep up with them. Know what I mean? The Coffee Kick?"

"Gotcha."

"Well, help yourself," she smiled.

"Oh, cool, and a Keurig with lots of choices," Gary cheered. "Yes! Plus Italian roast. Just what I need! Thanks, Clara."

Gary waited for his coffee, knocked politely, walked in and sat down with Mel and DJ. And Clara was right about the coffee kick. Mel was already flying like she had just been shot out of a cannon. She's just a fireball anyhow, but when Gary walked in she did not wait a second for pleasantries. No, ma'am. She just dove right in.

"Gary, to be honest, I don't need any more time to think about your proposal or even talk about it. It's pure genius, and it sounds fabulous!"

"Wow! I'm glad you like it, Mel."

Mel always knew how to encourage Gary, but this time she had some of her own ideas as well.

"Like it? Gary, this is wonderful, stupendous, magnificent, sublime, majestic, terrific, remarkable, incredible, astonishing and pretty darn cool! Plus," Mel went on, "considering that art critics around the world have already dubbed you history's greatest ever disciple of Leonardo's *sfumato* techniques, it seems like a natural for you to give the Mona Lisa a shot. I mean, the museum could make quite a splash out of that with an eight-year documentary for PBS and publicity world wide." Melanie laughed, but Gary's eyebrows popped up in alarm, mostly about the eight-year documentary.

"Eight years? Really?"

"Just kidding about the eight years. But, Gary," Mel said settling down to serious note, "I'm not kidding about this: that proposal is so perfect, it is just begging for tons of international press, TV scrutiny and top notch art critiques. Are you ready for that? It could be brutal, what with everyone a self-styled art critic spouting off good and bad on social media with you as their target. You're going to need a team of therapists to get you through it."

"Hmm. Got that covered with you two, if you're available."

"Well," DJ added laughing, "what are friends for if not to bind up your wounds, heal your soul and get you back in the ring when the art world tears you to shreds?"

"Whoa. You really think it could be that bad?"

"Gary, I know it's before your time, but have you ever read about the scrogging Roger Maris took when he broke Babe Ruth's home run record?"

"Yes, I have. It was indeed brutal and lasted for years."

"Yeah, and that wasn't Leonardo, the world's most famous artist ever with some hot shot Americano trying to duplicate the best painting in the whole history of art."

"Good point. But, still, it sounds like fun to me. I mean, I'm not trying to out hit Leonardo. I just want to copy his style and see how I do. Besides there are new X-Ray techniques that have digitally pulled apart the layers of Leonardo's painting from charcoal to *sfumato,* so all I have to do is paint by numbers and *voila!* Do you know that they even found his finger prints from when he cast aside his brushes and finger painted *sfumato* glaze? So let the cameras roll, and let's have a party that will draw everyone in the world to a once-in-a-lifetime worldwide art festival demonstrating how what Leonardo da Vinci accomplished in the Mona Lisa is unmatched in the history of art and impossible to duplicate."

"Until now, that is," Mel quipped.

"No, no, no, no! Impossible! But here's the real draw: I will learn so much, and in front of the cameras I will talk about what *I'm* learning and demonstrate it as I go. Viewers can watch all of us try our best to match the Master! 'Match the Master!' It'll be a blast, Mel!"

"Well, Gar," Mel admitted, "if you can carry on with that kind of transparent humility, candor, excitement and enthusiasm...."

"Plus," Gary interrupted, "my unbridled, over-the-top admiration for history's greatest painter and the world's greatest painting. Add that to the mix."

"Gary," DJ said much more calmly than Mel, "if you maintain that kind of excitement mixed with humility and your total admiration for Leonardo and the Mona Lisa, the whole world will be cheering you on."

"There's not a phony bone in my body about this. Not one."

"Then," Mel added in conclusion, "I'm for it."

"*Magnifico!*" Gary shouted kissing his fingertips to the sky. "Let's go for it! Of course we'll have to start by informing all the studio participants of our change in plans, and hope they like the new direction. But let's not scare them with the eight years business. Heavens to Betsy, I'll be an old man by then!"

"Agreed," said Mel, who then caught herself, "but not with the old man part. You will still be young, eager and fun!"

"Hopefully. But do you know what? It will be the greatest art show on earth, don't you think?"

"I do!" cheered Mel.

"Plus, Gary," DJ offered, "if you make your DNA test public, and I hope you will, there's also Dario Siciliano, maybe your great, great, great, etc. grand-relative with his fingerprints possibly squarely alongside Leonardo's on Mona Lisa's *sfumato*. That, by itself, could kick off the most delightful, energized and contentious art treasure hunts and debates in history to go along with your studio, Gar. You and Dario combined will expand the draw of your art event beyond art lovers, treasure hunters, critics, investors, the Mona Lisa Society and museums to students and professors in university art departments in every country in the world, plus millions of ordinary people, all eager to participate in the greatest art show ever. Ever!"

"Wow, DJ," Gary declared, "I have never seen you so worked up. This is fun already, and we've only just begun!"

They all raised their coffee mugs.

DJ toasted, "Here's to the
Greatest Art Show on Earth!"

Chapter 27

The Greatest Art Show on Earth

G ary and Mel hustled out of the Holy Oil Can, crossed the MLK Parkway and headed toward the old main entrance of the Cleveland Museum of Art. They bounded up the marble steps and past the 30-foot Corinthian columns that supported the Greek temple portico leading to the museum's main floor exhibits. They flew past the medieval armor displays, and by the time they got to their offices two floors down they were breathless — partly from exertion and partly from excitement.

"I'll take care of consulting art museum management. Why don't you contact everyone in the studio?"

"On it, boss!"

Off they went to begin planning the "Greatest Art Show on Earth," for that is exactly what they had come to call it.

Although Gary's job sounded easier, Melanie was done in less than two hours. Gary had to talk about art *ad infinitum* with every one of the artists, so it took a long time for Gary to excitedly, but patiently, explain the new parameters of the studio. But it was worth the effort. Every single person he talked with bought into Gary's enthusiasm and totally loved the new wrinkle — even the name, "The Greatest Art Show on Earth!"

His friends in France enthusiastically volunteered to teach master classes in classic French Impressionism, and CMA's own *sfumato* expert, Paulo Ringetti, simply loved the idea of offering an added choice to the studio artists. They could paint Old Tony *sfumato* style, Laughing Old Tony impressionist style, classical Mona Lisa with *sfumato* OR — and this came from Gary's French colleagues — Mona Lisa impressionist style, or even modernist style. Since, because of the time difference he had to call his French colleagues first, Gary got caught up in their enthusiasm. Everyone else he called got all four choices right off the bat, and they were thrilled at the ideas — especially Angelina, whom Gary called last.

By the time Gary had made all his calls it was supper time, and he was famished. To his delight Mel had asked the museum cafe folks to set up for Gary and her a last minute meal in the conference dining room. They reluctantly agreed, but when Mel explained the Mona Lisa ideas they were hatching, everyone perked up, volunteered for overtime and encouraged Mel with, "Great ideas, Dr. Zurkos!" "You go, girl!" "Can we all be on TV?" Everyone continued the happy chatter all through dinner as well as the clean-up, especially because Gary and Mel both pitched in. Exhausted, but with smiles all around, everyone called out joyful "Good nights" as the cafe staff went to their homes and Mel led Gary down to her office for a little debriefing.

"So," began Mel, "what do you think, Gar?"

"I'm amazed that not one person questioned our sanity."

Mel laughed, but she wholeheartedly agreed, "Now that you mention it, there are only two things that make "The Greatest Art Show on Earth" *not* insane, especially considering that there have probably been a million artists over the centuries who have already tried to paint the Mona Lisa *ala* Leonardo with various levels of artistic success and PBS couldn't have cared a lick."

Gary smiled, "True. So what makes us different?"

"Number two, Old Tony." Tears stopped Mel from going on.

"Number two? Mel? You all right? What's number one?"

Mel fought through her emotion to answer. "Gary."

"What?" Gary asked confused.

"Number one. You are the number one reason, Gary, that PBS will pick it up. Your artistry, your love of Leonardo, your humility, your infectious joy in art. Heavens to Betsy, Gary, it's your hope—a whole life style of hope—on the heels of personal tragedy. It's you, Gary. You are the difference maker. You and you alone can paint a Mona Lisa worthy to stand next to Leonardo's. Not surpass it. That's not what I'm saying. But with your humble character, immense talent and dogged perseverance you will paint a Lisa who will brim over with life, beauty and charm and dazzle the art world just like Old Tony did. Just like Leonardo envisioned for all his paintings, but especially the Mona Lisa."

Mel took a breath and dried her eyes. She looked straight into Gary's eyes and said, "Gary, I'm so proud of you first as an MFA student, then as an artist, and now? Now as a man. You make my heart sing, Gary Siciliano, arias of admiration. Old Tony gives you art creds, but you, you will paint the art world back to Leonardo back to the Mona Lisa, and then back to The Virgin of the Rocks, St. John the Baptist, The Last Supper, Virgin and Child with St. Anne, back to an awesome renaissance of Renaissance painting and the master Renaissance Man himself. And, Gary, all of it will be your miraculous gift back to your hometown of Cleveland, and all the people here will cheer you on. Including me."

"Thank you, Mel," Gary said through his own red-eyed emotion.

"I am proud to be the teacher surpassed by her student!"

When Gary got to his car he called Annie on his cell.

"Hi, Big Guy," she sassed on the edge of flirtation.

"Hi, may I speak with Annie the realtor," Gary laughed back.

"Oops, I forgot. Hello, this is Annie of Dunlop Realty. How may I help you?"

"Whoa! You're good."

"I know how to be good. But, Gary, with you I'd rather be bad."

Gary laughed. "You're such a tease."

"No, no. I'm dead serious. One of these days you're gonna be glad I can be bad. Whoa! That rhymes! Glad To Be Bad. Wow. Sounds like a great T-shirt, doesn't it?"

"Annie, you are so much fun. And I love you."

"What?! Say that again, will ya. Start with the "Annie" part. I want to record it in my heart. Pleeeease?"

"Okay, you silly girl. You ready?"

"Ready," she answered softly, afraid to speak any more loudly lest she start bawling.

"Annie?"

"Yes?"

Gary was really getting into Annie's little game. He enjoyed it every bit as much as she did. "You okay?"

"Not really."

"Good. Turn on your heart recorder then. Mine's on."

"Roger."

"Here goes. Annie, you are so much fun," Gary said softly. "And I love you. Did you get that? Did you record that in your heart, because that's exactly where I want it to be."

"Whoa," Annie croaked. No sass. Just grateful, hopeful and filled with love. "I got it, Gar. Every bit of it."

Then quiveringly she added, "Gary, it's recorded on my heart. Plus I recorded it on my phone. I hope you don't mind. It's the absolute nicest thing anybody has ever said to me. Ever."

"Ever?" Gary asked softly.

"Ever."

"Good. But if you ever forget — or if you accidentally erase that recording, I'll say it again for you. I will. Again and again."

"Oh, Gary, it's in my heart. Forever and ever." That did it. The flood gates opened, her eyes cried rivers, but her face? Her face smiled. Smiled a really big smile with happy tears sparkling her face. If only Gary could have seen how beautiful she was at that moment....but best he didn't. Some day maybe. "I better hang up," she croaked through her tears.

"Okay. Bye, Annie."

And she blew him a two-finger good-bye kiss with loud sound effects. "I just blew you a two-finger good-bye kiss. Did you get it?"

"I sure did. I heard it too. So here's a great big Cleveland cowboy kiss back at ya. Got it?"

"Great big?"

"Yep," said the cowboy. "Great big. Too big for ten seconds, that's for sure."

"Good. I got it. Wow! You're a great kisser."

Gary laughed. "Glad you think so." He choked back a sob. "Bye, Annie."

"Bye, Cowboy."

Click. Click.

"Good thing we were miles apart," Gary said aloud. Then he just sat in his car and smiled, heart thumping a mile a minute. "Yep, pardner, good thing," he said. "But some day," he said. "Some day for sure."

And he meant it.
Every word.

Chapter 28

The Three Wise Men

When Gary got home he noticed cars parked across the street in front of the mission. Quite a few actually. He was pretty sure the Honda was Melvin's, if he remembered Joe's description correctly. But the other two? Black like movie star SUVs. "Who could that be?" he wondered wanting to go across the street and ask. He didn't want to be nosey, but still, he *was* curious, curious enough to walk across the street and check things out. Besides, he wanted to ask Joe if he was planning a Christmas worship service of some sort. So he hustled out of his compact SUV into the house, dropped off his notes and computer, picked up his mail off the floor and scooted over to the mission to poke his nose in the business of his friends — including Melvin, who just might become a friend. Never know.

He ran across the street, and as soon as he walked through the mission's front door, he realized the number of voices inside was way more than he expected. Craning his neck to get a better look-see, Gary spied an unfamiliar-looking young couple with what looked like a two-year-old little boy. Plus, craning a little more, he spotted three official looking men he had never laid eyes on before. Coats and ties, black top coats, the whole nine yards. Official looking.

"Hmm," he said quietly to himself, "this snooping around gets more interesting by the minute."

He made a lot of noise walking up the steps to draw, he hoped, Joe's attention. It worked.

Joe zipped right to the foot steps and smiled broadly when he saw it was Gary. "Gary, my friend! Good to see you. What's up? Can I help you?"

"Good to see you too, Joe. I just stopped by to see what was happening, to ask if you're planning a Christmas or Christmas Eve service and if there's any way I can help."

"Yeah, well, Gar, we're trying to put it together right now."

"Joe, buddy, it's tomorrow, pal. Tomorrow!"

"Oh, yeah. But, Gar, things are crazy here. See those three guys in there, see 'em? They all have guns."

"What?!! Real guns? In church?!"

"Yeah, real guns. Look, Gar, you may be walking into more than you bargained for. Just saying. This could be a real hornets nest. Still want to come in?"

"Are you kidding? After that warning, now more than ever, especially if one of them is named James, as in 'Bond, James Bond!' Show me the way, Pastor."

"Okay. Walk this way," he said mimicking the old pop song with strained humor. "But just remember, you asked for it. You may think you were joking just now, but this is no joke, my friend."

Joe led Gary toward the voices in the gathering area behind the worship center. Gary could feel tension in the room even before he could actually make out the words people were saying. He quickly recognized Carmela, Angelina, Melvin, Dr. Don and, to his surprise, Gandy. "Gandy? What's he doing here?" he asked under his breath.

Joe heard him. "Gandy? Now *that is* a surprise. Just wait."

The three suits were talking about some sort of danger, and Gary heard the tall man furthest from him say, "Folks, you just don't know what you're getting into."

"Gary — excuse me gentlemen — this is my good friend Gary Siciliano. Gary...." He didn't have a chance to get out another word, because the stranger who had just been talking stopped abruptly, turned to Gary and exclaimed, "Gary Siciliano?! The famous artist?... YOU painted Old Tony?"

"Don't mind him," said one of his partners, "he's an art geek, God help us!."

The unexpected exchange miraculously, though temporarily, broke the tension and had everybody smiling, especially Gary. It was at that very moment that DJ walked in and, never bashful about butting into somebody else's conversation, shouted out, thinking he was being funny, "Don't arrest him for that! Old Tony died years ago, and he was a naturalized citizen from Slovenia. Right, Gar?" That just sucked the air right out of the room. "What?" he asked turning his palms out. "What'd I say. I was just trying to be funny."

"Boss," Joe responded, "you just hit into a triple play and totally lost the funny game."

"Oh. I'm so sorry, but when I heard Gary and Old Tony in the same sentence from an F.B.I. special agent, I...."

DJ never finished his sentence, because as soon as he said "F.B.I." pandemonium broke loose. People were panicking.

"What now?!"

"F.B.I.?!"

"Who are you guys?"

"I thought they were here to play the Three Kings!"

"Yeah, right. Me too."

"Well, that's what they said. 'We're the Three Kings,' they said.

Joe tried to get back some decorum. "Hey, everybody, settle down. They'll answer all our questions. That's why they're here. Gandy, help!"

"Yeah, Gandoff," said the shortest stranger with a twist of sarcasm, "Help us if you can, we're feelin' dow-wow-wown!"

"Gandoff?" Joe asked. "What's going on Gandy? Are we in Middle Earth?"

"Might just as well be, Joe," quipped Dr. Don. "The Dark Tower looms."

Gandy raised both arms to pat down the panic, and then asked everybody to get a chair and have a seat. "My name is Gandy or Gandoff, and I live just down the street at 3615 Divine with my wife and daughter. But my day job is as the Supervisory Special Agent of the F.B.I. here in Cleveland."

That triggered another round of chaotic shouts and even a bit of anger.

"Whoa!"

"What the heck is going on here, Joe?"

Gandy raised his arms again, patted the air, and everyone hushed as quickly as a room full of second graders when the principal walks in.

Gandy continued, "I'm the one who asked Joe to call this meeting. Also, I invited these three Special Agents to help us. We have all been in contact with F.B.I. and D.E.A. analysts in D.C. to track Jose, Maria and Jesus from El Paso as well as assassins from the Copper Canyon Cartel near Juarez who are trying to kidnap Jesus and kill the other two. Right now we are way more interested in arresting the two thugs and saving lives than sending a little boy back to Juarez and certain death."

"Gandy, please, hold on. Why would a cartel want to kill a two-year old boy named Jesus and his young parents? At Christmas no less," asked Gary, with a bit of disgust on his face.

"Yeah!"

"What's going on here?!"

"I thought this was a Christmas Eve rehearsal!"

"Ho-ho-hold on everyone," Gandy commanded. "Good first question, but I'll let Maria answer it."

"Well, first off, my name is not Maria, or Mary, any more than these three gentlemen are the Three Kings. We took Christmas names to protect ourselves while hiding from the BCC assassins, Bando de Canon Cobre, or the Copper Canyon Cartel. Joseph's name really is Jose. My name is Cristina Maria, and this little man's name is..." she paused and turned to the little boy, "Can you tell everybody your name?"

"Me llamo Miggy!" he said proudly.

"Miggy, or Miguel. His father, Marcos, named him after an American baseball player. Marcos' dream was for Miggy to play big league baseball in the USA. But the cartel murdered Marcos and his wife Teresa, Miggy's mother, because they identified the men who killed the brother of the man who owns the orphanage we work at, Jose. So now the cartel has sent more thugs to kill us, steal Miggy and teach everybody a lesson not to betray the cartel. Also they intend to train this beautiful little boy to be an innocent courier of drugs and money. That's what they do with children — train them to be gangsters. But Jose and I got him out first. We want to hide him in a safe place in Canada."

Gandy jumped in. "And since we have been tracking cartel activity we discovered that two Copper Canyon assassins are closing in, we believe, to steal back the child and kill Cristina and Jose.. That's why our three agents are here, to protect Mary,

Joseph and Jesus — and now all of you as well — from Herod's assassins, if you will, as well as arrest or otherwise get them out of circulation. I don't mean to make light of our situation, but like Mary, Joseph and Jesus in the Bible story, you are all in grave danger. Because of that very serious threat, we have been working with the D.E.A. to form a joint S.W.A.T. team to intercept the assassins before they get to Jose, Cristina and Miggy, and before they get here. Those D.E.A. agents should be here any minute. Shepherds, I suppose," he said with a grin.

Everyone snickered at Gandy's gallows humor; however, no one underestimated the danger of their situation.

That's when Gary saw Annie peek inside and ran to intercept her, take her back outside so he could explain to her what was happening. On their way out they passed two more strangers. "Must be the D.E.A. guys Gandy told us about," Gary said as he and Annie walked toward the house.

Back inside the mission DJ asked, "So are we all confined to this church building?"

"Yes. We hope you'll be safest here for now. And, please, use no cell phones to talk, text or e-mail anyone. Anyone! Understood?" Yes's all around. "The cartel thugs have ultra-sophisticated technology, and I promise you they have the ability to hear us and track us just as we can hear and track them. The bad guys use all the same cell towers and the same satellites we use, though most of the time that works to our advantage."

"Most of the time?" Joe asked.

"Yes, most, but, unfortunately, not always."

Melvin asked, "Sir, are *all* the actors here."

"If you mean the assassins, no, not yet, not on the property, but we believe they are on the Near West Side, perhaps within a quarter mile. Nor are the two D.E.A. agents here who will be joining us. So, just in case, we'll go outside to meet the D.E.A.

detail. We already have a plan with the D.E.A. which we will implement before the cartel thugs even get on the property. Understood?"

"Understood," some said. Others simply nodded unsure of the whole thing.

"Why don't we just leave?" Angelina asked.

"You can if you want," Gandy answered. Since Angelina saw Gary and Annie leave to go across the street, Angelina left and Dr. Don went with her. Like Gary and Annie, they also walked past two men in suits they also figured were the D.E.A. agents. Then they crossed the street to Gary's house. Dr. Don walked down the street to his own house.

Inside the mission, Gandy continued, "In at the meantime, you folks just practice your Christmas program like you planned. And don't worry. We'll get those thugs. How about somebody get on the piano and everybody else sing "Joy to the World" to get you in the mood for Christmas. The Wise Men are already outside where they can connect with the Shepherds. I'll join them in a minute. We'll get this cleaned up in a jiffy." 'I hope,' Gandy thought to himself.

Carmela said, "I can play!" and she rushed down to the piano and began pounding out "Joy to the World." DJ pretended to direct the choir encouraging everyone else to start singing at the top of their lungs.

"Melvin? That's your name?" Gandy shouted over the choir.

"Yes, sir." Melvin snapped to attention and saluted waiting for an order. A soldier's willingness to receive and follow orders never goes away, but the salute surprised even Melvin.

So Gandy smiled, saluted and gave the order, "Melvin, guard the child until the D.E.A. detail arrives. Oh, and all right, here they are."

Two more men in suits walked in nervously looking around.

"Gandoff?" a huge man asked Gandy.

"Yes. Here. Melvin there has the boy, and you have everybody else. Those two…" He never got out another word as the two supposed D.E.A. men pulled out their weapons and opened fire. Gandy was the first to fall badly wounded. In a flash Melvin dove on Miggy and rolled the screaming child to relative safety under the pews of ancient oak which were already exploding under the assassins' assault. Carmela dove underneath the piano. Everyone else dove into the pews when suddenly even more gunfire barked out from all the doors into the sanctuary as F.B.I. and D.E.A. agents, realizing their plan had failed, rushed in firing at the assassins both of whose heads suddenly exploded into bloody gore leaving two headless corpses crashing down in hellish disfigurement while covering pews with a grotesque bloody mash. Then as if to an unspoken command, just as suddenly as it all started, the gunfire stopped — creating a cold, breathless silence, save for women sobbing, a child screaming, wounded men cursing and the bullet riddled piano still ringing with the overtones of "Joy to the World."

Immediately sirens wailed ever closer. Dr. Don ran in the front door. Having heard the fusillade of gunshots before he even got home, the former Army doctor immediately called 911 then ran to the danger, proving that heroes come in all shapes, sizes and ages.

"Holy Mary, Mother of God!" he exclaimed and prayed with the same words. He immediately went to a still breathing Gandy lying near two headless corpses. Even though Gandy had numerous wounds over his body, he still gratefully welcomed Dr. Don whom he had only just met a couple of weeks earlier.

"Dr. Don," he choked out, "praise God you're here."

"Gandy, let's get you some help. DJ," Dr. Don called, "please help me with Gandy."

DJ rushed to Dr. Don's side, and together they gently slid Gandy to a flat surface where the good doctor could assess the damage, which looked considerable even to an experienced war medic like DJ.

At the same time Joe ran to help Melvin who still lay on top of Miggy within the pews to protect him from the deadly chaos. But when Melvin was shot he fell full weight upon the boy and was now crushing the two-year old Miggy under his considerable inert body weight. The combat medic in Joe quickly sized up the situation. Yes, Miggy was safe and unharmed beneath that good, good man, but Melvin was in serious trouble with bullet wounds and oak shrapnel puncturing him in dozens of places over his body.

By then Cleveland police and emergency squads had arrived thanks to Dr. Don's quick thinking. DJ quickly explained the situation to the first responders, and they moved into action. Angelina and Gary ran in the front door to help, spotted Carmela hiding but moving behind the piano, bloodied from piano shrapnel and paralyzed with fear. Gary ran to Carmela, while Angelina helped Joe and Jose pull Miggy out from under Melvin. On their heels came two EMT's with a spine board stretcher, a saline drip and bandages. They secured Melvin to the board and carried him out to the EMS rescue vehicle where they could work on him in a more sterile environment to clean wounds and stabilize him while they transported him to Metro General's ER. An EMT was already on the phone talking with the ER doc, giving and getting instructions especially for treating the many fragment wounds from pews and the piano.

A second team had arrived and helped Dr. Don secure Gandy to a spinal board while they sterilized and loosely bandaged his wounds to stem the bleeding. As they carried Gandy to the second rescue vehicle, Joe told Dr. Don, "This feels a whole lot like an ambush in Iraq."

Knowing Joe's war experience, Dr. Don, himself a Vietnam War vet, asked Joe, "You all right?"

"For now I am. We'll get done what needs to get done, you know. I'll take care of my sh— after that."

"That's how it is, soldier."

"Yes, sir. That's exactly how it is. Although I'm not sure Melvin's gonna make it."

"Well, I'm going with the EMTs. They'll do their best, and I'll help where I can. He and Gandy are both in trouble."

"F-ing crazies. Thanks for hustling here, Doc. God bless you."

"You're welcome. I know you have a special bond with both these men."

"Yes, sir. They're both good, good men, Doc."

Dr. Don turned to follow the stretcher out. "See you later, Joe."

"Yes sir, Doc. Later," Joe said. "Feels like war," he added quietly to himself.

The Cleveland police officers had begun interviewing the F.B.I. and D.E.A. agents as well as gathering and interviewing bystanders trying to make some sense of such carnage and destruction in a church in their city. They were stunned at all the property damage — more than they remembered seeing on video of the Mother Emmanuel mass shooting. Fortunately here, while there was much more property damage, there appeared to be only two fatalities — so far — presumably the would-be assassins. Since Joe and DJ were in charge of the mission, they were sure to get interviewed on down the line.

But in the meantime, since they had both served as military medics in war zones, they went to see how they could help any of the others.

The EMTs wanted to load Carmela into a rescue vehicle strapped to a gurney, but she insisted on sitting in wheel chair.

"I'm not an invalid!" she shouted.

"Yes, ma'm," they said shaking their heads but complying with her demands. They secured her in a chair with an IV, secured the chair in the rescue vehicle, signaled the driver and off they went to Metro's ER. Dozens of oak, wire and iron piano fragments had punctured her, some quite deeply embedded. However, she was conscious, lucid, mobile and quite feisty.

Melvin, on the other hand, was not conscious. Although he had many fewer fragment wounds than Carmela, he also had several serious looking gunshot wounds and had lost a lot of blood. Both squads sped out, sirens blaring, lights flashing toward Metro General.

Chapter 29

Chaos and Fear

No one else seemed injured or wounded, at least not at first glance, so, with police approval, Joe and DJ shepherded the others down into the church basement near the food and clothing give-away area where they cleaned off a couple of tables, made coffee and tea and set chairs around them for praying, talking, sobbing or simply resting. And that's just what they did. Prayed, talked, wept and slept.

By that time Annie had wound her way back through the growing crowd outside the mission, talked her way past the police officers and went into the church building. Gary and Angelina, already inside helping, saw Annie arrive and saw how stunningly unprepared she was for the grisly sight that met her.

Annie hesitantly inched forward, afraid she would see even more, but still driven to move ahead.

"Holy cow!" she exclaimed, her knees suddenly wobbling as she talked to herself. "Will you look at all that blood, all that mess! Look at that piano. It's been shot to smithereens. Good Lord, God, help us all."

Gary watched, got ready, and in an instant ran to catch Annie as she wobbled forward turning white and green and collapsed into Gary's waiting arms.

"Annie, are you all right?" he asked holding her from falling.

"No, Gary, I can't stay in here. I feel like I'm about to get sick." And she did, right on Gary who accepted it as a token of his love for Annie.

As Gary held her, Annie cleaned her mouth on the sleeve of her coat and Gary's shirt. "Gary," she sniffled, "I want to go back to the house. With you."

"Absolutely."

But at that instant DJ called Gary, who turned to look and momentarily lost his grip on Annie who was miraculously saved by a soft voice and a strong hand.

"Sir, Ma'am," came a soft voice. A Cleveland police office had quietly walked up beside Annie to catch her. "May I help you?"

"Thank you," said Gary.

"Please," Annie sobbed, grabbed onto the officer's arm who led her out the door blindly, and unknowingly, right into Dr. Melanie Zurkos, vomit and all.

"Oh, she blubbered, I'm so sorry. Oh! Mel! It's you!" And she burst into uncontrollable sobs. She pulled loose from the policeman's arm as Mel gathered Annie into her arms.

"Oh, Annie, this is so terrible."

"Mel!" Annie sobbed, "Gary, Angelina and I just walked into the most horrific sight I have ever seen in my life. The whole church is shot up and there are giant puddles of blood on the floor and splattered all over the pews. And there's two dead bodies. It is just terrible."

The officer interrupted to ask Mel, "Ma'am, this is Annie? Correct?" he paused to be sure he was correct.

"Yes. Annie," she said.

"I'm to take her back to her house across the street."

"Oh, I can do that, if it's all right with you," Mel offered.

The officer looked for approval from Annie and Gary, who both nodded. Annie said, "Thank you, officer, I'll go with Mel."

"You're welcome, sir, ma'am." He turned away and walked back into the chaos, while Mel kept her arm securely around Annie's waist guiding her back to Gary's house. But when Annie burst out sobbing, grabbing onto Mel with the whole of her body weight she nearly knocked them both to the ground. Mel stiffened her back, held Annie even more tightly, "Annie, oh, Annie, I am so sorry. Would you like to sit down right here, or shall we walk to the house."

"I'm sorry, Mel, to be such a bother, but let's get to the house. I could use a cup of tea, for sure. I can make it. And we can clean up."

"That sounds like a good idea." And off they went with Annie slowly getting her legs under her, though unable to stop weeping.

When they got into the house, washed up some, made tea and sat at the table, Annie got control, dried her eyes and took a couple of shaky semi-deep breaths. "Thank you so much, Mel. I think I'll be okay as long as I don't have to go back in there. But maybe you might be of some help to the others instead of staying with me. You could even bring them back here into the house and out of the chaos?"

"Great idea, Annie! Are you sure you'll be all right till I get back?"

"I think so. I'm sitting. And I've got my tea." They smiled at one another, both realizing how they had become such good friends. "You'll be a tremendous help anywhere, Mel. Go on. And thank you again."

"Good to help a friend."

"Yes. Good to have a friend. See you in a little bit."

"In a little bit, Annie."

As Mel walked back toward the mission she stopped to talk and comfort stunned, crying neighbors and strangers, pausing to embrace them and to listen. Cleveland Police cordoned off the entire mission yard with crime scene tape and posted guards at the doors. They then barricaded Harbor and Divine Streets from any traffic between West 41st to West 45th from Lorain to Divine. They allowed only two reporters and one photographer inside the mission building, and told everyone else to stand behind the tape and barriers which they kept expanding to accommodate the first responders, the growing number of reporters and a large number of gawkers and neighbors. More emergency vehicles and police SUVs arrived along with the Cuyahoga County Coroner's personnel and vehicles all packing Harbor Street, even parking in Gary's drive and front yard. Curious, frightened neighbors turned on their house lights, threw on winter coats and then gathered to watch police, EMTs, reporters, videographers, two massive television trucks, no, three, now four... five. It had the vibe of a disaster film movie set, but with an absolutely real disaster. More police and sheriff's deputies drove in, including the Cuyahoga County Sheriff himself who took charge with a bullhorn full of calming instructions to quell the chaos and fear.

Finally DJ walked out of the mission's front door bringing a sudden hush to the gathering crowd. The sheriff turned to meet him and, holding the bullhorn, asked, "Sir, who are you?"

"I'm Dr. DJ Scott, the United Methodist Cleveland District Superintendent. This is one of our missions."

"I'm sorry Reverend, this must be quite a shock." the sheriff empathized. "But, sir, can you tell us all what happened, and speak to the crowd as you explain things to me?"

"Yes."

"Thank you," and he passed DJ his bullhorn.

However, CNN TV techs quickly sized up what was about to happen and brought live mics and stands to DJ and the sheriff.

"Thank you," DJ said and then proceeded splendidly. He told the crowd and the television cameras the wild, true story of an insane shootout between drug cartel assassins and agents from the F.B.I. and D.E.A. "The two assassins were shot to death," he said causing a huge cheer to explode from the crowd. "Our local F.B.I. Supervising Special Agent and a second brave man protecting a young child were both severely wounded. They are now both alive, but in critical condition at Metro General Hospital. The pianist who was playing "Joy to the World" while the rest of us sang was wounded as she played, and then wounded even more as she dove for cover from the hail storm of bullets. She is also in Metro General and in fair condition." DJ took a deep breath leaving just enough time for a reporter to shout out, "And who are you?"

"I am Rev. Dr. DJ Scott, Superintendent of the Cleveland District of the United Methodist Church. This is one of our inner city missions, and I just happened to be visiting here, at an auspicious time, I guess. It's a terrible mess in there." Turning to the sheriff, DJ asked, "What do you think, Sheriff, maybe room for one video feed for everyone? Your call."

The sheriff started directing the television crews. "CNN? You set up a video for all the crews. Though, to tell you God's truth, it's not something you want any of your viewers to see, so please be sure you all edit it before you broadcast."

Off to the right of the sheriff, DJ looked around for any clerical collars. Seeing a few he moved to the mic and asked, "Are there any other clergy here?" Six or seven hands went up. "Thank you, friends, for being here." He took a second to fight down his emotion from his love for his brothers and sisters in ministry.

Speaking to the clergy he asked, "Would you be so kind as to spread yourselves out with your hands held high and gather groups to pray for all of us, for our churches, for the wounded and the dead and their families, for Cleveland and for whatever else God puts on your hearts? And would all the rest of you join them in prayer? *Please?*" A hearty cheer of "Amens" and applause rose up, followed by a quiet rustling of people gathering in groups. Saintly voices of the clergy prayed as believers in worship called out their amens, sanctifying the scene with sacred solemnity and healing balm.

Meanwhile the sheriff continued to direct the setting of barriers, stringing crime scene tape and giving verbal directions to everyone while walking among the bystanders.

With a grateful heart, DJ had given the mic back to the CNN techs and went to find Mel whom he had seen walking Annie toward Gary's house. After he checked on them, certain that Annie was going to be fine, he and Mel walked back into the church to check in on the others to pray and counsel with them. But when they got to where DJ had left them in the basement, they were all gone. A police officer told them, "They left out the back door about ten minutes ago with the real D.E.A. agents and said to tell you they were going to Gary's house across the street."

"Thank you. That's good. Where are the F.B.I. Special Agents?"

"One is inside here in the basement conferring with the Cleveland Chief of Police and over a zoom feed with the

F.B.I. and D.E.A. in D.C. The other two are out making sure there are no more cartel thugs. Please stay nearby and keep me informed of your whereabouts, in case the investigators would like to talk with you. Agreed?"

"Yes, sir. And thank you for being here."

"You're welcome. And, Reverend?"

"Yes?"

"You take care. You're an awesome man of God. All of us here could feel it and were blessed."

"Thank you."

And right there DJ bowed and prayed for Officer Jacobs (he saw his name pin), as well as for all the other first responders, the neighbors, Carmela, Melvin and Gandy in Metro General.

He looked up, shook his head, cleared his throat of emotion and said to Officer Jacobs and Mel, "Wow, what a mess! Gotta get it cleaned up for Christmas, for sure."

Officer Jacobs smiled, nodded and agreed it was quite a mess, but then he told DJ, "But, sir, not for a while." When DJ looked confused, Jacobs explained, "The clean up."

"Oh?"

DJ still didn't get the point, so Jacobs spelled it out, "Investigators will probably spend the whole night combing through the debris for evidence. Heavens to Betsy, look, they even shot up the piano."

"Oh, yeah," the light dawned. DJ added, "I think they were trying to shoot the pianist and the kid. Carmela got nicked mostly by piano shrapnel, but Melvin totally saved that kid. Not even a scratch on the boy. But Melvin? Melvin took some hits. I sure hope he pulls through."

"Me too, sir," agreed Officer Jacobs. "He was a very brave man."

"For sure. Officer Jacobs, my colleague and I are counselors, so we're going to check in with the others again, but we'll be back shortly to find out exactly when we can start putting God's house back together for Christmas." He scanned the devastation of the beautiful old sanctuary built by German immigrants more than a hundred years ago in the 1880's, shook his head, sighed and said, "What a shame."

"Yes it is," Jacobs agreed. "But, you know, it's kinda like the Bible story when King Herod ordered his thugs to kill all the baby boys two and under in hopes of killing God's King."

"You know, you're right. In that light, we could worship right here in the middle of the mess, minus the gore, and remember those terrible days for the Holy Family, and thank God for how He saved them."

"And," Jacobs said, "how just now He saved us."

DJ and Mel turned to leave, but DJ said over his shoulder, "Thank you, Officer Jacobs. We'll go to Gary's house to check on the others. We'll be back in a few."

"In a few then, sir, ma'am."

Chapter 30

"O Come, All Ye Faithful"

Excuse me. Dr. Scott?"

DJ turned to see a man with an angelic, tear-stained face looking back at him. "Yes?" he said rather curtly before he noticed tear-glistened, sad eyes, black clothes and the white collar of a priest. "Oh, hello, Father. I'm sorry I was so rude."

"Your upset does not offend me in the least," the angel face said. "I'm Father Ed O'Brien of Saint Patrick's just down Divine Street. And I'm terribly sorry for your tragedy."

"Thank you, Father," DJ choked out. "It's been a helluva night."

"Well said," Fr. Ed responded. "But you handled things splendidly. I'm sure God is proud — especially when you asked all the religious to lead the people in prayer. I wish you could have heard the earnest prayers of the believers for you, for the mission, for the wounded, for our city and for the angels God has sent to help. It would have made your heart sing with Christmas joy on such a night of darkness as this."

"Thank you, Father Ed. Just hearing you tell me about it does make my heart sing. How can I help you?"

"Well, all of the prayer groups and clergy leaders," he motioned to the hundred or more people behind him whom DJ had not noticed until that moment, "we all thought we should forgo our own individual church Christmas Eve services and instead worship all together with you."

"Oh my, how kind," DJ said noticing that the crowd was quietly listening to every word. He paused, took a breath and went on. "But I doubt we will be ready to receive any guests for worship by tomorrow night," DJ responded with a twisted grin and a shrug. Fr. Ed and most of the crowd tittered with restraint at DJ's boyish candor.

"Exactly so. That's why all of us would like to invite you and your mission along with the entire Near West Side of Cleveland to St. Pat's for Christmas Eve worship when we will thank God for the Holy family and for seeing us all through the terrors of this night. And," he added with a saintly smile, "when all of us, all of our churches worship together, we all decided that we want to dedicate our entire Christmas Eve offerings to cover your mission's expenses from tonight's tragedy."

The growing crowd cheered, and started singing "Joy to the World," when just then DJ noticed Gary, Annie, Mel and the others singing as well. Experiencing the unequivocal support of neighbors and friends in faith was an overpowering emotional moment for all of them. When the singing ended Father Ed continued speaking into the microphone, "We'll begin at 6:30 with hundreds of candlelight processions of the faithful from every home and every church down the city's streets right through the open front doors of St. Patrick's for Christmas carols together until 7:30 when we will all celebrate an open mass of lessons and carols with the sacrament served to all who come forward. Will you accept? And, Pastor, will you help me serve? The other clergy have already said they would love to join in."

DJ couldn't get his "yes" out fast enough. "Yes! Absolutely, Yes!" And turning to the crowd said, "With joy and gratitude for all of you. Thank you! Thank you." An open invitation to the sacrament in a Roman Catholic Church is a very special gift, and DJ knew it. It would be a perfect Christmas celebration for the whole Near West Side of Cleveland and perhaps beyond, he thought, taking special notice of the TV broadcast trucks.

In gratitude DJ threw his arms around Fr. Ed. As the two embraced, cameras rolled and the crowd cheered erupting into a spontaneous in-the-streets rendition of "O Come, All Ye Faithful" joyous enough for the angels in heaven to hear.

DJ thanked the people, prayed for them, thanked God for mercy and safety through the perilous night and then said to his new friend loud enough for all to hear, "Father O'Brien, it will be magnificent. Thank you."

Father O'Brien smiled at DJ, blessed the crowd with the sign of the cross, shouted out "Grace and peace to all until we meet tomorrow night at St. Pat's," as if he were leading a high school pep rally, and amazingly the crowd cheered back at him. So the good father egged them on to join with him and DJ all together blessing one another in pep rally style:

"In the Name of the Father and of the Son and of the Holy Ghost. AMEN!"

The two men waved, smiled, left arm-in-arm, totally exhausted, saying to one another,
"Amen indeed!"

Chapter 31

Look at All the Heroes

Meanwhile at Metro General Hospital, just five minutes south of the West Side Market on West 25th Street, the ER was already packed with the usual Friday night mix of injuries from auto accidents, bar fights, household mishaps, and, unfortunately, family abuse plus heart attacks and strokes when the EMTs rolled in the gurneys carrying Melvin, Gandy and Carmela and rushed them into operating suites where emergency teams were already preparing for their arrival. Dr. Don put on scrubs and joined Gandy's OR team, all of whom had worked with him previously and welcomed his expert assistance.

At first the triage nurse had assigned Carmela, who insisted upon walking into the ER on her own power, to a small ER cubicle. However, when the nurse practitioner saw all of the piano fragments embedded in her body like so much shrapnel from a wartime roadside IED, she quickly directed staff to wheel the increasingly weak Carmela into the remaining operating room, and then summoned another team of docs over the hospital p-a system. Carmela had absolutely no time to look in on Melvin, because she was in serious danger of a systemic infection unless all her dozens of wounds were treated immediately. In fact, her vitals already indicated that her body was under attack and in need of IV saline and antibiotics. Besides, since she walked into the ER so heroically, she had quickly become exhausted, dizzy and confused, all warning signs to ER personnel.

Out in the ER waiting area Angelina, Gandy's wife Lydia and daughter Angel along with DJ, Mel, Gary and Annie all checked in at the ER desk and now sat waiting for progress reports on their three friends. Joe joined them ten minutes later, while Fr. Ed had offered to keep watch in the mission and pray for the wounded while serving as the mission contact person for the investigation teams. He enjoyed being helpful and loved chatting with Officer Jacobs.

The DEA agents remained with Jose, Cristina Maria and Miggy in Gary's house. Sandy, Dr. Don's wife, stopped by to offer help getting food, running errands and even providing one of her spare bedrooms for Miggy to sleep. But when the agents consulted their Cleveland office, their supervisor ordered the D.E.A. agents and the three refugees to stay put until the F.B.I. and immigration officials decided what to do with them, since they were all still targets of the Copper Canyon Cartel as well as being possible illegal aliens with illegal credentials themselves.

At the hospital 90 minutes later Dr. Don came out to give family and friends an update. "All three patients are stable, but all of them, including Carmela, are in guarded condition and undergoing extensive surgeries: Gandy has many bullet wounds, several of which are quite serious involving major organs; Melvin has two bullet wounds as well, but dozens of oak shrapnel wounds, some as large as knife blades; and

Carmela also has two less serious bullet wounds along with scores of shrapnel wounds of wood, cast iron, ivory and plastic which pierced her body through her clothes in addition to peppering her exposed skin on her head, face and neck. Carmela's condition would actually require many more separate surgeries than Melvin's, but neither of Carmela's bullet wounds had struck major organs like Gandy's had done."

Everyone was concerned for them all, but Joe's face was very troubled. "Dr. Don," he said, "I'm not surprised at Melvin and Gandy,'s conditions, they were both unconscious when they arrived here, but what in the world is happening with Carmela? She actually walked into the ER under her own power."

Dr. Don took a breath and then explained, "Joe, the piano is mostly wood, but it also has a cast iron harp, copper, brass and steel strings and pins, plus plastic, bone and ivory keys all of which don't just splinter like oak, but rather explode into sharp, lethal, fragments–some knife-sized and some very tiny, smaller than BBs but similar to the small pieces that shatter from plate glass broken on a hard floor. Unfortunately," he explained, "Carmela has many dozens of those small fragments embedded in her beautiful face, head, neck, arms as well as the rest of her body that was covered by clothing. We have a call out for two plastic surgery teams who can work simultaneously to help us. Fortunately no pieces entered her eyes, though some are as close as her eyebrows. But, like I said, she has no wounds into or threatening major organs, besides her skin. Friends, it will be a long night, to be sure. However, on a brighter note, look at all the angels God sent to help!"

"Amen," the rest said.

At that, he turned and walked away, and everyone else's shoulders slumped in resignation, aware of the difficult struggles all three of their friends would face through the night and into the days to come. Most said things like, "Wow," "Holy cow," along with one sarcastic, "Merry Christmas."

Joe summed up his frustration with, "I wonder if that Cristina and Jose ever considered the price other people would pay for their heroic efforts to save Miggy. Just sayin'."

DJ started praying aloud. Everybody else bowed their heads but some wore angry scowls on their faces. Like Dr. Don said, it will be a long night. For sure.

After the Amens, DJ said he would go back to the Mission at Harbor and Divine to give Fr. O'Brien some relief. Mel said she would stay until the next round of medical updates before she would go home, but everyone else agreed to stay the night.

Gary summed up what they were all feeling, saying, "Way to start Christmas Eve, huh?"

Chapter 32

Christmas Eve Day

Next morning Joe was up first. After a night trying to sleep but not sleeping on ER waiting room chairs, Joe admitted it wasn't hard to be the first one awake.

"Pssssst," he whispered to Angelina. "Wanna go with me to get coffee and Egg McMuffins for everybody? My treat. And I'll drive."

"Sure, why not. I've been doing the sleep five minutes / awake five minutes routine all night. Although, I admit," she paused, "I don't want to miss any updates about my mom and dad. I mean, the last one was encouraging, so I half expect them both to dance out those fancy doors together and sing us the next update as a duet! Like, 'Everything is beauuuuti-fullll on Christmas Eve Day. Everyone is hea-hea-healing in their own way.'"

Joe laughed as he walked to check to see if the two women at the desk would like some breakfast.

"Yum!" they cheered together and, "Thank you very much!" as they gave Joe their order of two sausage McMuffins with cheese and two large peppermint flavored coffees.

When he got back to Angelina Joe asked, "So, you coming or staying?" as he hustled out the door.

"Coming," she sang, still in song-and-dance character as she vine-stepped toward Joe's car. Then, when she caught up to him, she ordered Joe in a snooty, prim English voice, "Cheeves, take me to McDonalds."

"Yes, Miss Daisy. Hey, Angelina, I didn't notice, but was DJ back?" Joe asked.

"I didn't see him. It wouldn't surprise me if he stayed there all night and went for coffee and McD's just like you. You two are a lot alike, you know."

"Never thought about it, but I'd like to think I'm at least half the man DJ is—pastor, decorated war hero, Methodist Superintendent, mission worker and full of love for everybody. Well, just about. I'm not sure he has much love for those thugs who tried to gun us all down."

"Probably not. You know my dad was awarded the silver star twice and a few purple hearts."

"That's wonderful, but not surprising with how he risked his life to protect that little kid Miggy. He's one courageous, self-less man. If I had a medal, I'd sure give it to him. 'The Medal of Christmas!'"

"Yeah. But you know what?"

"What?"

"He hates 'em."

Joe looked confused.

"The medals; he hates 'em. Calls them trash, even though he saved the lives of two soldiers and got shot up both times for the effort."

"Yeah. He told me that same thing when we were talking at his house. He did admit, however, that he liked saving those two guys, not to get some award, you understand, but because that's what a good, good man does for his friends."

"That's my dad," Angelina said brushing away a tear.

They drove on in thoughtful silence.

"Hey, here we are. I'm going for those sausage egg McMuffins with cheese. How 'bout you?"

"Sounds perfect. Plus the peppermint coffee. Yum!"

"No peppermint for me. That's a girly drink."

"Hey, that's not nice... but... it is true." She smiled.

"Although I think I'll get a variety for folks to pick from — McMuffins and coffee. Even peppermint. Sound good?"

"Perfect. Maybe a few extras for the docs?"

"Great idea," Joe said to Angelina. "And, hey, you know what? You're all right. You are going to make a great mission co-worker. Now don't get a big head or anything, but you're a pretty good singer too."

Angelina punched him.

"Hey, what's that for? I'm just sayin'."

Angelina smiled, "Thanks."

"A punch in the arm is thanks? Whoa, I'd hate to be around when you *really, really* like something!"

Angelina just kept smiling, thinking, 'I am really going to like working with this man.'

Joe pulled up to the drive-thru, ordered everything on his list plus a few more and in five minutes they were on the road back to Metro General. They pulled into the ER parking lot with perfect timing, because as soon as they walked into the waiting room all six docs walked out of surgery looking totally exhausted, but with big smiles on their faces and gave updates.

"Good thing I got extras! You go, girl!" he said to Angelina. "Great idea of yours to buy for the docs."

Like feeding the five thousand, they passed out breakfast to the grateful, hungry masses, took their seats, then between bites and sips the docs told them non-stop good news about all three of their patients. Almost as good as hoofing it out of the OR and singing it to them.

"And in about 45 minutes," Dr. Mason told them as he looked at his watch, "you can visit, but only for five minutes, no more, and one at a time, please. Oops, I guess I talked for 15 of those 45 minutes. So, make that in a half an hour. Us docs, we are going to finish this delicious breakfast—thank you—clean up a bit then get to our rounds."

At that everybody stood up, applauded and cheered. "Thank you, doctors!" "You guys are the greatest!" You're the best!" "Praise God for you guys!"

Gary mused out loud for everyone to hear, "I was just wondering if doctors could also be angels? What do you think?"

With mouths full of McMuffins absolutely nobody answered, but some nodded.

The half hour wait flew by, and everybody lined up at the recovery room door with smiles on their faces like they were getting on a ride at Cedar Point, unable to keep bubbling over with happiness and relief. Of course, once they got in and saw all three hooked up to multiple IV drips, ventilators, heart monitors and who knows what else, tears returned and worry reset their brows. Timidly they approached the bedsides; quietly they spoke the names of people they loved; hopefully they repeated the good news from the doctors; and sadly they realized all three had long, uphill climbs to get healthy again.

Five minutes was way too short to witness any improvement, but at the same time it was way too long to watch them struggle. Nevertheless, they all left after five minutes, tearfully saying "Good-bye," "I love you," "Stay strong," "Get better."

Then turning toward the door, they walked away as silently as Trappist monks heading to lauds, filing through the waiting room and out into the bright December sunshine.

Once in their cars, Lydia and Angel headed to their home on Divine Street. Gary and Annie drove away to Gary's house dropping off Dr. Don at his home on their way. Joe and Angelina went to the mission. They all reminded one another to process from their homes or the mission at 6:30.

What a harrowing 24 hours.

What a frightening Christmas Eve 'Eve!'

As Gary drove up to his house, Annie said, "Gar, I'm totally exhausted. Do you mind if I stay here to clean up and rest. Your couch is calling me."

"Annie, that's a great idea. I'll get you some towels and such."

"Thank you. What a hard night. I don't even want to look across the street. It makes me remember everything that happened, how terrible everything was, and how, when I first walked in, all I wanted to do was throw up, run away and hide." But she did look. "Gary, isn't that DJ's car? Do you really think he stayed all night?"

"Probably so. Hey, while you clean up — you can help yourself, you know, to coffee or anything — I'm going across the street to see how DJ's doing. Hey, but," he suddenly noticed, "there are no police cars or black SUV's. And look, there's a huge Service Pro van. I wonder if they're already cleaning the place up. You think?"

"I hope so. That would be great."

"Okay. I'll be back in a little bit and bring you the news if you're still awake. See ya."

"See ya." But she turned to Gary and embraced him. Not a five-second hug style, but with a hunger for loving comfort as she burst into sobs all over again. "I'm so sad, Gary. I thought church would always be a safe place. But last night, it was like we all got robbed of our child-like trust in goodness by a couple of murderous thugs. A church just gets shot up and good people simply gunned down." She pushed herself away. "I'm sorry. I'll be all right. You go see how things are coming along. I'll be eager to hear some good news when you come back. Okay?"

"You bet. But here's some Good News til then: Even with murderous King Herod on the throne, Jesus was still born at Christmas." Gary walked away, but turned back worried about his best friend.

Annie blew him a troubled, but sweet, two-fingered kiss.

Gary started to shoot back his cowboy gun thing to her, but he couldn't. "Can't do that any more, Annie. Even a finger gun means something different now. Something terrible." He turned to go, then turned back again. "How 'bout a cowboy tip of the hat instead?"

Annie smiled, "Try it, cowboy."

He did. "Later, ma'am."

"Later, cowboy."

It worked. Smiles chased away the worry lines from their faces.

Growing love has its ways. Thank God.

Gary crossed Harbor Street and made his way into the Mission at Harbor and Divine looking around for a familiar face, finally finding DJ asleep in an oak pew while the men and women on the ten-person cleaning crew worked their magic.

And magical it was! They had already torn up all the blood stained carpet runners especially from where Gandy and the assassins were shot; removed the most damaged of the pews; thoroughly washed down and sanitized all the rest of them; removed the shot up, demolished piano; dug bullets out of the walls and remaining pews; washed all the floors and oak wainscot on the walls; and who knows what else. They replaced the smell of blood and death with the aroma of Murphy's Oil Soap, and that was a good, a very good tradeoff. Still, the look of chaos remained waiting to be replaced by a look and smell of fresh hope.

Maybe soon. Maybe after Christmas.

Gary walked toward DJ who jerked awake like the old Marine he was. The only thing he didn't do was reach for his weapon, which wasn't there anyhow. "That's some progress," Gary said considering DJ's long struggle with PTSD.

"Oh, Gary, it's you. Good morning. And what'd you say?"

"I said, 'That's some progress,' because when you jerked awake you didn't reach for your weapon."

"Huh. I guess I'm slipping, eh?"

"Yeah, but that's a good thing, is it not?"

"Sure is. But it took another fire fight to get me there."

"That's true. But anyhow, good morning to you, Rev. Dr. Captain DJ!" And then with a wry smile he added, "I see you're supervising the clean up detail from your usual reclining position. Nice job!"

"Nothing like a good helping of breakfast sarcasm to start the day! But, really, they are doing a great job, aren't they?"

"Sure are. I didn't think the investigators would even let them get started until tomorrow, or even Monday, and they've already gotten so much accomplished. It's great."

"Yes, it is. Unfortunately they still have so much left to do. But, Gary, tell me, how are the wounded doing?"

"According to the doctors, really well. But, honestly, I've got to tell you, when we went into the recovery rooms to visit them, well, they looked downright pathetic all wired up, hooked up and intubated. Still, the good news is they are all stable, and only Gandy has major damage — lungs, ribs, liver. Missed the heart and major arteries, thank God. So the docs said even he is going to recover. All good news.

"But, DJ, how about you? How about Jose, Miggy and Cristina Maria? I can't believe all of you escaped without injury."

"Well, to be honest, I did get grazed by a bullet from somewhere and I did get pelted by blasts of oak shrapnel. Same with both Jose and Cristina, I think. I didn't go to the hospital, because somebody had to hold down the fort here; however, Jose and Cristina didn't want to go to the hospital because they were afraid once they walked into the hospital and signed into the system, I.C.E. would find them and either ship all three of them back to Mexico, or arrest the two of them and turn Miggy over to Children's Services. Of course, not going to the hospital did not save them from I.C.E. The F.B.I.'s report contained all the details I.C.E. needed to drop in on them this morning at Dr. Don's place where they stayed the night, so when Sandy answered the door this morning at seven, well, what could she say other than, 'Come on in and have a cup coffee.' The two I.C.E. agents took over from the two DEA agents, Dr. Don got home, and the eight of them have been drinking coffee and confabbing over what to do with Mary, Joseph and Jesus ever since — like most of the rest of the world for 2,000 years. Maybe we should walk over there and see what they decided. Want to?"

Just then the front door opened followed by more sets of foot steps up the stairs and in strode Joe and Angelina.

"Hey, Joe, Angelina. Good to see you. Did you stay at the hospital to get a second visit with the wounded?" Gary asked.

"Yes, but we also decided that since we were hanging around waiting, I'd check in at the ER desk and get my cuts and scratches treated. No sense in risking infections. Angelina was kind enough to wait for me."

"Makes sense. How did that go?"

"Well," Joe began, "I have dozens of oak shrapnel wounds, which I thought really didn't amount to much, until they started pulling out all those little suckers and scrubbing them — yes, scrubbing! — with extra-stinging alcohol and antiseptics. Ouch!"

"Wah-wah!"

"Such pastoral empathy you have, Rev. Dr."

"Sorry," DJ said as he smirked. "Not sorry!"

"Then, comes the easy part, they shot me up with antibiotics and told me to go home. No sutures and, really, not that many ouchies, DJ. I just embellished the story to entertain your highness."

"Except," Angelina interrupted, "Macho man here did have a bullet in his leg."

"Ouch!" winced DJ in real empathy.

"Yeah, but," Joe said all set to tell another story, "it must have ricocheted ten times before it got to me, because the bullet didn't even tear through my pants on its way into my leg! Isn't that crazy? How does that happen? So all I had to do to get that bullet out was tug on my pants and 'pop!' out flies the bullet just as slick as goose grease. Had to have been a multiple ricochet. Anyhow, they were all so impressed that I 'dug out' the bullet by myself that I didn't tell them any different.

Got it right here, look at this little bugger. I guess what I did was so unusual they never figured out that I had a trick up my sleeve — er, up my pant leg — so they just cleaned out the hole like they would for any other hero, but left it open under a wrap that I'm supposed to change, clean out and douse with antiseptics twice a day. They gave me some oral antibiotics to take for a week. Plus, and get this, this beautiful nurse there cut out a purple heart and gave it me, and called me her hero. I think I'm in love!"

The others laughed, even the clean up team got some jollies out of that yarn and joined in with some whistles and hoots. Joe was in hero heaven. At least in his own mind.

"So, hey, Superman," Gary teased, "still want to go to Dr. Don's to check on Mary, Joseph and Jesus? I do. After all, it is Christmas Eve."

"Count me in," said the hero.

"Us too! Right, Angelina?"

"I'm in. We can have a mini-reunion."

And out they scampered in pretty good humor considering they were still walking out of the bloody scene of a shootout and a double homicide. They were already doing their best trying to forget the whole thing — with some success — sorta.

They got to Dr. Don's in a flash, since it was only the distance of a strong throw from right field to home.

"Well, there's the black SUV. What? It's ICE!" exclaimed Joe. "What's going on?" he asked just as Mary, Joseph and Jesus rounded the corner with sheepish looks on their faces accompanied by two very official and tough looking gentlemen.

"What's going on?" asked the toughest-looking guy in reply to Joe's query as he and his partner crowded in closer to their three customers not knowing what Joe and his posse had in mind. "Who's f-ing asking?"

Joe figured he better talk. "Oh, fellas, we're from the mission coming to see how things are going with the Holy Family, a.k.a. Cristina, Jose and Miggy. What's going on with you guys?"

The other agent laughed, "Holy Family, huh? That's rich. They were just hopping into their car to make for Egypt. Unfortunately for them, but good for us, I removed their battery cable, so they couldn't even have made it to Lakewood, assuming they would be headed for the so-called underground railroad from Juarez to Canada. I'm Agent Jason Slocum, and this here's Agent Mitchel Thomas." They both displayed their id's. "We're I.C.E. agents assigned to safely transport these good folks downtown to federal court for temporary custody until people smarter than we are can figure out how to keep this little man safe and these two supposed do-gooders from breaking the law. That's about all we can tell you, and we're outa time. Nice to meet you folks, but we gotta go." He tipped his hat and said to his partner and the other three, "Okay, let's load up." They had handcuffed Cristina and Jose, so they had to help them into the middle row of seats and belt them in. Then one agent took the wheel and the other took Miggy into the rear seat, belted him in, tapped the roof and said, "Let's go, Mitch." And off they drove. So much for the fantasy of Mary, Joseph and Jesus joining them for Christmas worship.

Dr. Don and Sandy walked onto their porch, and Sandy said, "Good morning, everyone. And that's what happens when even well-meaning people break the law."

"I guess so," agreed DJ. "But let's not waste our good intentions. How about a trip to visit our friends in Metro General?"

Everyone agreed, including Dr. Don and Sandy who climbed into their own car, while the rest headed back to the mission to load up into theirs. Gary took a detour to get Annie on the way.

When they walked into the main hospital waiting room, miraculously, there sat Carmela waiting for them with a mischievous glint in her eyes as the group ran up to her all excited.

"Carmela! You're here!"

"Are you released?"

"What's going on?"

"I got released! And Gandy and Melvin got transferred to the step-down unit."

"Hooray!" cried Angelina rushing to give Carmela a hug.

"No-no-no-no!" Carmela warned holding her hands out to ward off her well-intentioned but momentarily-stupid daughter.

"Oh, yeah. Sorry, Mom. I forgot."

"That's okay. I appreciate the thought. But I still feel as though I've been dragged a mile behind a semi on an old gravel road! And, so, sorry to say, I was just kidding about being released."

"Boo," said Joe, "I wish it had been the truth, but, really, it's miraculous you're even up and about."

Angelina, more upset than Joe with her mother's ruse, said in a pout, "So you're *not* going home with us?"

"Oh, no. They just helped me come out to surprise you."

"Pooh!" Angelina said. "I miss you."

"Angel, I miss you too, but I'll be home before you know it. I've still got to be hooked up again to IV's and have all my wounds abraded and disinfected every morning and every evening for another two, maybe three more days."

"Double ouch!" winced Joe. "That hurts just to think about."

"Oh it's not so bad. I get breakfast in bed, laundry service, and THEY do the dishes!" Carmela said with a smile that she turned into a pouty frown to match her daughter.

"Oh well! As Fr. Ed might say, 'Bless you, my child!'" Joe chuckled. "But, hey, why not come with us to check on Melvin and Gandy before visiting hours are over and they kick us out. Wanna come?"

"I'm sorry, I can't do that either," sighed Carmela. "I need to go straight back to my room. In fact, here come my helpers now. The doc said no visiting, not even Melvin for now. Tomorrow maybe. But thank you all for coming. You brightened up my day, and I'm sure you'll cheer up Melvin and Gandy as well. And, Merry Christmas!"

"Merry Christmas, Carmela," they all said. "We'll see you again tomorrow."

Angelina added, "I love you, Mom. Get better."

"Thanks, Angel. I love you too. Good-bye, all."

They went to visit Melvin and Gandy for a few minutes, and, in no time at all, they were on their way back to the mission.

Considering how damaged all three had looked earlier that morning, they all appeared remarkably improved in just the last few hours, not just Carmela, but Melvin and even Gandy. Melvin was able to talk with them, but not Gandy since he was still on a ventilator. He did, however, respond by blinking his eyes — one for yes, two for no. Plus he managed to smile with his eyes and made everybody misty eyed.

As they were leaving for the mission, Joe called out for pizza delivery for dinner at Gary's house. Of course, everyone was so tired that once they got to Harbor Street and Gary invited everyone in to take a load off, drink some Coke or coffee, talk about the day together (or catch some z's) and wait for the pizza, everybody nodded off, totally zonked. That is to say, nobody heard the pizza delivery guy until the persistent driver knocked his knuckles raw and rang the door bell count-less times finally waking up Gary who stumbled to the door, got the pizza, paid the bill and blessed the driver with a hefty tip for the extra effort. The noise woke everybody else up, so in no time the whole gang was digging into the pizza, slurping coffee and Coke and chattering about how Cristina, Jose and Miggy had come and gone leaving behind terrible memories, profoundly injured people and a sanctuary filled with the spirit of evil, chaos and death the night before Christmas Eve.

"Just saying," Joe concluded, "but I'm sorry they came and I'm glad they're gone. I wish DJ, Dr. Don and I had sent them packing right away, but we felt so sorry for them, and I know, for one, I had no clue how much darkness they would bring into our lives. Stupid, I was." He paused to think for a few beats then said, "Except in Iraq, in a war—*WAR*—I'm telling you, I've never known two people who caused so much chaos, violence and woe as quickly as Cristina and Jose did. Thank you, Lord, for taking them away."

"Amen!"

"Agreed."

"You said it, Joe!"

"Hear! Hear!"

"On the other hand, all they were doing was trying to 'help.' Oy!"

Joe summed it up with: "And all God's people said," and the others joined in with a resounding,

"OY!"

All, that is, except Angelina. She kept her thoughts to herself about the high price at least some people have to pay so that children grow up safely because the rule of law abides and peace reigns. Good, good women and good, good men everywhere have got to pay a steep, steep price. She smiled to herself thinking, 'Mom and I are so blessed to have such a man who willingly risks his life and has ended up paying steep, life-long prices to save others.' Then out loud she said "Father God, please heal my dad. Please."

Joe heard a bit of what she said but still asked, "What was that, Angelina?"

"Oh, I was just praying for my dad."

"Let's all do that. What do you say?"

"I've got this," said DJ. "Let's pray."

And they did.
They all knew God heard their prayer,
but they hoped that perhaps, somehow, Melvin did too.

Chapter 33

Christmas Eve
Joy, Peace, Hope and,
Oooh-la-la, Love!

D J, are you hanging out to walk with us to St. Pat's?"
"Not sure yet, Joe. I need to check with Mel. Either she'll
drive her car back here, or I'll have to drive out to pick her up.
Hey, how about I call her right now, so you know."

"Okay. Sounds good, but, DJ, either way, I really hope
she wants to come. It feels important to me to have all of us
together tonight, all of us, including Mel."

"I agree. And I think she will too. Let me call." He walked
out onto the porch for a quick chat, then quickly back into
the house to report. "Mel says she'll drive out and be here in
about an hour."

The group cheered, then one by one began to nod off.

Joe piped up and asked, "Before everybody falls back to sleep, anyone want to make a Christmas Eve visit to wish Gandy, Melvin and Carmela a "Merry Christmas?"

"I'm exhausted," said DJ, "but count me in."

"Me too," added Angelina. "Mom's going to need some cheering up, for sure. Dad too."

"Annie, do you want to go? Gary?"

"Yes," Annie answered. "I'd like to be part of a cheering up expedition. With so much violence, and death, and crying in the last two days I believe a little Christmas joy is in order."

"Count me in, Joe," Gary said. I'll drive Annie and me."

Joe smiled, "That's the Christmas spirit!" And he started singing, "Dashing through the snow, in a one-horse open sleigh, o'er the fields we go, laughing all the way! Ha-ha-ha!" And everybody started singing and laughing as they dashed out to their cars in the Christmas Eve cold complete with lake effect snow.

Joe, DJ and Angelina left to pick up Dr. Don, who had already told Joe he'd love to check in on Melvin and Gandy if anybody else would be driving. Angelina had texted Dr. Don, Joe pulled in Dr. Don's drive, the good doctor hopped in the back seat with Angelina, and off they drove.

Joe cleared his throat auspiciously, then said, "Just to keep things real, so no one is blindsided, do you both realize we could still all be charged with aiding and abetting a whole host of crimes?"

"Like what for example?" Angelina asked. "And who says?'

"Our F.B.I. saviors say. And, with apologies to E. B. Browning, let me 'count the ways' we could be getting into deep do-do," Joe answered, "all of them having to do with helping Cristina, Jose and Miggy.

"Number One, and I'll put 'aiding and abetting them' in front of each one just to keep things real. Ready? Here goes:

"Number One: aiding and abetting them in child abduction.

"Number Two: aiding and abetting them in international kidnapping;

"Number Three: aiding and abetting them in crossing multiple state lines while committing a felony;

"Number Four: aiding and abetting them in falsifying Miggy's birth certificate;

"Number Five: aiding and abetting them in child endangerment;

"Number Six: aiding and abetting them in double homicide;

"Number Seven, all on our own: failing to report the abduction of a child.

"Get the picture? We are at the mercy of federal, state and municipal authorities, especially the four of us, including Dr. Don."

"But, Joe, we were only trying to help!" pleaded Angelina.

"Sure, I think they all understand that our complicity in the whole business was not meant to deceive the authorities. But yet we did deceive, and therefore we are still culpable on every charge, especially since we were not forthcoming, at least not right away. Not until Gandy approached me about the meeting, and, yes, then we did bend over backwards to help, getting all shot up in the process. Still, get ready to be grilled all over and over again whenever that may happen — maybe even later today or even on Christmas Day, I don't know. But I do know this is a big honkin' deal not only in Cleveland, but nationally, and internationally. Mexico is already involved, hotly so, as I understand. And the headlines in today's over-hyped media, 'F.B.I. Shootout in Cleveland Church: two dead three more hospitalized,' aren't going away any time soon. And neither are the TV crews camped outside the mission. In fact, someone is following us right now."

They all turned their heads to look. The guy waved.

"He waved!" Dr. Don chortled. So he turned around, smiled and waved, and the guy waved back at him again. He did it again, then said, "It's not at all like he is trying to nab gangsters red-handed. Know what I mean? Just friendly, finger-wiggling wave. Friendly guy! "

"Sure, Don," admitted Joe. "But still, no matter who asks questions — media, F.B.I., Cleveland Police, please: number 1, keep in mind that this is serious stuff; number 2, keep in mind we really did indeed do it; number 3, cooperate and be pleasant, honest, forthcoming and transparent. Make sense? Oh, yeah, and number 4, always speak truth."

"Yes, sir, Joe," DJ totally agreed. "This is a big deal for all of us as well as for the church where it all happened, a church, I might add, under my jurisdiction."

"Not to mention my medical license," stewed Dr. Don.

"Not to worry, Doc, they never interviewed you, did they?"

"Hey, Joe, you're right," Dr. Don realized. "They didn't."

"Well, stop waving, because I think that means you're not even on their radar."

"Yeah, but now I'll be on the radar of whoever is tailing us."

"Well.... Maybe not."

"I hope not. I hear those kinds of interviews are seldom, if ever, pleasant!" Don fretted.

"You may be right at that, but really, those guys have bigger fish to fry than a bunch of out-of-their-lane-do-gooders from the Mission."

"I sure hope so, Joe,"

"Me too," chimed in Angelina.

"Me three," agreed DJ.

A few minutes later, the somber looking foursome arrived at Metro General, parked the car next to Gary's SUV and silently walked into the main entrance. Dr. Don went in through the physicians' entrance, and the others through the visitors' main entrance to check in. Because Joe said he was a pastor and wanted to pray with Gandy he got admitted to intensive care to visit him. Then because Angelina was Melvin's daughter and DJ a pastor, they both got to visit Melvin in the step down unit. Gary and Annie needed no special pass to visit Carmela, but because she was in a secure unit with an armed guard, they did need to identify themselves, state their business and show their id's. It all went smoothly and all three patients were elated to see their holiday visitors.

However, when Joe took one look at Gandy who was as pale as a ghost and all hooked up, all he could do is shake his head and ask the ICU nurse how things were going for Gandy and if he could pray.

She smiled said, "Gandoff? He is doing remarkably well, considering all the trauma and surgeries he's been through."

Quietly Joe turned to look at Gandy one more time, shook his ahead again and said to himself, "You coulda fooled me."

The nurse heard him, so she half smiled and told Joe, "Sir, I'm not saying he doesn't have a ways to go, but I am saying that for all I understand he's been through in the last 24 hours, all of us here think he's doing remarkably well. Worry less, pray more," she added. Then she asked Joe, "Do you mind if I stay and pray with you?"

"Mind? No, ma'am. In fact, I would love you to pray with us and even take a turn leading if you'd like."

"Thank you, I would like that very much."

On their way out, the five visitors shared how their patients were doing. Since Joe noticed that Gary, Annie, Angelina and

DJ had smiles on their faces, he said, "How 'bout you guys go first."

Gary and Annie had nothing but good news about Carmela, reaffirming all the positive reports she had shared with them earlier in the day.

"I'm happy to go next," Angelina chirped, "because my Dad is doing very well, really well. He even talked with us, cracked a joke, but he couldn't laugh because he said it hurts him too much, so we laughed for him, but that made him laugh even more plus wince in pain which, for some reason made him laugh more yet. I think he loved the laughing so much he didn't mind at all the price of pain he had to pay."

DJ added, "And the nurse said he'd be moved from step-down to some kind of special floor. Did you catch what she said?" he asked Angelina.

"Not really, just that Dad was super happy about it, and said something about having a police guard. Maybe it's the same unit my mom is on."

Joe's eyebrows went up. "Really?" he asked. "A guard?"

Angelina's smile faded, she eyed Joe worried-like and then asked, "Joe, I never thought about it that way. Do you really think there's a chance we could go to jail for helping those three out?"

"I don't know. I don't know a thing. I don't even know who the guard is for, to keep Melvin from leaving or to protect Melvin from somebody else. I just know that the special agents were concerned for us. I think they like us, but the law's the law, and it looks like we broke it to smithereens. I never thought that our personal safety might still be in jeopardy. But maybe it is. So how 'bout we focus on your mom's and dad's good news for now. Other things will come as they come, and God will be our Rock."

"Amen," said DJ. "But Joe, what about Gandy?"

"He's still got a long road ahead of him."

"Do they think he'll make it?"

"Hey, we were standing right next to him, and who knows what he can hear or understand. But the nurse did say that for all he's been through she thinks he's doing very well."

DJ nodded saying, "I'll take that. Yeah. So you prayed?"

"We did, and the nurse even jumped in with her own prayer to give Gandy a spiritual lift. I liked that. She gets my vote for nurse of the year!"

They kept walking toward the main door, where Dr. Don stood waiting for them. "So, how did your visits go?"

Joe answered, "Really well. The docs and nurses think all three of them are model patients, and Melvin said he's getting moved to a regular room with a police guard. It sounds good, but scary. A police guard? Know anything about that, Doc?"

"All I know is that he just got moved to the same high security unit Carmela's in. They must have moved him right after you left, and they didn't want me to tag along. But his docs told me he's doing very well, even though they were mum about when he might be released."

"Hmm. More mysterious by the minute," DJ pondered. "What did you find out about Gandy back in the Secret Doc Cave?"

Dr. Don smiled at the Doc Cave quip as he replied, "He had eleven hours of surgery and he's not out of the woods by a long shot. Oh, sorry, but you get what I mean."

"*No ai problem*o. But eleven hours? Isn't that a lot?" asked Joe.

"It sure is. His left lung and his liver were both torn up, maybe by the same bullet, so he's on a ventilator and receiving blood plus the usual IV cocktails of saline and meds. The surgeries were all successful, but he's in very serious condition, and far from healed, far from out of the woods. Even the entrance and exit bullet wounds were such extremely delicate surgeries, that they actually needed my extra set of hands to help. By the end of the day all of us surgeons were exhausted to say the least. But today they and all the other surgeons are pleased that Gandy made it through the night, which, they said, is a very big deal and a good sign. And I agree."

"Well, yeah," said Joe with a dash of sarcasm. "But, I've got to tell you, in spite of the Recovery Room nurse's optimism, he looked really rough to me. Oh, and yeah, on another note," Joe shifted gears, "I almost forgot. Doc, would you and the missus like to walk with us to St. Pat's for lessons and carols and an open communion table?"

Dr. Don's eyebrows went way up as he asked, "Meaning anybody, not just Catholics?"

"Yep. That's a once in a blue moon invitation."

"Right! I know! That makes it a hardy 'Yes!' from both of us. We'll be there. What time?"

"6:15 at the Parish House — the mission."

Their conversation had taken them all the way to the cars, and they were still talking until they loaded up and drove back to Gary's house, forgetting all about their tail, who had not forgotten them.

Inside they swapped more stories and scarfed down most of the remaining pizza. Around 6:15 they got bundled up for the one mile walk to St. Pat's and headed out the door joined by Dr. Don and Sandy. As they crossed Harbor Street together, a man dressed in a black top coat walked straight toward them.

Everyone slowed down. The man did not. Joe and DJ stepped out from the group to meet the stranger.

When they got face to face, Joe asked, "Can we help you?"

"Oh, sorry. I didn't mean to alarm you. I'm Lieutenant Albion Carter of the Cleveland Police Department. I have been your tail, and I would like to walk with you to St. Pat's, if you don't mind." He spoke loud enough for the rest of the group to hear, all of whom let out a collective sigh of relief that he was there to help.

"Mind?!" Joe exclaimed. "We'd consider it a gift to have you walk with us, Lieutenant Carter. We're just about ready to leave."

"Great. I'm ready to go."

"Oh! But would you be interested in the last two pieces of our pizza? Pretty sure they're still there, and it's Mamita's best! We'll wait."

"I'd love to. I'm famished."

"All right then." Turning to the rest of the group he said, "Let's go back to the house for a sec." Then to Lt. Carter, "There's some coffee and Coke in there too if you'd like some."

"I'd love it all," said the grateful policeman. "Thank you!"

Joe smiled, offered his hand and said, "You're welcome. Nice to meet you, Lieutenant. I'm Joe Whitehorse, director of the mission here, and that's my boss over there, the Rev. Dr. DJ Scott. And, really, we're glad you'll be walking with us."

"Thank you," Carter answered with a pizza smile that didn't tell Joe that they really had no choice in the matter. Just as well, no? "Oh, and there may be a few more of us join in along the way. Still good?"

Joe just kept right on smiling, "Yes, sir, it's all good."

Lt. Carter finished the pizza and coffee on the way out the door, stuffed the empty paper cup and napkin in his pocket, and again told Joe, "Thank you very much! I'm ready now for another shift! Let's go!"

"A few more along the way" was a gross understatement, but how was Lt. Carter to know that not only were there 25 extra policemen including two horse mounted officers, but also half of the Near West Side all wanting to walk to St. Pat's with the folks from The Mission at Harbor and Divine.

It seemed that, as they walked, every ten or fifteen seconds someone new would walk up to the mission group to ask, "Do you mind if we walk with you to St. Pat's?" or "Okay if we keep you guys company along the way?" or, as one older gentleman put it, "Merry Christmas, folks. I just want to say I'm proud to be your neighbor. Okay if I walk with you along the way?"

It was as if the gates of heaven opened and all God's angels poured out into the streets of Cleveland. Then when one of them started singing, "Joy to the World, the Lord is come..." the entire heavenly host joined in, and the inner city streets of Cleveland's Near West Side rang with the angel chorus of healing and hope all the way from the corner of Harbor and Divine to St. Pat's.

Joe turned to Gary and Annie both whose eyes already sparkled with tears, and he said, "Can you believe this? Look down the street. They're lining the street waiting to walk with us! We may be on our way to jail, but we're getting a glimpse of heaven on the way!" And he joined in singing, "...and heaven and heaven and nature sing... He rules the world with truth and grace and... ."

They were still five blocks away from the church but the street was already packed to the curbs and sidewalks beyond. Just then down the middle of the crowded street, coming straight toward DJ and Mel, who, at the moment, led the way, Joe spotted the St. Patrick's crucifer, a robed young man holding the crucifix high above his head surrounded by three more robed young people. One carried a huge open Bible needing two strong arms; two more with giant candlesticks waiting to be lit in church and a fourth one, a not so young Fr. Ed O'Brien, wearing a smile bright enough to light the night, all come to escort the mission folks to St. Pat's. Joe broke ranks to run and embrace the priest, shouting, "Look what God has done in Cleveland, Ohio. Fr. Ed! It's a miracle!"

Fr. Ed smiled and said, "Joe, it's Christmas! What else would you expect from God at Christmas? The Super Bowl? In Cleveland?"

Joe laughed. "Well, while He's at it, why not?" Fr. Ed chuckled then turned the robed cadre around 180 degrees to head back toward St. Pat's, and at that instant it started snowing. The whole crowd of hundreds and hundreds cheered and filled the glittering night with shouts of "Merry Christmas!" Fr. Ed took it as a heavenly sign and shouted even above the crowd, "Let's all sing to our neighbors!" And he led,

"We wish you a Merry Christmas!
We wish you a Merry Christmas!
We wish you a Merry Christmas
and a Happy New Year!"

That morphed into "O Come, All Ye Faithful/Adeste Fideles," then "Hark! the Herald Angels Sing," and soon the wave of Christmas joy transported them all to the open doors of St. Pat's where a magnificent organ pumped out "Joy to the World." The pews filled, standing room folks packed the side aisles, and the murder and mayhem of yesterday lost its swagger under the Christmas carol power of joy, love, peace and especially hope. Bethlehem's Christmas story was not to be forgotten that night, especially by the twelve hundred who packed St. Pat's massive sanctuary to hear Christmas Bible readings, sing carols and share all together in the Sacrament of Holy Communion.

At the end of worship, at the very instant Fr. Ed blessed the congregation and wished everybody, "Merry Christmas and Happy New Year," the grand organ erupted in a raucous, joyful rendition of "Joy to the World" propelling twelve hundred joy-filled, carol-singing Christmas revelers out the doors and onto Divine Street to be greeted by a thousand more frolicking, cheering saints singing in the gently falling, cool lake snow and shouting "Merry Christmas!" *"Feliz Navidad!" "Freuliche Weinachten!"* and Christmas greetings in a dozen more Near West Side languages.

When Fr. Ed had initially welcomed everyone to worship, he singled out The Mission at Harbor and Divine folks, announcing that all the Christmas Eve donations would go to the mission, drawing a huge cheer from all the congregants who, now outside, greeted Gary, Annie, Joe, DJ, Mel and the rest of the Mission team with fervent best wishes and more than a few fifty and one hundred dollar bills stuffed in their handshakes.

As they made their way up Divine Street back toward the mission and to Gary's house, Annie asked, "Well, Gar, does this feel like home yet?"

"More than ever, Annie, especially with this wild swing from last night's disaster to this night's elation. To have steady friends to walk with through life's monumental ups and downs takes me back to all the church friends we had back when Dad was at his worst."

"Drinking, you mean?"

"Yeah. We'd come here at Christmas Eve and at first Dad would be great, joking, celebrating, hugging friends until Christmas Day when our relatives and friends would go back to their homes and we'd be alone together, and he'd start drinking again. Sounds strange to say, 'alone together,' but when Dad felt alone, that's when he would drink himself sideways. Even though all of us were there with him in the same apartment up there on the seventh floor, he'd start carrying on, yelling one minute, crying the next, throwing dishes, even breaking our brand new Christmas presents. That's when I remember feeling so very alone, afraid and vulnerable. And that's how I felt last night after the gunfire–alone, afraid, vulnerable. But since Dad's been sober we've had many beautiful Christmas Eves together filled with the peace, joy and hope as well as a secure kind of love. Just like tonight. Does that make sense, Annie?"

"Sure does. I feel the same way about today's joy and hope after last night's dark despair. And, Gary, for me, you are a huge part of that secure kind of love in my life."

"I'm glad. As you are in mine, Annie."

And they stopped right in the middle of Divine Street and kissed one another as the soft snow fell on their faces anointing their kiss with Christmas joy. Behind them a small cheer arose from their friends, all of whom knew how much they loved each other, but how difficult it had been for them to overcome their careworn pasts and commit to a new life together. They both turned to smile at their wonderful new friends.

"They're cheering us on, you know," Gary told Annie.

"I know. Reminds me how life grows new joy with seeds planted in the rotted compost of the past."

"Well put, Annie. For both of us, huh?"

"Yup. It's a Christmas kind of thing. Love we get that we don't deserve. But here it is. And, Gary, here you are."

They hugged again, and kissed to the delight of an even larger crowd, as a hundred more people stopped to stand and watch God once again unfold His Christmas gift of love and hope to a hurting world. They cheered. They whistled. And they shouted, "Oooh-la-la!" Annie looked up, smiled shyly, blushing for such an audience as this.

Gary too looked up, way up, remembered Dianah in France, smiled broadly and said "Thank you." Yes, thank you to God, for sure. But to Dianah as well, his once shy wife, who was, it seemed to Gary, again smiling her approval of Gary's growing love for Annie. Years ago Dianah blushed at the very thought of Gary's French artist colleagues viewing and critically ana-lyzing Gary's lush impressionist paintings of beautiful Dianah, which they did with relish. In fact, Gary told her back then, that they whistled. "Yes, they did," he told Dianah, "wolf whis-tles." Gary had loved it. Plus they cheered too. They even kissed their fingers, raised them heavenward in an artistic toast to love and beauty while enthusiastically exclaiming, "Ooh-la-la! Ooh-la-la!"

Later that night long ago in France when Gary had arrived home from his French Impressionist master class, he told Dianah all about what his colleagues had done in graphic, joy-filled detail. The more he told her, the more Dianah blushed. The more she blushed the more Gary embellished his story until she giggled, and laughed and *really* blushed throwing herself into Gary's arms.

Gary remembered her blushing as if it were only yesterday.

But this night, this Christmas Eve night, it was Annie, with her love for Gary on full display for all to see. This night it was Annie who blushed, and Gary smiled with a grin as wide as Cleveland's Bob Hope Bridge, so broad that it spanned the flats from the West Side Market right into Downtown Cleveland. That's when he noticed something. It was no longer the beautiful Dianah Brownbear stirring his heart with love, joy and hope. No. This night it was the enchanting, joyful Annie

Dunlop whose middle of the street kissing not only stirred her beloved Gary, but rallied the crowd to cheer and shout out,

"Oooh-la-la!"
"Merry Christmas!"

Chapter 34

Christmas Day
Bells of Hope

Gary woke up that Christmas morning feeling oddly at peace. "Whoa," he said to himself, "that's strange. Haven't felt this normal since... hmph... yeah, since before Dianah and Lily died." He shook his head and took a deep breath, "Don't go down there, Gar." Instead he put on his happy game face, swung his feet out of bed; and then he just sat there feeling out this first Christmas Day alone in, what, fifteen years. "Strange," he said reviewing the insanity of the last two days, "alone, yes, but I don't feel lonely any more. Hmmm."

Right on cue his over-the-top ring tone started, "If you're happy and you know it clap your hands..." It was the three of them, Gary, Dianah and Lily, singing, like they did a hundred times on road trips. He'd kept that ring tone all this time since they died, even though it broke his heart to hear it. But this morning? This Christmas morning? "If you're happy. IF?" he challenged himself. "Hmmm. Am I? Come on now, Gar. Are you happy?!" And in that instant the joy of Christmas, this

263

Christmas in particular, enveloped him in a grand embrace making him shout out at the top of his lungs and clap his hands, "Doggone it, I AM Happy! And I DO Know It! I do! I do! I do... I think...." His flood of joy gently morphed into a stream of consciousness thanks. "Thank you, Dianah! Thank you Lily! Thank you, Jesus, because now I have a thousand new friends who love me, and all of whom I love right back!" And frantically he began naming them: "Like Annie. Yes, especially Annie. And DJ. And Mel. Yes, yes. And Joe, and Carmela, and Melvin — please heal him, Lord — and Angelina and Gandy, yes Gandy, Lord. Please heal him too! And Little Angel and Lydia. And Dr. Don and Sandy. And Clara, oh yes. And Father Ed. And Lt. Carter. And Dr. Mason. And my dad. And my mom."

Then, in a halting, emotion-filled voice, even though the phone had stopped its singing, quietly Gary sang it to himself. "If you're happy and you know it clap your hands!" And he did. He clapped his hands ever so softly. He stomped his feet a little louder. He soft-shouted, "Amen!" Then he sang it all over again louder and stomped louder and shouted louder, "Amen!" And again, "Amen! Amen!" He sang and shouted, sang and shouted, sang and shouted until his mania subsided into exhaustion, until his breathing slowed his heart rate, until finally, very quietly, so very softly he said, "Amen." Only then did he really admit to himself that the phone call wasn't from Dianah. Of course it wasn't. But it felt like it for a minute or two, and that was thrilling. So he smiled through Christmas blurred eyes, his vision glancing at his phone.

"Hmmmph. Somebody did leave a message," he said aloud to no one, but he couldn't read the number. "Obviously not Dianah. Still it's got to be good news on Christmas morning, right? Maybe Jesus is calling. That'd be sweet," he laughed, ruminated and added fantasy upon fantasy. "Maybe, maybe not. Hmm. Probably not. What would be second best? Hmm." Shrugging his shoulders he picked up the phone again and listened to the message replay.

"Hello? This is Melchior! Merry Christmas!"

"WHAT???? Is this a joke?" Gary, confused at first, shouted at the phone. "Gary, you idiot, that's the message." So then he listened as three manly voices completed the message.

"And this is Caspar! Merry Christmas!"

"And this is Balthasar! Merry Christmas!"

"I'll be! It's the Three Kings! A great second best, for sure!" he cheered. His smile grew past his cheeks as he listened to the rest.

"We'll be at the mission this morning at 9:00 with Christmas gifts of Love, Peace, Joy and Hope. Please be there with all your friends. And once again..." all three shouted, "Merry Christmas!"

"Oh, my goodness," Gary laughed. "Imagine that! F.B.I. special agents leaving a Christmas morning message. Who'd a thunk it? This really is Christmas!" So with the excitement of a five-year-old unwrapping Christmas morning presents he commenced to call everybody, starting with Annie and including his mom and dad, to wish them Merry Christmas and tell them the Wise Men would be coming to Harbor and Divine at 9:00 with Christmas gifts of Love, Peace, Joy and Hope. He knew they would all get it.

And they did.

Every single one laughed, some got teary but everyone said, "Merry Christmas! I'll be there!"
And they were.

265

Joe arrived first dressed in an elf get-up to unlock the doors, shovel the walks and, of all things, to ring the bell on that sunny Christmas morning. And ring it he did, hard and loud and long! He rang and rang, and though he didn't plan it as such, he kept ringing far beyond, he was certain, whatever might be the prescribed time for Christmas bell tolling. Until suddenly, that is, he heard St. Pat's bells, which made him cheer, "Whahoo!" and ring all the harder until his muscles ached while his heart soared as if he were answering Fr. Ed's morse code of bell-ringing joy. Then one by one even more bells began ringing from every direction causing the whole Near West Side of Cleveland to wake up to the exciting sound of Christmas bells ringing out the Love, the Peace, the Joy and the Hope of Christmas, just like the Wise Men said. Neighbors even smiled their way outdoors drawn to the bell tolling epi-center at Harbor and Divine. Even the NBC and CNN tele-vision vans came to life with Christmas morning curiosity.

"Good morning, everyone, and Merry Christmas from our NBC family to yours! This is Lesley Wilson back in Cleveland's Near West Side where this morning we were startled by the sudden tolling of Christmas Bells coming first from The Mission at Harbor and Divine, the very same church building where less than 36 hours ago a tragic shoot-out gave birth to everything but peace in this beleaguered inner city neighbor-hood. But like last night, from this same Harbor and Divine location, there began a healing with a Christmas Eve proces-sion through these inner city streets with thousands of carolers singing their way to St. Patrick's church nearly a mile away, where Christmas lessons and carols brought divine balm to a community devastated by tragic violence.

"And now today, once again at the corner of Harbor and Divine, the joyous hope of Christmas seems to be throwing bell-tolling haymakers at any remaining darkness—any and all. Take a listen." And Lesley Wilson directed her microphone and the cameras right at the bell tower to broadcast around the world the bells of Christmas hope from The Mission at Harbor and Divine in Cleveland, Ohio.

Those same bells surprised Gary in his home across the street; made him jump up and down cheering, laughing and shouting, "Way to go, Joe!" who, Gary was certain, had to be the Christmas morning bell ringer. Throwing on his winter coat and hat, Gary ran out the door and followed the bells through a gathering crowd of carolers singing in the Christmas sunshine at the foot of the bell tower.

"Merry Christmas!" Gary greeted the singers one by one. "Merry Christmas!" he said again and again as he ran into the mission where he, indeed, found Joe in the bell tower ringing like Quasimodo but with the smile of angels beaming from his face and no hunch back.

"Hey, Joe, great job! Merry Christmas! You know you've got hundreds of people outside singing Christmas carols, with, guess who, the Three Kings dressed in top coats and Burger King crowns leading the songs."

"For real? Hundreds? The Three Kings? Our three Kings? And hundreds singing with them? No way, Gar! Absolutely no way!"

"Yeah way. For real! Hundreds. It is so cool. Hey, how 'bout I take over the ringing for you and you go out and take a look for yourself at the best Christmas morning service ever on the corner of Harbor and Divine. EVER! Go on. Take a look. You've just got to see it!"

"All RIGHTY THEN! Thanks, Gar! I am exhausted, but it's been like the bells of a dozen other churches are sending one another ding-dong Christmas code messages of Joy and

Hope. I love it, though I am exhausted. How in the world did Quasimodo do it?"

"Well, you have awakened the world to Christmas! Maybe even Paris, Madrid and Moscow! The TV trucks have broadcast your bell-ringing all around the world. You *should* be exhausted! Go out there and celebrate! I'll give you ten more minutes of bell ringing."

"Yes, sir! And, Gar?"

"Yeah?"

"Thanks and Merry Christmas, my friend!" Joe said as he passed the tolling rope to Gary who rang and smiled and rang and laughed!

"Merry Christmas, Joe!"

Joe turned to go outside, opened the door, but stopped stunned by how amazing the bells sounded, turned back to Gary, and asked, "Hey, Gar, did it sound this good when I was ringing?"

"Better! Louder! I mean, Joe, you woke up the whole Near West Side of Cleveland, for crying out loud! And they're all right out those doors. Maybe thousands by now. I don't know. Go on out and see for yourself."

So Joe ran out into the stunning sight of a sunrise Christmas celebration with the Three Kings leading hundreds, maybe even a thousand, of Joe's new best friends in singing carols and shouting Christmas cheers. The CNN cameras were already rolling, and a TV tech was setting a microphone for TV and loud speakers in front of DJ and the Kings.

"Hey, Joe!" shouted DJ. "Merry Christmas!"

"Merry Christmas back at ya!"

"Recognize these guys?"

Up came the Three Kings. Right on cue Gary stopped ringing the bell, and Joe stood tall on the mission steps, raised his arms for quiet and he and the Three Kings shouted out to the crowd,

"Merry Christmas!"

"Merry Christmas!" the caroling crowd shouted back and then they cheered. Then in a quick thinking ad lib Joe and the Kings shouted out, "We love Jesus, yes we do! We love Jesus, how 'bout you?" And they pointed out to the crowd.

The crowd got it right away shouting back in rhythm with a singular, thunderous voice, "WE LOVE JESUS, YES WE DO! WE LOVE JESUS, HOW 'BOUT YOU?" The whole mission staff jumped up on the steps in front of the mic with the Kings and together they tossed their love of Jesus back to the crowd. Back and forth it went until Joe and the Kings called it, pointing to their sore throats, then raising their hands, as Joe stepped up and shouted at the top of his lungs, "Ladies and Gentlemen: The Three Kings!!" To which, it seemed, the whole world cheered with the crowd for the top-coated men with Burger King crowns. And through CNN maybe the whole world did cheer.

Some big voices in the crowd started chanting "Jesus! Jesus! Jesus!" and the hundreds joined in, until yet another group began singing, "We Three Kings," and everybody joined them in the singing, at least through the first verse that everybody knew.

Then the Kings stepped forward, raised their hands to the immense cheers of the crowd. One of the Kings stepped up and called for quiet with his hands. When he had it, he introduced himself in a big, big voice, "Merry Christmas, I'm Melchior." More cheers. "Next to me is Caspar." More cheers yet. "And next to him is Balthasar. And together," all three totally hammed it up, "we are three wild and crazy kings!"

Frenzied cheers and laughter erupted. Had there been a house, they'd surely have 'brought it down' as the crowd chanted, "Jesus! Jesus! Jesus!"

"Who's leading them?" asked Gary emerging from the bell tower.

Joe leaned over and shouted into Gary's ear, "This is incredible. Must be Christmas angels, Gar. You ever seen anything like this?"

"Never. Especially considering the two days of darkness we've just had."

As Melchior caught his breath, broadcaster Lesley Wilson made sure the cameras kept rolling, for what she thought was a once-in-a-lifetime broadcast. She smiled when she realized all systems were 'go.'

"However," Melchior continued as one of the broadcast team set a microphone in front of him. Melchior acknowledged the help with an Elvis-like, "Thank you, thank you very much," and continued. "In our day jobs we are not really kings." (Awww's and groans.) Then pointing to the heavens he called out, "We have only One King. Right?" And the Jesus chants picked back up until Melchior brought them down again.

"Man," Gary said to his father, Guy, who had walked up from Gary's house to join him on the steps to his old family church, "this fella really knows how to work a crowd, doesn't he?"

Guy nodded, "He sure does. Just what is his day job?"

"You almost missed it. But wait a sec. You'll soon find out."

Melchior picked it up again, "For our day jobs we are Special Agents of the F.B.I." The unexpected roaring cheers took the Special Agents in Burger King Crowns all by surprise, but they instantly recovered shouting into the crowd, "and we were right here, we were here in this building two nights ago to witness the heroism of the people of this Mission at Harbor and Divine. They are true Christmas heroes!" he shouted over the cheering din of the Christmas crowd, as the CNN cameras kept rolling.

Annie tugged at Gary's sleeve shouting in his ear, "Sounds like Jesus Himself is making an appearance right here, right now, Gar. This is Fab-u-lis-tic! Incredible!"

DJ walked up to Melchior, asked for the mic and thanked their heroic special agents once again with, "Friends and neighbors, give it up one last time for the Three Kings!" who then pointed glory to God like Leonardo da Vinci's St. John the Baptist as they got cheered off to the side and made room for DJ.

DJ stepped up to the mic and invited everyone to join in singing "Silent Night" led by him, his mission teammates and the Kings.

Yes, Annie was right, that Christmas morning Jesus did make an appearance. Love, peace, joy and hope were born again on the corner of Harbor and Divine for thousands of hurting people living each day of their lives mostly on faith, love, prayer — and especially hope.

That Christmas morning hope reclaimed the soul of a desecrated mission church standing once more as a witness to struggling neighbors that they are worthy of the Love of God; they are worthy of the Healing, worthy of the Hope, worthy of the Joy and worthy of the Peace that Christmas brings into their private, struggling worlds.

That Christmas morning Gary, with his own soul once torn asunder by grief, fell to his knees on the stone steps to the church as if they were the Holy Grotto of Christ in Bethlehem, in total surrender to Mary's Baby Boy, saying, "Thank you, thank you, thank you, Lord Jesus, for this new life, and these new friends, and this new home. Thank you, thank you, thank you for being born to us this day."

Annie knelt beside him, then Joe and DJ, Mel, Dr. Don, Sandy, Angelina, the Three Kings with Burger King crowns and tears in their own eyes not knowing at that moment a thousand more people behind them were falling to their knees to worship the Baby born to be the King of Heaven and Earth, the Lord of love and the Giver of hope right there on the corner of Harbor and Divine.

"All is calm, all is bright," they sang. Some lit their Bics. Some raised their lighted cell phones. They sang and swayed until the last words, "Christ the Savior is born; Christ the Savior is born."

DJ stood at the mic, faced the crowd, some kneeling, some standing, and he prayed. Yes, knees were wet and cold, so DJ was brief, but still he invited them to a Christmas life change, to a new hope and a new birth with Jesus, ending with "God bless you all. Amen. And..." Joe, anticipating the moment, had run into the bell tower and at "Amen" cranked on that bell rope for all he was worth just as DJ, the mission team and the Three Kings called out,

"Merry Christmas!"

Chapter 35

An Epilogue of Hope

Like Cinderella's coachmen who, at the last stroke of the midnight bell, became kitchen rats once again, so at the last stroke of Joe's Christmas morning tolling, the Three Kings removed their Burger King crowns and became, once again, three Special Agents of the FBI. Okay, true, some might say that coachmen turning back into kitchen rats is far more dramatic than Three Kings with Burger King crowns turning back into FBI Special Agents. But those life-saving Special Agents made the best ever Three Kings from the East. Ever. After all, they did save lives, they defeated the denizens of darkness and they brought new hope to the Near West Side of Cleveland.

Acting Supervisory Special Agent Adams, no longer a king, became the newly minted supervisor of his Cleveland F.B.I. unit since Gandy was still hospitalized in Metro General's Intensive Care Unit and headed toward a very long recovery. As such, newly minted SSA Adams invited all the mission staff to walk indoors with him for their previously arranged 9:00 AM powwow, postponed by what SSA Adams called "the most awesome Christmas morning worship ever! Ever!"

he emphasized, then added, "and I've been a Christian my entire life, and I'm telling you salvation was born right here on the corner of Harbor and Divine in Cleveland, Ohio this Christmas morning!" The mission team cheered "Amen!" "Right here!"

And Angelina cocked her head and asked SSA Adams, "Are you sure you're not a preacher? Because you sure sound like one, and a good one to boot!"

"That's the truth!" Gary added. "So, really, aren't you a little out of character, you know, from the TV F.B.I. hard guys?"

"I suppose so. But you folks in the mission and the community have really been through hell this week, and we got permission from Gandy and headquarters to have some Christmas fun with all of you. After all, bringing hope, love, and joy into a dark world is what Christmas is all about. Right?"

"Preach it, now, Special Agent Man!" cheered Joe.

Agent Adams raised a hand for quiet, and said, "Thank you. But," he began already smirking, "in fact, of all the 11,987 excellent reasons to postpone (or even cancel!) a meeting, ANY meeting, that Christmas morning worship, that Christmas mountain top experience with God on the corner of Harbor and Divine was absolutely the best ever reason to cancel a meeting. However, there does come a time. So let's get started."

Everybody groaned and laughed all the same, and started into the old German-built sanctuary, scarred for sure, but filled once again with the love and hope of Christmas.

The chatter of the women going into the building caused all three Special Agents to smile, because they knew something the others didn't.

Angelina didn't know, so she asked Annie, "Do you think they are going to bring charges against us?"

Annie was aghast: "Oh, I certainly hope not. You mean like arrest us, throw us in jail?"

"Shh," Mel told them. "They'll hear you.".

"So what? I'm scared. My armpits are sweating, and I NEVER sweat in my armpits!" Angelina shout-whispered.

Special Agent Gomez just about blew his cover trying to stifle his laugh by turning it into a terrible, gut-wrenching sneeze. "Haa, haa, ACHOOO!" If hernias are born of such abdominal strains, Gomez had just ripped open a doozie.

"See?" Mel whispered. "That wasn't even a good fake sneeze! He's on to you! Both of you! You're both going to Sing Sing, you know!" Mel teased mercilessly, then cleared her throat to cover up her own laugh. She felt a little guilty, but she loved it. As a psychotherapist, Mel had worked countless times with law enforcement officers of all stripes and knew that a chapel was not in any way the official setting to grill, charge or arrest suspected criminals. "No," Mel knew and said to herself with a smile on her face, "this is a time for heart-felt thanks and praise all around the table." Mel knew.

So, as much as she loved the teasing, she recanted and said, "Ladies, ladies, nobody's getting charged or arrested or any such thing here today."

"How do you know?" Annie asked sweetly.

"Annie, I've been to dozens of those harsh meetings, and not a single one was ever held in a mission chapel or any place other than a police station, a jail, a court room or a judge's chambers. Take a deep breath. You're going to love this. Guaranteed."

Annie, already known to her new friends as "The Weeper," well, Annie and Gary both, Annie shed tears of relief. "Thank you, Mel," she said as she plastered on as good a smile as she could muster while the rest of her face cried holy relief.

SSA Adams stopped walking and just stood there, right in the middle of the still damaged, but mostly cleaned up chapel. He turned to the rest, leaned lightly against a pillar. "Folks, let's just stand here and look around for a minute. Not long. Just long enough to remember two nights ago."

So there they stood. They stood and looked around remembering those terrible sixty seconds of chaos and bloodshed and the terror of desolation they all felt afterward. Even the men had to fight back emotion to stay dry-eyed at their memories: Gandy lying bleeding, close to death; Carmela hiding behind the piano, her bleeding face and upper body peppered with oak, wire and cast iron shrapnel; Melvin lying as still as death atop that little two-year-old boy from Mexico he barely knew but whose life he had surely saved. The assassins with their totally unexpected murderous onslaught both shot dead in the center aisle. And to think everyone thought they were going to be the shepherds called by angels to witness the birth of Jesus, the Lord of Life.

And then there were the Three Kings, those Special Agents plus the two DEA agents storming that citadel of worship and praise that had been overrun by the darkest evil. They all remembered the din of the armored assault that turned those two assailants into headless corpses, keeping everyone else alive. Like the army of Egypt at the Red Sea, the death of evil upon the seashore is not joyous sight, but always welcome; not miraculous, but necessarily harshly violent; not so much a gift, as a well-fought-for victory.

With her face washed in tears of soul-deep gratitude, fed by the terror that was still strangely alive in her soul, Angelina choked out, "Thank you, gentlemen. From the bottom of my heart," her voice quivered, "thank you for saving my mother's life, my father's life and the lives of all my friends standing here, plus Gandoff. We would not be here today, were it not for your quick thinking bravery and your skill with weapons. You became God's shield about us, standing between us and certain death. Thank you, thank you, thank you." She could say no more. But it was enough.

Just then two men walked into the chapel looking, at first glance, every bit like the two assassins from two nights before. In a flash chaos once again sprang loose as all of the mission staff yelled "Get down!" or screamed "Under the pews!" or "Dive for cover!" Or they just stood there, catatonic, unable to utter a word or move a muscle.

SSA Adams yelled his loudest, **"Everyone! STOP! STOP!"** And they did.

"There is no danger." He went on to explain: "These men are the D.E.A. agents who helped us dispatch the assassins. Agent Rossi. Agent Pettigrew. They're the good guys," he said unable to restrain a great big smile. Rossi and Pettigrew both nodded as Adams continued. "I invited them to join us this morning, not suspecting that this would happen. I'm very sorry. But maybe it's a good thing, because what some of you just experienced were classic Post Traumatic Stress Disorder, PTSD, behaviors. Chances are you will experience them again, perhaps many times. Sudden loud noises; car backfires; fireworks; even the confusion of large, noisy crowds, may all transport you instantly, in your mind, right back to the trauma you experienced two nights ago, triggering any of a wide variety of responses including fear, anger or terror. I strongly urge you to seek counseling, which really shouldn't be too terribly difficult for you, since you have, on your own mission team here, two of the very best PTSD counselors in all of Cleveland: Dr. DJ Scott and Dr. Melanie Zurkos. Do any of the rest of you have other past experiences with PTSD and the disruption it can cause in a person's or a family's life — in a marriage, on the job?"

DJ, Mel, Joe, Gary, Annie, Angelina all raised their hands.

"Wow. More than I thought. Maybe your life experiences taught you more than you ever realized about having courage in the face of violence, fear and danger, and how they change a person deep down, soul deep, fearfully deep. You know then. You can also add to your list of fellow PTSD survivors all the government agents you see before you plus Gandy."

"And," interjected Angelina, "please include my father, Melvin Anderson, who dove on top of that little boy to save him. As a combat veteran, my dad has struggled with PTSD for 20 years. He is a good, good man always battling the dark."

"Thank you. He certainly proved his merit to all of us, didn't he."

A chorus of, "Yes!" and "Amen!" and "He sure did!" gave further testimony of Melvin's valor.

"Friends," SSA Adams continued, "this has already been quite an eventful morning, but can you afford to give me ten more minutes, no more, so I can say what I had planned to tell you when we called you in the first place?"

Everyone nodded and said things like, "Yes," "Of course."

"Thank you."

Then Adams stood respectfully looking in turn at each and every person there. Into their eyes he gazed as if searching for hidden treasure and then smiling when he found it. SSA Adams cleared his throat. "You are amazing people. Look at you, including Melvin, Carmela and Gandy. You are ethnically and culturally diverse, like America; you are male and female; young and old, rich and not so rich, like America; you are filled with the values that built this nation and continue to build it. You look like America. If only America could be filled with people just like you what a wonderful land this would continue to be. In an inner city mission you, on behalf of the hurting, lonely, broken people who live here, every day you wake up to battle the darkness that threatens them. Do you not?"

"Yes, we do," said Joe. "Just like you, Agent Adams."

"Yes, we are much the same in that regard, rising each day to battle the dark. But today, this Christmas Day, we came here to thank *you*. To thank you for setting loose the miracles of hope that lift up struggling people. We came here to thank you for modeling how to give back the love and joy and peace to your neighbors, that once were gifts given to you. This morning, those were your grateful neighbors who literally answered the bell and gathered to celebrate the goodness and the courage you demonstrated within these very walls two nights ago. You were heroes, heroes to every person on the Near West Side of Cleveland and, through television, to a nation living in constantly encroaching darkness, you were, and you are, heroes of the Light, the one true Light that shatters this world's darkness and brings hope to us all.

"We in law enforcement do what we do, choose a career of willingly mucking around in the nation's dens of deepest darkness because there are people like you. You, your character, your love of the people who are your next door neighbors, you make all the difference for us.

"As we walked in here a few minutes ago some of you speculated that we called this meeting to put you in jail, because," SSA Adams grinned and shook his head, "because you wanted to help an orphaned two-year-old whose parents were gunned down by drug lord assassins. You wanted to help that little boy get a fresh start in America. Jail? For that? A reprimand for your foolish risks, maybe. But jail? Oh, my. Never!

"It's because of people like all of you and Gandy, Melvin and Carmela, because of good, good people like you, this nation under God is worth fighting for. Because you stand in the city's trenches of urban poverty, family brokenness, cultural despair and racial hatred; because you put hurting people on your backs, feed their children, befriend the lonely and stand tall for justice in the land. Because of all that, you give us reason to get up every morning, strap on guns every day and battle the drug lords of this dark world." He took a shaky breath and went on. "You give us hope. You stiffen our spines. You bless our hearts. And all we want to say to you today is 'thank you.'" The tough man's eyes got moist, but he continued to look straight into their eyes and call each one by name to say:

"DJ, Joe, and Gary, thank you. You are worth fighting for.

"Annie and Melanie, thank you. You are worth fighting for.

"Angelina, thank you. You and Carmela and Melvin are worth fighting for.

"Lydia and Little Angel, thank you. You and Gandy are worth fighting for.

"Guy and Phyllis, thank you. You are worth fighting for.

"Dr. Don and Sandy, thank you. You are worth fighting for.

Each and every one of you."

SSA Adams paused while he and his two partners picked up the three Burger King crowns from a nearby pew which they then clutched as cherished medals of honor, while Adams finished his thanks.

"Each and every one of you gives meaning to our lives, purpose to our work and value to our risks.

You are all–so–worth fighting for. Thank you."

At that, with crowns in their hands, Melchior, Caspar, Balthasar and their two D.E.A. teammates said, "Merry Christmas!" and walked out the door.

Merry Christmas, indeed!

finis

Acknowledgements

Cathy Poremba, my wife and best friend, who endured all my conversations about my 'new best friends' in my Harbor and Divine Series of books of fiction. In <u>Hope at Harbor and Divine</u> she read everything at least seven times to find mistakes, come up with better ideas while handing me enough "atta boys" to keep me going.

Everett Stoddard, long time good friend, brother in faith, newspaper editor, pastor, counselor and encourager who gave me generously of his time, effort, advice and counsel about what makes sense and what does not as well as what honors Christ.

Robert Capes, confidant, jokester, encourager, brother in faith, friend and one-time fighter pilot who has the encouragement gene from Barnabas.

Gerald Lewis, friend, brother in faith, who gives criticism wrapped in humor and tied up with ribbons of Christ's love.

Walter Isaacson's book, **<u>Leonardo da Vinci,</u>** introduced me to the mind, soul and art of the quintessential Renaissance man. Dr. Isaacson's admiration of Leonardo's *sfumato* techniques inspired my creative thinking about artificial lines that divide us one from another and what it is that brings us together.

Joseph Campbell and his transformational book, **Hero with a Thousand Faces**, which taught me that heroes, men and women of all nations and races, change their world by traveling boldly upon the path set before them, relying upon angels and spirit guides along the way and then returning home to bless those once left behind. The hero cycle is one of the templates for my Harbor and Divine series of books.

Jesus Christ, my Hero and Savior, as well as those who followed Him: **Mary His Mother, Paul of Tarsus, the Apostle John, sisters Mary and Martha, Francis of Assisi, Dr. Martin Luther King, Jr.**, friends of the Sea Islands Rural Ministry, who taught me the meaning of love across the artificial boundary lines of class, race and ethnicity.

Lastly the real life missionaries of Cleveland's Near West Side, **Gary, Jack, Doug and Charles** who lived into the fine spiritual art of serving the poor, the outcast, the lost, the lonely, the broken, the hungry, the stranger and the different, just like Jesus did. They also showed me what camaraderie in faith looks like—working, praying, laughing together while totally loving one another and the people they served.

All my helpers at Xulon Press.

And to all my readers: Thank you all from the bottom of my heart for finding and then actually reading this book! I hope you fell in love with my characters as much as I did.

T. W. Poremba